"I have feelings for you, Iris," Shane said. "They came out of nowhere, much like you did. I've never—"

"Don't," she ordered and surprised them both with the strength in her voice. "Don't tell me you've never felt this way about someone before."

"Even if it's true?"

Especially if it's true. How many nights had she longed to hear those words from someone? Even when she knew she wasn't emotionally equipped to deal with them. But she'd let go of fairy tales a very long time ago. "I don't do family, Shane. You know this. I don't know how to..."

"To what?"

I don't know how to love you.

Instead, she said, "You know I can't stay."

"No." The patience in his voice had her wanting to hold on to him forever. "I don't know that, actually. What I do know is you're scared, and honestly, that gives me this weird feeling of hope. Because this... thing that's between us, it scares me, too."

Dear Reader,

If the third time's the charm, then the fourth time is extra lucky! When Melinda, Cari, Amy, Carol and I first conceived of the Blackwells, we had no idea we'd still be writing them all these years later. Personally, I think this is our best round yet.

The Blackwell Belles are a complicated group of sisters, each dealing with their unique upbringing in very different ways. My sister, Iris, has opted to be a loner. No one to rely on, no one to rely on her. An open road, working how and when she wants to, with only her dog, Cosmo, along for the ride. What better hero to present to Iris than a rancher with more roots than a forest of trees. It took tragedy to bring Shane Holloway home to care for his nephews, niece and curmudgeonly father, but now that he's back, he's come to understand just how important family truly is. And he's more than a little determined to prove that to Iris. Add in some familiar return characters and a shelter full of rescue pups and, well, those are all essential ingredients to a Blackwell romance.

I hope you enjoy Iris and Shane's journey to happily-ever-after and that this branch of the Blackwell family finds a place in your reading-loving heart.

Anna J

A COWGIRL ON HIS DOORSTEP

ANNA J. STEWART

Harlequin

HEARTWARMING

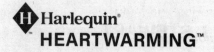

Harlequin®
HEARTWARMING™

Recycling programs
for this product may
not exist in your area.

ISBN-13: 978-1-335-05121-9

A Cowgirl on His Doorstep

Harlequin Enterprises ULC
22 Adelaide St. West, 41st Floor
Toronto, Ontario M5H 4E3, Canada
www.Harlequin.com

Printed in Lithuania

MIX
Paper | Supporting
responsible forestry
FSC® C021394
www.fsc.org

Bestselling author **Anna J. Stewart** honestly believes she was born with a book in her hand. After growing up devouring every story she could get her hands on, now she gets to make her living making up stories and fulfilling happily-ever-afters of her own. Her dreams have most definitely come true. Anna lives in Northern California (only a ninety-minute flight from Disneyland, her favorite place on earth) with two monstrous, devious, adorable cats named Sherlock and Rosie.

Books by Anna J. Stewart

Harlequin Heartwarming

Hawaiian Reunions

Her Island Homecoming
Their Surprise Island Wedding
A Surprise Second Chance

Butterfly Harbor Stories

The Bad Boy of Butterfly Harbor
Recipe for Redemption
A Dad for Charlie
Always the Hero
Holiday Kisses
Safe in His Arms
The Firefighter's Thanksgiving Wish
A Match Made Perfect
Building a Surprise Family
Worth the Risk
The Mayor's Baby Surprise

Visit the Author Profile page
at Harlequin.com for more titles.

In Blackwell tradition, for my writing sisters
Melinda, Cari, Amy and Carol.

And our fearless leader, Kathryn.

May we never run out of ideas!

PROLOGUE

"WE'LL BE THERE in a couple of weeks." Elias "Big E" Blackwell paced along the length of his ragged RV, wincing at the slight crackle coming from the phone connetion. They'd made their first stop about a hundred miles south of Falcon Creek, Montana, after Big E had gone home for his great-granddaughter Rosie's birthday celebration. "Don't want to put too many miles on the old girl." The poor vehicle had had a rough couple of months what with circling Montana, Wyoming, and Texas like a jetliner waiting for clearance to land. "Keep a light on for us. And the grill fired up!" He ended the call and with a patience-gathering sigh, slipped his cell phone into his flannel shirt pocket. "Flora!"

Instead of Flora, Big E's sister Denny Black-well came ambling out of the convenience store, using the cane for once that she insisted on calling a walking stick. With her thin frame and thick silver braid worn long down her back, Denny defied every one of her eighty-plus years with grit and determination.

He suspected the paper bag she carried crumpled in her free hand was hiding a package of beef jerky she wasn't supposed to be eating. His baby sister was plenty old enough to take care of herself and she was well aware of what she could eat given the limitations of her chronic kidney condition. Didn't mean Big E wasn't tempted to point out the error of her ways. That said, he was a man who had learned when to pick his battles and he certainly didn't want her running commentary on his nightly shots of whiskey.

"Cut out your hollerin'," Denny ordered goodnaturedly as she made her way toward him. "Flora'll be along in a minute." She pointed to a small area located next to the convenience store. "She's letting Zinni get her zoomies out of the way before we sardine ourselves back into this tin can of yours." She lifted her cane high enough to tap against the metal siding. "Stop frettin'. We've got plenty of time. Nobody's punchin' daylight but you."

"Never known one tiny puffball to throw a well-planned schedule completely out of whack." His mutterings only earned him a raised brow and critical eye.

"Don't go taking your worry out on that dog." Denny stopped beside him, turned around and together they scanned the open grass area beside the small market stuffed to the gills with travel snacks, air fresheners and first-aid supplies.

"Whatever happens with Iris, we'll get through it." Denny leaned forward to catch his gaze. "What's botherin' you? We've done pretty well so far with the girls. We've got Maggie and Violet on board to rejoin the Belles for Flora's Cowgirl Hall of Fame induction, not to mention Violet's agreed to return Ferdinand the Bull to Maggie. We'll find a way to get Violet what she wants as well."

"But we knew what we were walking into with those girls." Big E's mouth twisted. "Flora was more than forthcoming about her relationship with those two. No telling what storm's brewing with Iris. You ask me, Flora's purposely avoiding any questions we ask."

"Wish I could shed some light," Denny said. "I even called my son to ask for some input and all he'd say was that Iris and Flora's mother-daughter relationship has always been…what did he call it? Complicated."

Big E took a long, deep breath. If they had any hope of rebuilding the Blackwell Belles and bringing this branch of Denny's estranged family back together, he needed to get his head in the game. "Bet that means Iris is going to be a challenge."

"Course she is," Denny scoffed gently. "She's

a Blackwell. Difficult is in our DNA." The fact Denny agreed with him didn't make him feel better.

"I'd best go see about wrangling Miss Flora and Zinni." Big E said as his sister turned toward the RV. Elias Blackwell believed in three things in this world: horses, ranching and family. And not necessarily in that order.

Dedicating his life to horses and ranching meant he'd made his fair share of mistakes over his eighty-six years, but he'd been doing his best recently to make up for the family side of things. That said, whatever optimism he'd carried with him on the first two legs of this reunion journey wasn't to be found where Iris Blackwell was concerned.

While he and Iris had met a handful of times in her thirty-plus years, he knew very little about this grand-niece. Other than the fact that she made up one fifth of the sisters who once upon a time performed as the trick riding, spotlight stealing rodeo troupe known as the Blackwell Belles. From the online videos he'd watched of the Belles there was no mistaking Iris's riding talent. She was an absolute natural when it came to horses and clearly taking on whatever role was necessary within the group.

The work she did now honestly impressed him more. Just thinking about the renovation business she'd built from the ground up, which included produced videos of her rebuilding inside and out worn down RVs, trailers and fifth-wheels gave him a burst of pride. She was someone who knew her worth and was making the most out of the abilities she possessed.

The question was, where did Iris's heart lie where her sisters and family were concerned? More importantly, was it going to be more difficult to convince her to come back into the family fold? Or part with Aunt Dandelion's custom hand-crafted saddle?

"Definitely going to be a challenge," Big E muttered as he crossed the parking lot to where a rhinestone accented Flora Blackwell rode herd on her teeny terrier, Zinni. Flora had nearly caught up with the pooch. Dog and owner skidded to a comical stop, looked at one another, then Zinni launched herself through Flora's legs to hide under a weathered picnic table.

"Dang it." Flora planted her hands on her rhinestone bejeweled hips, tilted up the cowboy hat that matched her bright blue boots. "Don't know what's gotten into her today. Big E, would you—"

Big E stuck his thumb and index finger in his mouth and blew a sharp whistle. Zinni poked her head out, blinked twice and toddled over to plopp her butt down right in front of him.

Flora swooped in from behind. "Gotcha!" She

scooped Zinni into her arms. "Thanks, Big E."
She nuzzled the dog who let out an odd noise that
wasn't quite a growl, and not quite a bark.

"Let's move out." He pointed to the RV. Flora
winced.

"I need…uh, water. No! A soda. Be right back."

"Thought you already—"

Flora shoved Zinni into his arms and raced off
to the convenience store. Grumbling, and doing
his best not to take this as a sign, Big E carried
Zinni to the RV and climbed on board.

"Flora's acting strange," he told his sister as he
set Zinni into her bed under the table and headed
to the driver's seat. "Stranger than usual," he
clarified at Denny's look. He removed his hat,
hung it on the hook behind his seat and lowered
himself behind the wheel. "She's anxious about
seeing Iris again."

"She hasn't been around Iris in twelve years,"
Denny reminded him. "I'd be nervous too. Don't
worry. We've earned our wings as buffers and
peacemakers. Whatever problems they have to
work out, we'll be there to ease the way."

"Hope so." He turned the engine on, waiting
for Flora to buy her soda. Five minutes later she
finally emerged. She sauntered as if she thought
they had all the time in the world.

"She's afraid." Denny's murmured comment

had Big E looking at his sister. "Never really seen this side of her. Flora's usually unflappable."

It was as close as Denny would ever get to admitting Big E was right.

"Like you said," Big E told her. "We'll be there for her. For all of them. Whatever is going on between her and Iris, we'll work it out."

"Hmm." Denny didn't sound convinced.

"All right. There's my good baby!" Flora pulled the door shut behind her and flopped into the bench seat at the table. "Okay, ready to go?"

"Been ready for some time now," Big E muttered. "Should take us a while to get there." He glanced at the rearview mirror and caught Flora cringe before she looked out the window. "Plenty of time for you to give us all the details about Iris before we arrive."

When Flora remained uncharacteristically silent, Denny turned in her chair to look at her daughter-in-law. "Flora?"

"I'm sorry," Flora said. "I… Iris is a bit of a blank slate for me. I've tried over the years but…" She shook her head. "I don't know how this is going to go. But the truth is, more than anything I want my girls there at the ceremony for my big day."

"Yours and Dandy's big day," Denny reminded Flora about the sister who had been the other half of the Blackwell Belles before Flora's daughters had become the act. "I think I'm beginning to see what the issues are," Denny murmured to Big E, who nodded in agreement. "Okay then. Cottonwood Creek, Texas, here we come!"

"For better or worse." Big E tooted the horn and shifted the RV into Drive.

CHAPTER ONE

IRIS BLACKWELL CRANKED up the volume on her truck's sound system and belted out, "Gonna fly me away in a big metal plane, soaring the roads and sky. Ain't no place to be but where I wanna be and there's no one to tell me I cain't."

"Can my cousin Chance write a song or what, Cosmo?" She reached over and scrubbed her hand into the thick fur of the Border collie she'd rescued off the side of the road four years ago. "Ain't nothing ahead of us but sunrises and sunsets. On our terms," she told him with a wink. "What do you think of that?" Cosmo woofed and turned his attention to the open road of Northern Texas as the wind from the open windows made him look like he was in front of a fan machine.

"I think you're humoring me," she teased. "I know your sense of humor, Cosmo, and yep. You are definitely teasing me. Oh! Hey, that's our exit."

Iris glanced in her side mirror, catching the reflection off her 2010 Jayco trailer before she eased over one lane and veered off onto the Piston Hills turnoff. Piston Hills was about as North Texas as you could get before hitting the patch between Oklahoma and New Mexico.

She'd been on the road for a good four hours. After spending the past six weeks refurbishing a rusted-out motor home for a newlywed couple in eastern Arkansas, Iris was on to her next challenge. And her next client.

Her backside was definitely beginning to feel every bump in the road, and she was regretting not stopping at that last gas station about thirty miles back.

"Gonna have to find a grocery store after we settle in at the Holloway Ranch," she told Cosmo. "Especially since you scarfed down the last of your kibble this morning before we left."

Cosmo glanced at her, blinked, sighed and then looked back out at the road.

Iris powered up the windows, flipped on the AC. October wasn't normally plagued with the summer temps that this part of the state was known for, but the past few days were definitely hotter than expected. She longed for a cool evening breeze, and honestly, Iris was more than looking forward to parking and popping open one of the last bottles of ice-cold beer nicely housed in her fridge.

Life was good, good, good. After four months

of constant remodeling jobs of trailers and motor homes, her bank account was full, her savings account was flush and the promise of a hassle-free holiday season loomed large. She could only hope her creative juices kept flowing. The preliminary pictures she'd been sent of the trailer that was next on her list of jobs would have discouraged a less challenge-obsessed designer. But Iris had always been the kind of woman who thrived on the impossible. The bigger the obstacles, the happier she was.

The Holloway remodel would be the last of the year. It would take her most of the month—how could it not when the reported 1976 vintage Holiday Rambler had to be stripped down and rebuilt from the wheels up? And when it was completed, well, who knew where she'd be headed next.

It was, she told herself with a smile curving her lips, the absolute best way to end the year.

The music cut off as her connected cell phone rang. Iris glanced at the dashboard screen, her smile fading along with her good mood.

"Not today, Mom." She hit the decline button and struggled to keep hold of her good humor. "Don't look at me like that," she told Cosmo, who gave her "the look."

"I have nothing new to report, and if someone had died I'd have heard from J.R." More likely Violet, the family peacemaker. Maybe. Iris flinched. Well, one of her four sisters would have called her. Or, perhaps her father. She made sure to chat with him at least once a month, if only to make sure he was doing all right.

Their last conversation revealed her parents were giving their long—some would say ill—suffering marriage another go. Iris's sarcastic eye roll was nothing new. Try as she might, she could not figure out that relationship. Her father had the patience of a United Nations negotiator, but despite her parents'…*difficulties*, and no matter how frustrated or dejected Barlow got, he always circled back to the fact that he loved Flora. And that, for him at least, made it worthwhile to try to overcome those challenges.

Personally, in all of her thirty-two years Iris had yet to find a way to interact with her mother in a constructive or positive way. Flora lived her life on her terms, doing what she wanted when she wanted, and she was not going to change. It had taken Maggie getting shot with an arrow during her sisters' trick riding performance, and the subsequent head-in-the-sand attitude of their mother, and the resulting breakup of the Blackwell Belles to finally accept that, but it had been an epiphany that had freed Iris to finally follow suit and live her own life, in her own way.

There were times the resulting ten-year-plus estrangement from her family—parents, four sis-

ters, grandmother Denny and umpteen cousins—
didn't sit too well, but she would not trade her
solitary, vagabond life for anything.

"Two years, six months and twenty-two days."
That was the last time she'd spoken with Flora.

Cosmo huffed.

"Hey, she was the one who hung up on me last
time," Iris defended herself to her dog. "And, as
expected, all she could talk about was the so-
called good old days." Sure, there had been fun
times as one of the Blackwell Belles, but even
those memories had been tarnished with age.
"She was the one who expected me to drop everything I was doing to come see a new rodeo
act with her. I was three hundred miles away. I
mean, I know I'm the best at rebuilding these
trailers and motor homes and all," she continued,
surprised to catch sight of a sign that said Holloway Cattle Ranch, Ten Miles. "But even I can't
make any of them fly. Besides, I had committed
to a job, and you know my motto, Cosmo. Take
a job, do the job, finish the job." She pointed to
the promo key chain dangling from her rearview
mirror. "Even put it on my saddle logo."

The call had been typical of her mother. Whatever Flora wanted, everyone within spitting
range was expected to drop everything and come
running. Flora had been born with a silver spoon
of expectation in her mouth and had spent a hefty

portion of her life corralling her five daughters into whatever configuration would get them the most attention. Usually with sequins, saddles and more and more risky stunts.

Well, Iris was definitely past the age of doing what she was told, and was most definitely old enough not to have to do whatever was expected. She'd walked away from the Blackwell Belles, her family's all-female rodeo performing troupe years ago. There was nothing—not one thing— that would ever pull her back into it.

Admittedly, she'd come close to surrendering back in August, when her father had called to tell her about the big Blackwell family reunion Grandma Denny was hosting in Eagle Springs, Wyoming. Thankfully, Iris had her usual excuse of not being about to leave a job to agree to make an appearance. A surprising twinge of regret twisted inside of her. It might have been fun, seeing all the extended Blackwells, reconnecting with some of her sisters, not to mention her grandmother. Iris didn't know the woman well, but Denny Blackwell had always come across as steady, strong and reliable. As a woman in a male-dominated profession herself, Grandma Denny had been enthusiastic when Iris had started Saddle-Up, her fifth wheel renovation and custom design business. Iris supposed that constituted an emotional connection between them. Not a very strong one, but that seemed to be the way their gnarled branch of the family tree bent.

When the notification for a voicemail popped up, Iris quickly deleted it and turned off her phone. Whatever Flora Blackwell had been calling about for the past week and a half wasn't remotely interesting to Iris. She'd left all the drama—and her family—eleven, no, make that twelve years ago.

She pressed her foot down on the gas and powered through those last miles, doing her best to outrun the guilt she suspected would land on her like a ten-ton cow pie when she gave herself time to think.

As the dust plumed up from under her tires, she took the turnoff onto a long dirt road bordered by a significant amount of fenced-in land. The summer grass was just about dried out. She'd spent enough time on ranches and farms to have a feel for schedules. The Holloways would be busy enough on the property to stay out of her way so she could do her job.

The overhanging sign up ahead had a giant *H* and smaller *olloway* in a lasso-type font, the metal edges shining against the midday sun. Passing beneath it, she soon found herself pulling her battered blue truck and hand-painted trailer to a stop near the yellow two-story ranch house. She killed the engine, disconnected her phone and shoved it into her back pocket as she climbed down out of the truck.

"Come on, Cos." She didn't have to say much more than that before the dog shot out of the cab. Within seconds he'd laid claim to at least three fence posts as Iris made her way around the front of the truck toward the ranch house.

She caught sight of three bicycles sprawled haphazardly across the ground in front of the large wraparound porch. The house itself looked well cared for. Recent paint had freshened up the railings and trim. A selection of soccer balls, footballs and various other sports equipment sat piled around the bikes. An old dusty plastic play-house with a crooked roof had been shoved under the porch and was half covered with a drab olive green fabric.

The front screen door bounced open and two boys stood in the doorway, looking first at her, then at Cosmo.

"Hi." Iris stopped where she was, hooked her thumbs into the back pockets of her jeans. "I'm looking for Butch Holloway."

"That's our grandpa," one of the boys declared and earned an elbow in the ribs from the other boy. They both had dark curly hair and brown eyes. One pair of eyes was filled with curiosity. The other? With suspicion.

"Can we tell him who's here?" The one who had done the elbowing cleared his throat and stood a bit straighter. The oldest, Iris told herself. Just like her sister, J.R. There was always something about how the oldest sibling presented themselves that spoke of responsibility, protection and caution. J.R had always shouldered so much. Iris wondered if this boy did as well.

"I'm Iris Blackwell. This is Cosmo." She reached down and petted Cosmo's head again, at which time the dog promptly dropped his backside to the ground. "Your grandpa hired me to fix up his trailer."

"You're going to fix that monstrosity?" the older one said.

Iris's lips twitched, wondering who might have dropped that word where the trailer was concerned. "I am indeed."

"But you're a girl." The younger boy looked genuinely perplexed.

"Girls do all kinds of things," Iris told him. "For instance." She pointed to the broken iron sconce beside the front door. "I've got some welding equipment in my truck that would fix that right up. Is your grandpa around?"

"Uh-huh." The older one frowned. "I'm not supposed to let strangers in the house."

"Not a problem." She pointed back to her truck.

"You tell your grandpa, and I'll just be over there. It was nice to meet you both."

"I'm Miles," the younger one announced and glared at his brother when he got another elbow. "Ouch! Stop that!"

"No need to start a tussle," Iris said easily, catching sight of one of the curtains falling back into place. "It's nice to meet you, Miles."

"And this is my brother, Eric." Miles's cheeky smile widened when he darted away from another elbow. "He can go tell PaPa you're here. Can I pet your dog?"

"Sure. Let him—"

"Get a good sniff first, yeah." Miles crouched down and held out a hand. "We had a dog. Thumper. He died last month."

"I'm sorry to hear that." Her heart twisted at the flash of sadness in the little boy's eyes. She gauged his age at around seven or eight, his brother only a little older. "It's the hardest thing about having a pet. Losing them."

"Yeah. Hey!" Miles beamed up at her as he sank both hands into Cosmo's fur. "He likes me."

Cosmo pushed his nose up under Miles's chin, looked back at Iris as if saying, "See? I am a good boy!"

Iris saw that Eric had disappeared into the house, so she headed back to her truck, not surprised to have Miles right on her heels, Cosmo walking beside him.

"You're really going to make PaPa's trailer okay? It's a heap of junk. That's what Uncle Shane says."

Ah. The monstrosity declarer. "I'm going to do my best. I like a challenge." She pulled open the back passenger door to the cab and dragged out her cooler. "Do you happen to know where the nearest grocery store is around here?" She ducked down, dug around the chilly water bottles for something—anything—edible.

"Closest store's in town. About five miles north."

Iris popped up at the deep voice. She had to inch up her chin, not once but twice, to finally find a face. A handsome face with a curious expression that reminded Iris an awful lot of Eric's.

"Who's your friend, Miles?" the man asked.

"This is Iris," Miles declared. "She's going to fix Grandpa's trailer." He stepped closer to the man and whispered, "And she's a *girl*!"

"Yes," the man said. "I noticed." He pulled off his hat, brushed it against the side of his dusty jeans. Iris wasn't often caught off guard. Growing up with four sisters, it was virtually impossible to ever be surprised by anything, but if there was a perfect example of a Texas cowboy—from his tousled dark curly hair, to the black T-shirt covering his very broad shoulders, the exquisite fit of those very worn jeans, right down to a pair of boots that looked as if they'd been around a stone's age—this man was it. The five o'clock shadow on his angular face added an extra little zing that for a good long time had lain dormant inside Iris.

"Well, you're too young to be anyone's grandpa." Iris grinned, surprised at the sudden tightness in her throat. Being on the receiving end of this man's laser-focused gaze unnerved her in a very unexpected way. "I'm guessing you must be Uncle Shane. Iris Blackwell." She held out her hand.

"Shane Holloway, yes, ma'am." He returned the greeting. "Blackwell." His eyes flashed. "Any relation to—"

"To whatever Blackwell you're about to mention?" Iris teased even as she tried to ignore the sudden tingles in her fingers. "Probably. My father's side of the family is from Eagle Springs, up in Wyoming. Me, I'm from a bit of all over."

"You're one of Denny's then."

"I am." Regret surged once more. Denny Blackwell's reputation carried far and wide, especially in the ranching world. Iris shouldn't have been surprised that he knew of her grandmother. "Is there someplace around here I can park this thing?" She patted a hand on her truck. "Preferably close to wherever the monstrosity is."

"I don't think—"

"A water and power hookup would be a bonus," she plowed on as if she hadn't heard him hesitating. "Not necessary, of course. Although I'll need some of both when I boot up my power tools." She widened her smile. "Whatever you've got will work just fine. I'll try to stay out of everyone's way."

"I'm afraid there's been some kind of mistake," Shane said, holding his hat with both hands. "My father didn't tell me anything—"

"Excuse me, but I'm a grown man still in possession of his faculties." A louder, deeper voice boomed at the same time the screen door banged open. Heavy booted footsteps echoed, and a somewhat frail, silver-haired man stepped off the front porch, Eric standing right behind him. "I've been talking for years about restoring Cassidy. Friend of mine sent me a video of this young woman on one of them tube-y video things." His gaze gentled when he glanced at her, but Iris could feel the tension snapping like downed power lines between him and his son. "Only a few minutes in and I knew you were the right person for the job. I'm Butch." He approached, all but ignoring Shane as the younger man stepped aside. "Butch Holloway. Welcome. Appreciate you coming this distance. We are so glad you're here."

Yeah. Iris bit the inside of her cheek and fought a grin. She wasn't so sure about that. Miles abandoned Cosmo to come stand beside his uncle. Shane rested a hand on his nephew's shoulder.

"I'm looking forward to working with you, Butch." Iris cast a quick eye across the area, noted the large stables, a pair of barn-type buildings and a spacious corral and paddock. "What kind of ranching do you do out here?"

"You name it, we've done it." It was impossible not to note the slight snap in his voice. "Once upon a time we trained and housed quarter horses, but that's a trickier market than cattle. Right now we've got about five thousand head rotating on a hundred and fifty acres of pasture."

"Beef or milk producing?" Iris took a step back, narrowed her eyes at the well-built stables just around the corner.

"Beef," Shane said. "The market's getting pretty tight, though. We might need to look into some new ventures. Maybe go back to quarters."

Butch harrumphed. "This one here's trying to convince me to add sheep to the rotation." The older Holloway didn't look remotely convinced or even interested.

"We've got a huge barn out there on the western slope going unused." It was obvious this wasn't the first time Shane had made this argument. "Sheep are the perfect solution and would be an added income stream."

"Generations of Holloways bought and added to this land near back over a century ago. Been cows and horses for as far as the eye can see every day of my life. They'd be rollin' over in their graves knowing their kin would be looking to add sheep to this land. Next thing you know he'll be suggesting goats."

"Not a bad idea, though. It's forward thinking." Iris cast her gaze across the expansive pasture. "Sheep and goats are natural grazers and keep the ecosystem in balance. Plus, they're entertaining," Iris added with a cheeky grin aimed specifically at Shane. "And they're super cute when they're little."

Butch's mouth twisted. "Hmm." He eyed her RV. "You do all this work yourself?"

"Every bit of it." Pride straightened her shoulders and had her stepping out of the way so Butch could admire her skill. "If I don't know how to do something, I do it on my own vehicle first, just to work out the bugs. Took me about a year and a half to get her finished." She followed the older man as he walked around her trailer. "I went to design and mechanic school during the day, fixed up Wander at night."

"Wander?" Miles's face scrunched.

"Wander Woman." Iris always got a kick out

of that name. "Because she never stays still and she's always changing direction."

Shane's eyebrow quirked.

"I found her in a junkyard about eight years back," Iris explained to Butch. "Biggest rusted-out piece of promise you could ever imagine, and that's exactly what I wanted. Figured if I could rebuild her, I could rebuild anything. And that's what I did, from the chassis up. Main thing I kept was the framework. Changed out the fiberglass for sheet metal siding. Makes it a lot more hospitable to every climate."

"Must have added some weight," Butch mused, resting his hand on the smooth, tan-painted finish.

"Some. I compensated with a bit of welded reinforcement. But we can get into all that after we take a look at… Cassidy, was it?"

"She's out back behind the stables," Butch said. "Haven't moved her in more than five years now. She might disintegrate when you touch her."

"You said she's a classic '76 Rambler, right?" Iris appreciated the admiration she saw in Butch's dark eyes as he peered at one of the windows. "Those babies were built to survive an apocalypse. I'm sure she's got life left in her. Probably more than most people would expect. How about you let me see her and—"

"Dad." Shane cleared his throat and purposely

looked anywhere other than at Iris. "I can see you've got your mind made up about this, but realistically, I don't think we're set up—"

"Deposit's already been made, Shane." Buck spoke as if he'd been rehearsing his response. "Nonrefundable, wasn't it, Ms. Blackwell?"

"Ah." Iris blinked, but jumped on Butch's unexpected verbal train. "Afraid so, Butch. And it's Iris, please. I'm afraid I spent the deposit already on getting out here. You know, gas? Food. Supplies." Her mind raced. "I won't intrude if that's what you're worried about," she insisted to Shane. "I grew up around horses and ranches. Heck, I've probably lived on more ranches than you've got here in Texas. I know how to stay out of the way. Trust me." Her smile brightened. "You'll hardly know I'm here."

CHAPTER TWO

YOU'LL HARDLY KNOW I'm here.

"Somehow I don't think that'll be the case."

"Is she staying, Uncle Shane?" Miles tilted his head back and narrowed his eyes as he looked up at him. Shane's heart hopscotched over that familiar beat of grief when he looked down at his younger nephew. The boys' dark eyes—identical to those of Shane's brother and their father—shimmered with confused curiosity and excitement.

"Looks that way." Shane bit the inside of his cheek. In his thirty-four years he'd never been able to win an argument with his father. His luck wasn't going to change now. When Butch Holloway made up his mind about something there was very little—if anything—that would ever change it. And apparently putting a shiny new coat of paint on Cassidy was what he planned to do.

"Her dog's really nice," Miles said in that not-so-innocent way he'd perfected over the past few weeks. "His name's Cosmo. He likes me."

"All dogs like you," Eric said as he came over. "How long is she gonna be here for?"

Too long. Shane sighed. "Not sure. Guess we'll find out." He plastered on an overenthusiastic smile. "At least she'll keep your grandpa out of trouble for a while." And maybe out of Shane's hair. There. He'd found a silver lining in this unexpected arrival after all. "I've got some things to tend to in the stable. Why don't you two round up your sister, and when I'm done we'll head into town for some shopping. Maybe grab dinner there? Sound okay?"

"Can we have pizza?" Miles asked.

"You always want pizza," Eric grumbled.

"So?"

"We'll see what everyone else wants," Shane promised, giving silent thanks that Destry's, the main eatery in town, offered a wide variety of menu choices. "I'll just be a little while."

"We can help!" Miles started to race toward him, but Eric grabbed his arm. "If it's to do with the horses or cleaning up the stables, Dad always said—"

Eric shushed his little brother in a way that sent Shane catapulting back to his own childhood. To when Wayne would step in when needed, like big brothers were meant to do.

"I know you can help," Shane assured his nephews. "And thank you for doing your chores this morning. But what I have to do is mainly office work. Go clean up and we'll head out in a bit." He walked away before he could see the disappointment he knew was there, in the pained expressions both boys wore more often than not.

Shane situated his hat back on his head. His long-ago broken-in boots crunched in the gravel and dirt leading around the house toward the main stable. The building, originally built more than three decades before, was spacious and, save for a handful of horses, used mainly for storage and as Shane's office. He'd turned one of the paddocks into a workspace almost the day he'd returned to the ranch last year.

The Holloway Ranch had indeed been a family business for generations. It was never meant to be Shane's, however. Being second born, three years behind his brother Wayne, meant the Holloway legacy was already firmly in place by the time Shane came along. It had taken Shane a good long while to understand that this was a good thing.

There hadn't been a day that he and his father hadn't butted heads. His mother used to say one was always bound to set the other off. More than likely because they were too similar in temperament. She'd been right, about setting each other off at least. His mother had been the perfect foil between them until she'd passed when Shane was seventeen, and then Wayne had stepped into the role.

Instead of feeding into Shane's long-held belief he had a responsibility to the family business, Wayne had encouraged Shane to pave his own path, away from the ranch. To find his true calling and not feel beholden.

Shane was a problem solver. A fixer of sorts. It had taken him the last ten years to embrace that and build a reputation as a go-to when ranches, farms and other agricultural businesses found themselves in dire straits. He traveled around the country to consult and work, not with the intention of shutting things down, but with the purpose of finding the solution that would preserve the business in question. Professionally, his success rate was stellar, his reputation gold.

Personally?

He hung his hat up on the hook by the sliding door, scrubbed his hands down his whisker-roughened face. Personally he was barely holding on by his fingertips. He never would have guessed how hard it was to function with a broken heart. Try as he might, there didn't seem to be a solution as to how to make this family—his family—whole again.

Shane dropped into the squeaky antique desk chair that once upon a time resided in his grandfather's office. He'd kept the decor of his refuge to a minimum, free of clutter and chaos. A practical desk, a solitary filing cabinet and a souped-up laptop that, until earlier this year, had accompanied him as he'd focused on keeping struggling businesses afloat.

He sat there, legs stretched out, leaning back, the muted voices of his father and their visitor echoing dully through the walls.

Trouble had arrived on the Holloway Ranch and its name was Iris Blackwell.

She seemed to have an answer for everything. Didn't matter what he'd said—or tried to say—she'd come right back at him with that smile and spark of challenge in her dark eyes. Eyes that had him paying attention to something other than his juvenile charges or the four-legged creatures that inhabited the ranch.

Looking into her pretty, tanned face was a bit like stepping from a black-and-white spur-clattering Western into a full-on color musical extravaganza. He half frowned, half laughed as he pinched the bridge of his nose. He'd been watching too many movies with the kids. There was nothing romantic or entertaining about adding another person to his responsibilities. He had enough to do around here. He didn't need to include Iris Blackwell on his list of things to keep an eye on.

Although…

Shane perked up, a new thought catching hold. The RV/trailer/monstrosity that was Cassidy had become a sore point between him and his father. It had been parked somewhere on the property for as long as Shane could remember. Once upon a time he and Wayne had used it as a fort or as headquarters when playing cops and robbers. It had been a clubhouse, hiding spot, retreat and sanctuary until it eventually became a dangerous eyesore. Cassidy was a hunk of junk that deserved whatever trash heap it ended up on.

Not that his father was going to allow her to end up on one.

"We don't throw things away just because they're old and useless," Butch had told Shane in no uncertain terms after Shane made the suggestion to call Carver Wittingham to have it hauled off to his junkyard. "The right solution will present itself, but until it does—" Butch's tone had shifted to a warning one "—Cassidy will stay exactly where she is, if and until I decide otherwise."

Maybe with his father's focus shifting, Butch would finally ease up on Shane taking on the ranch. It wasn't so much he was standing in his way of doing things, more like the not-so-silent disapproval that occurred whenever Shane wanted to discuss business. "Fat chance that will change." Shane being in charge wasn't something

Butch was ever going to completely accept. Not when it should have been Wayne to take over.

Shane leaned his head back, rolled his eyes to the ceiling before his gaze came to rest on the small framed photograph on the corner of his desk. That familiar twisting of his heart, the twisting he both hoped to get used to even as he dreaded it, cut off his air.

"I miss you, man." Shane reached out a hand, stopped just short of touching the image of his big brother, taken on his wedding day. Wayne, with his flyaway curly dark hair and twinkle-eyed smile, along with Chelle, her equally dark hair tumbling around her lace-covered shoulders, stood laughing, frozen in time.

He'd loved them more than he'd ever loved anyone in his life. His brother, best friend and biggest champion. His sister-in-law, encouraging, sympathetic, with a spine of steel. The future of the Holloway family and business, with three great children, had been snatched away in a squeal of brakes and tires.

Losing them had been devastating enough. Coming home to deal with his father and three grieving, traumatized children he barely knew? Excruciating.

Discovering his brother had named Shane not only as his successor for the family business, but that he and Chelle had also made him guardian to Eric, Miles and Ruby Rose was sobering.

Instantly, Shane went from having only himself to look after to being responsible for his niece and nephews, his aging, persnickety father and the Holloway ranch and legacy.

Yeah. Shane took a deep breath. He really, really missed his big brother.

A feminine yelp echoed through the walls and Shane shot up in his chair. Instinct had him ready to jump to his feet until he heard the embarrassed laughter follow. The sound of his father joining in made Shane wonder, at least for a moment, if Shane had somehow been transported to an alternate universe where Butch Holloway took genuine pleasure in something besides his grandkids. Apart from a moment ago, he couldn't recall the last time he'd heard his father's laugh.

Unable to resist temptation, Shane got up and walked around to the side entrance of the stable. He stood there, not quite out of sight, and watched as Iris Blackwell carried what was left of the RV's door and tossed it on the ground.

"Guess I'm already starting demo." She slapped her hands together, offered Butch what Shane could only describe as an exhilarated smile and ducked inside Cassidy.

Shane's curiosity got the better of him once more and he moved closer.

"A lot of the flooring's rotted through in spots," Iris's voice echoed from inside. "Makes some of my job easier."

He heard stomping, and some kicking, and a healthy grunt as he approached his father, who looked as if he was a kid again being presented with the biggest gift under the Christmas tree. A decisive crunch sounded, followed by an "Oh, bother." Then another odd sound Shane couldn't quite decipher.

When Iris poked her blond head out once more, Shane looked down and noticed her jeans ripped at the cuff.

"Definitely rotted through," Iris said on another laugh.

"You okay?" Shane asked.

"I've been bitten by worse." Iris waved off his concern. "One reason I wear my boots during demo. They protected me." She wiggled her foot around. "So. Butch. Cassidy seems…" Iris stopped, eyes brightening. "It took me this long to get it. Butch and Cassidy."

"My late wife, Jesse, named her," Butch explained. "She was a Western movie buff." He pointed a thumb at Shane. "Even named our boys after her favorite characters."

"Shane and…" She inclined her head. "You have a brother?"

"Wayne," Shane said and wondered if the same

pinch happened to his father when he said it out loud. "He and his wife passed earlier this year."

"I'm so sorry." Iris shook her head. "I can't even imagine." Something crossed her face, understanding maybe? Sympathy, certainly, as she glanced back to the house, no doubt thinking about the kids. "I didn't mean to open old wounds."

"Not old," Shane said easily. "Still healing."

Butch shoved his hands in his pockets and looked away, the pulsing in his jaw visible.

"Well, about Cassidy." Iris cleared her throat. "I think that she and I are going to get along just fine. Depending on supply availability and the weather and, oh, life in general," she added with an assessing nod at the metal monstrosity. "Seeing it in person now, I've got some tweaks I want to make to the plans, pending your approval, of course, Butch. My estimation on timing is just about right. I should be able to have her rebuilt by the end of the month."

"We'll get you whatever you need," Butch said. "Carver Wittingham runs the local supply store in town. We can set you up with an account—"

Shane flinched, not liking the idea of giving this stranger carte blanche with the family finances. "I don't think—"

"*I'll* get you set up with an account," Butch

corrected himself with a barely restrained glare at his son. "This is my project. I'm paying for it."

"Whatever works best for you," Iris said. "First thing is to see what materials Mr. Wittingham has at his disposal." If Iris noticed the tension between father and son, she didn't let on. She glanced at her watch. "It's not quite four. What time does the store close?"

"Seven on weeknights," Butch said. "Nine on Saturdays."

"Oh, perfect, then. I'll head on into town and get the lay of the land so I can start work first thing in the morning. Do you all get deliveries out here or do you have a drop box in town?"

"Both," Shane said. "And Carver delivers free of charge on orders over two hundred."

"Excellent." That smile of hers was back on full wattage. "Then I'll head on out. Need to do a grocery run, too, if only so Cos has something to eat."

"We've got kibble, and canned dog food," Shane offered. "Even some treats. It's just been sitting in the mudroom since we lost Buster. Unless Cos is picky?"

"He is not." Iris's eyes softened. "Thank you. We'd both appreciate it. I'm going to bring my truck and trailer around if that works for you?" She did a quick survey of the area. "Okay if I just park myself there?" She gestured to the area behind Cassidy. "I have a ninety gallon fresh water tank, but I prefer to hook in to a clean water source when I can."

"It's all yours. Power, too." Butch pointed to the outside power box.

"Nice. I won't have to monitor my power rationing then." There was that easygoing tone again. "I prefer to keep close to my work. And, like I said, stay out of everyone's way."

Shane noticed she aimed her comment at him rather than Butch.

"I'm sure it'll all be fine," Shane said, having surrendered to his father's wishes.

"Okay, then." She backed away, gave them a little wave. "I'll go grab the rig."

Shane stood beside his father and watched Iris walk away.

"Fine-looking woman," Butch said in a tone Shane didn't quite recognize. "Spunky, too. I like her. Should have known, given she's a Blackwell."

"She related to Elias?" Shane asked, thinking of the ranching legend that was Elias Blackwell.

"Big E's her great-uncle," Butch confirmed. "Last time we talked he mentioned something about Iris's mother being inducted into the Cowgirl Hall of Fame later this year."

"Really?" That was a pretty big deal. Especially here in Texas. "What for?"

"Flora and her late sister started the Blackwell Belles." Butch turned disbelieving eyes on his son. "You remember the Belles, surely? Flora and your mother were friendly. We went to see them once, at a show in Lubbock. Of course, by then it was Iris and her sisters doing most of the performing."

Shane had a vague recollection of being dragged somewhere when he was about sixteen. He was annoyed, if not surly, if he remembered correctly. He'd had to miss a date with his then girlfriend Patsy Perkins.

"Were there five of them in these Belles?" Shane's memory caught. "Wearing sparkly costumes? Trick riding, wasn't it? With…fire?" Iris was a Blackwell Belle?

"That'd be them." Butch chuckled. "Those girls could do amazing things back then. They retired a while back. Guess Iris found a new direction. But making those restoration videos of hers is sort of in line with the family's famous showmanship. Flora still performs here and there from what I hear. Keeps her toe in the water, so to speak. Probably one reason she's getting inducted into the HOF."

"Is there any reason in particular you didn't tell me you'd hired Iris?"

"Didn't want to argue about it." Butch kicked at the metal door Iris had discarded earlier.

"There aren't many things in this life that are possible anymore, Shane. Before I die, I want to take Cassidy out, straight into the horizon. See where she can go. How far we can go. And I aim to do it in style and comfort."

"Dad." Shane shook his head. "One minor heart attack does not a deathwatch make. The doctor said you're just fine." Or he would be if he'd manage his stress better and get more exercise. The past year had taken a toll on everyone, but especially Butch.

"Doesn't change what I want," Butch insisted. "I can't have your mother back. Or your brother or Chelle. I might not be able to help you herd cattle any longer or ride—"

"Dr. Collins didn't say anything about you not being able to ride or herd cattle." To the contrary, his father's doctor had encouraged him to resume a healthy, outdoor-focused routine. As a result, Shane had spent the past six months trying to convince Butch his life wasn't over because of one medical incident, but it hadn't worked yet. "You're only seventy, Dad. You have plenty of friends older than you who are still running their ranches, Big E included if memory serves."

"Big E retired from the day-to-day," Butch said. "Turned it all over to his grandsons and their wives."

"Oh." Shane probably should have known that.

"Fine. In any case, I'd appreciate the help around here. It would save me from having to hire more hands come winter, and the kids aren't quite old enough for that much responsibility." The Holloway Ranch already had a pair of ranch hands who had stayed on to help Shane keep up with all the work that needed doing after Wayne's passing. "Dallas misses you riding him," Shane added, knowing his father still held a soft spot for the quarter horse Butch rescued from a derelict ranch a few counties over more than a decade before. "He tolerates me, but he misses you."

"Maybe tomorrow." It was Butch's usual response; one Shane had long stopped thinking would change. "Ah, there she is. Incredible, isn't it? How she manages that massive truck and trailer?"

Incredible was one word. Deftly and expertly were others. Iris expertly maneuvered the vehicles as easily as she had her horse back in the day. Iris left a good amount of space between Cassidy and her own trailer and enough room to pull the truck free.

"Shane, unhitch the lady's trailer," Butch ordered as Iris dropped out of the cab.

Shane had the impression Iris Blackwell didn't need his help doing anything. "Yes, sir." He joined Iris at the back of the truck just as she was unhooking the hitch. "Don't hold it against me," he said immediately. "My father told me to help."

"Understood." Iris grinned, tilted her head up to look at him. Her shoulder-length streaked blond hair cascaded over one shoulder. "Careful." She indicated one of the side latches. "It catches sometimes."

He released it without much effort. "Got it."

"Your Wander Woman's a beauty," Butch said as he walked behind Shane. "What is she? Twenty-five foot?"

"Twenty-eight and a half," Iris said. "In trailers and RVs every inch of space counts," she added on a laugh. "Come on back and check out the power system." She hoisted herself over the hitch and nodded for Shane to follow as well. "I just revamped the hookup, actually. We can do something similar for Cassidy if you think it'll suit your needs."

Shane marveled at the explanations and descriptions that came out of Iris's mouth as she filled Butch in on the details of power and water hookups. It was almost like another language. He'd taken a few engineering courses over the years, mainly so he could stay well-versed in the advances of ranching technology. It hadn't been his favorite thing to do, but necessary. He'd often felt lost, as if he was overreaching, but as he listened, he noticed Iris brought everything down to a level of understanding that even he could comprehend.

"So you have solar as well as general power?" Butch said.

"I do," Iris confirmed. "But that's more of a precaution, as sometimes I'm not sure I'll have a grid to hook into. It's more affordable these days, so doesn't add much to the overall cost." She patted the metal box on the outer wall of the stable. "I've got six four-hundred-watt…"

Shane tuned out, transfixed by the ease with which she uncoiled her power cord then plugged the water inlet hose onto the spigot near the ground.

"If your intent is to head on out without a plan, I'd recommend solar backup."

"Your recommendations are one reason I hired you," Butch said. "Works for me."

"Well, okay, then. We'll include that when I'm organizing my schedule tomorrow. Right now?" She touched a hand to Butch's arm. "I'm starving."

"I bet you are," Butch agreed. "Shane's taking the kids into town for dinner. You've been driving all day, Iris. Shane, you should take Iris along. Give her a break behind the wheel."

Iris's face went bright pink. "Oh, that's not necessa—"

"Happy for you to come." Surprising himself,

for once, Shane didn't ignore his father's suggestion. "We can show you around town, introduce you at the supply store. Destry's has good food and an arcade in the back for the kids. They've got school tomorrow so we won't be too late getting back."

"Sounds great. Butch?" She glanced at his father. "Since you're not coming with, would you mind keeping an eye on Cosmo for me? Maybe give him some of that food you've got in the mudroom?"

"I can do that," Butch said.

"I'll wrangle up the kids," Shane said as she disappeared inside her RV. "What?" he asked his father when Butch's lips twitched.

"Just glad to know you don't miss what's right in front of you, son," Butch said. "Sometimes you surprise me. In a good way."

Shane pinched his lips together, silencing the response that would no doubt start another argument. "It's just dinner, Dad. And maybe I want to make sure she's not running some kind of scam on you."

"How could she be?" Butch asked as they walked side by side to the main house. "She's a Blackwell. Plus, I'm the one who tracked her down."

CHAPTER THREE

IRIS COULDN'T RECALL the last time she felt so...
flushed.

Standing in the bathroom of her trailer, she
flattened her palms against her cheeks and stared
wide-eyed into the mirror. The warmth of her
skin pulsed against her hands before she shook
them out and, ducking, cupped cool water onto
her face. Dragging a brush through her hair, she
smoothed it into place behind her shoulders, trying her best to push the image of an all too handsome, far too distracting cowboy named Shane
out of her mind.

She'd quick changed out of her driving clothes,
opting for a clean pair of jeans and a blue long-
sleeve T-shirt. So far, most of her time at the
Holloway Ranch had been one surprise after another. Butch Holloway was pretty much what
she'd expected. Gruff, a bit cranky, but also excited at the prospect of getting his beloved Cassidy back up and running. He reminded her of
her uncle Elias in a way; a kind of oversize teddy

bear with a real stubborn streak. Big E had mellowed in recent years—reconciling with his estranged grandsons had gone a long way to fixing that—but the last time she'd met up with him, she'd been reminded of just how ornery men of his generation could be.

"Denny's just the same," she reminded herself, thinking of her grandmother. All that said, if it wasn't for stubbornness, neither Denny nor her brother would have succeeded in the businesses they had; nor would they have passed those businesses down to their offspring.

She opted for a fancier pair of boots tonight, dark blue with black embossing. Comfortable, practical, but with a bit of a fashionable kick. Even though she hadn't turned it on, routine had her checking to make certain the solar was turned off. And the water tank. After more than four hours on the road, the truth was she was anxious to tumble into bed and get a good night's sleep. But the promise of a meal and a look around the town she'd call home for the next few weeks overruled that desire and, for the moment, her excitement about digging in on the new remodel in the morning.

Iris left the trailer unlocked and grabbed her purse out from under the front passenger seat of the truck. Wallet, cell phone, a notepad in case she got a creative notion that needed to be sketched out. She carried a purse the size of a small country but, as she had learned early on, better to have as much with you as you might need in an emergency. Iris was a woman who prided herself on being prepared for anything.

Not that any amount of preparation could have gotten her ready for one Shane Holloway. With her hand still gripping the edge of the door of her truck, she stopped and blew out a long breath. "Get a hold of yourself, Iris." She didn't typically have her head turned by a handsome face, but then calling Shane Holloway handsome might be the understatement of the decade. Add to that the fact he was looking out for his father and nephews and, well, didn't that just spike his appealing meter into the stratosphere?

"You've been up on blocks too long." Times like this she missed having someone—like a sister—to confide in or commiserate with. To laugh with. But that was the price she paid for going solo. She'd walked away from her family, her sisters and the close connection they'd once had years ago. If that meant dealing with an unexpected attraction to a client's son, so be it.

She'd muddle through. She was a Blackwell. It's what they did.

Still… Iris slung her bag over her shoulder. Sometimes she missed the girl talk.

She made her way to the main house, committing the area and surrounding buildings to memory. The Holloway Ranch was nicely spaced out and surprisingly modern given how long they'd been there. The property didn't feel cramped at all, and the structures looked well-kept and up-to-date. She'd been on plenty of ranches and properties that were falling down around the owners' ears, but that definitely wasn't the case here.

The Holloways clearly took loving care of what was theirs. And their charges.

Speaking of charges.

Iris rounded the corner to the familiar sound of Cosmo's frantic, excited barks as he chased Eric and Miles in circles. The laughter emanating from the boys brought another smile to her face and lightened her heart. Miles had clearly been the more ebullient of the two, but it was nice to see Eric could do something other than scowl.

On the porch, Butch sat in a rocking chair, looking every bit the elder Texas statesman as he rocked slowly. "I'm not sure who's tiring who out more," Butch said as he nodded to Iris.

"Cosmo loves kids," Iris confirmed as she leaned against the railing. "He hasn't been around a lot of them. Most of my clients are older, so they're empty nesters. Not you, though," she teased. "You've got a full nest, haven't you?"

"I do indeed." There was no mistaking the pride in his voice. "They're good kids."

"I'm sure they are." She glanced over her shoulder just as Miles did a somersault and sent Cosmo into a yelping leaping frenzy of canine glee. "Why don't you come to dinner with us?" It dawned on her that, while it might be good to have a buffer between her and his son, it might also do the older man some good. There was no mistaking the sadness in his eyes. A sadness that no doubt had a lot to do with the loss of Shane's brother and sister-in-law.

"I don't get into town much these days," Butch said. "I appreciate the invite, but I'm happy here."

Shane's boots echoed as he stepped onto the porch. She wasn't the only one who had changed. He'd clearly taken time for a shower, as his hair was damp and slicked back from his tanned face. The black jeans and black button-down shirt seemed to accentuate that which Iris didn't believe could be further accentuated. When he put that hat on his head...

She blew out another long breath and silently prayed for control over her suddenly overactive imagination. Heaven only knew what her reaction would be when she saw him on horseback.

"All ready?" he asked her as he buttoned the cuff of his shirt.

"I was just trying to talk your dad into joining us," Iris admitted.

"And I told her I'll be just fine here."

"How about a burger from Destry's, Dad?" Shane asked. "The kind with the bourbon barbeque sauce you like?"

"Wouldn't say no to a burger." Butch shrugged in a way that made Iris wonder if Shane's father had even planned to eat.

He looked a bit gaunt, as if he'd lost a good deal of weight in a short amount of time. She wouldn't call him frail exactly. His silvered hair was thick and nearly as long as his son's, and they shared the same bright eyes. Although something told her neither would appreciate her pointing that out.

"You guys head on out," Butch continued. "Don't worry about me. Me and Cosmo will get to know each other, won't we, boy?"

Cosmo, upon hearing his name, froze in mid leap and immediately rotated, racing over to receive the affectionate pets Butch offered.

"Oh, he's definitely a good boy." Affection coated Butch's voice. "Nothing in the world better than a dog."

Cosmo angled his head to look at Iris, who rolled her eyes. "Don't inflate his ego any more than it already is, please. All present and accounted for?" she asked Shane.

"Almost, just waiting on…ah, there she is."

Iris watched as a little girl, no more than six, stepped cautiously out of the house and reached for Shane's outstretched hand. With round rosy cheeks and a smattering of freckles across her pixie nose, she wore her brown hair loose and untamed, curls springing around her face and shoulders. She wore jeans and an oversize yellow shirt, and around her wrist was a beaded bracelet that looked as if it had seen better days.

"Ruby Rose, this is Miss Blackwell," Shane introduced them. "She's going to be working on the ranch for a little while. Iris, this is my niece, Ruby Rose."

"Hello, Ruby Rose." Iris dropped her purse on the ground and crouched, held out her hand. "It's nice to meet you. I love your name. I have a sister named Jasmine Rose, but we call her J.R."

Ruby turned overly wide eyes up at her uncle, tightening her hold on Shane's hand.

"She's shy around new people," Shane explained.

"That's okay," Iris assured them. "I understand."

"Eric, Miles, help your sister into her car seat, please." Shane nudged Ruby on her way.

"Come on, Ruby." Miles trudged over and heaved out a sigh of dramatic proportion. "We'll buckle you in."

"You all have a good time," Butch said. "We'll be waiting for you when you get back."

"Last chance to join us," Iris offered but only

earned a stern look in response. "All right, then." She retrieved her bag, pointed a finger at Cosmo. "You watch him, okay, Cos? I want a report when we get back."

Cos barked once and plopped his butt on the porch floor as she walked away.

THE ROUTINE THIRTY-MINUTE drive into Cottonwood Creek was far from ordinary with Iris Blackwell in the passenger seat of his truck. Shane honestly hadn't thought she could improve appearance wise; she'd just about knocked him for a loop the second he'd spotted her. She'd worn the hours of travel effortlessly from the tips of her blond hair to the toes of her well-traveled brown boots, and those features in between? He blew out a slow, controlled breath.

He wasn't sure what kind of magic she'd weaved in that trailer of hers, but with her hair smoothed and her face bright with color, she practically glowed. Glowed brightly enough he found it hard to look away.

While Miles and Eric bickered over who had let the battery drain on their shared gaming device and Ruby Rose sat silently in her car seat, Iris may as well be sitting on a top.

"You keep looking around like that, your head's likely to spin right off your shoulders."

"Habit." Iris leaned forward, peered across

Shane as they passed the smattering of shops and businesses that stretched for a handful of blocks. "I love little towns like this. So much character and charm, especially during the fall and holiday season. I've never seen so many pumpkins! They're everywhere. Oh, look! A bookstore. And…is that an ice cream shop?"

"It is," Shane confirmed. "Run by the same family going back fifty years or so. It's a bit of a time warp. Hasn't changed much since it opened. Red, white and black decor with stainless steel countertops."

"Soda jerk behind the counter?" Iris teased. "White paper hat on their head?"

"Something like that." He and Wayne had killed many an after-school hour sitting in the back booth slurping up thick milkshakes topped with towers of whipped cream.

"What's a soda jerk?" Miles asked.

"Hank is," Shane said. "It's what they used to call the people in ice cream shops who pulled the soda levers. Like when you order a root beer float?" He glanced over his shoulder in time to see the dots connect for Miles. "Hank's about a hundred years old," he told Iris. "He'd probably get a kick out of hearing that title again."

"Soda jerk. Soda jerk." Ruby's soft voice sang as she knocked her booted feet together. "Hank is a soda jerk."

"Great," Eric grumbled. "Another one of Ruby's greatest hits."

Shane checked the rearview mirror and saw Ruby's eyes fill before she pinched her lips shut and looked out the window.

"Ruby's welcome to sing as much as she'd like," Shane told his oldest nephew, whose moods tended to run parallel to that of his grandfather. "I like her songs. Don't you, Miles?"

"Sure." Miles pretended to be a beatbox for about five seconds before his brother elbowed him. "Ow! Knock it off, Eric!"

"Both of you knock it off, please." Shane struggled to smile at Iris's twitching lips. "Sorry. Driving's always an adventure with these three."

"No apology necessary." She waved a dismissive hand in the air. "I'm the second of five sisters. I'm well aware of the perils of close-quarter travel. We moved around constantly when I was growing up and spent a good portion of our childhood crammed into one vehicle or another. I've still got elbow indents on my ribs."

"Four sisters." Shane shook his head and let out a low whistle as he pulled into a free space half a block down from Destry's. "Have a hard time wrapping my brain around that one."

"Don't even try," Iris said. "There's no way you can."

"Dad mentioned something about you being a part of the Blackwell Belles once upon a time."

The spark of light in Iris's eyes died down a bit. She ducked her head to avoid his gaze. "Did he?"

Uh-oh. He might have just stepped in something. "Actually, he reminded me we saw you all perform back in the day."

"Those days were a loooong time ago." She gathered up her bag and shoved open the door. "I'm starved. Someone needs to tell me what's good here."

"Pizza!" Miles shouted as he unbuckled his belt and dived out after her.

Shane got out and helped Ruby Rose from her car seat, held her hand as they circled around the truck to the sidewalk. It had become habit whenever they went anywhere. Ruby Rose had clung to him almost from the instant he'd come home. If he wasn't in sight, she might very well pitch a fit, and in public, that definitely wasn't something he liked to trigger.

"I'm getting a burger," Eric said solemnly as he trudged along behind his brother. "With onion rings. And maybe a milkshake."

"Sounds like you all have as big an appetite as me," Iris said.

"Lead the way, Miles," Shane told his younger nephew, who always appreciated being given even the smallest of tasks. "Time to show off our town to its newest arrival."

The classic country music welcomed them even before the front door came into sight. The closer they got, the stronger the aroma of a smoking grill. Add in that fresh toasty bun and oven-baked pizza and Shane's own appetite increased exponentially. Images of hot, melted cheese and crisp fried potatoes filled his head. He wasn't a bad cook, just a boring one according to his nephews and niece. Steak, check. Potatoes, check. And he could toss a mean salad. But his problem-solving and creative tendencies tended to be limited to the ranch, not the kitchen.

Stepping inside Destry's always felt like coming home. The dark wood decor accented with Western paraphernalia, antique framed photographs and quirky wanted posters featuring the long-time employees and owners added charm and humor. The telltale blasts and bangs from the arcade mingled with the twangy music.

"Twice in one week!" a female voice bellowed from behind the main counter right before her silver-streaked head bobbed into sight.

"Hey, Augie," Shane greeted her as Ruby's hand tightened around his.

"This must be a special occasion, as it's not a Friday. Hello, Holloways." She grabbed menus and winked at the kids. Her eyes widened a bit when she caught sight of Iris. "And guest. Shane? You been holding out on us?"

"This is Iris," Miles announced loudly and drew the attention of a few of the patrons scattered about the spacious restaurant. "She's fixing our grandpa's monstrosity."

"I'm in town to remodel Butch's trailer." Iris waved a hello. "Shane offered to give me a quick tour of the town so I could get my bearings."

"Not many bearings to get in Cottonwood." Augie's husky laugh filled the air. "Welcome, honey. While you're here, you're one of the family. His and ours. Come on. I've got a table for you all back here." She gestured for them to follow.

Shane let Ruby scoot in on their side of the booth first as Iris did the same across from them. Miles shoved Eric out of the way so he could sit next to Iris, not that Eric looked particularly offended. When he sat down, he practically dangled off the edge.

"They've got a great local beer, brewed out on one of the properties on the west side of town," Shane told her. "If you like beer."

"I do like beer, and I love local brews," Iris said as their server arrived with bundled flatware and a container of condiments and napkins. Shane ordered two beers for them and lemonade for Ruby Rose. The little girl carefully unwrapped her napkin and set her silverware into position.

"I'll have a root beer, please. Hold the jerk!" Miles said and earned a confused frown from their server.

"Don't ask," Shane said. "Eric? You want that milkshake?"

"No." Eric grumbled. "Just a Coke."

"So, what's good on the menu, guys?" Iris asked when their server moved off to fill their drink order.

"Honestly?" Shane said. "Everything. Never had a bad meal here."

"I like the pizza," Miles announced as if it was news. His boots banged against the bottom of the seat until Shane shot him a look that made him stop.

"What's the burger your dad likes?" Iris asked Shane as she opened the menu.

"The Bourbon Barrel. It's got a stack of onion rings on it."

"Excellent," Iris said approvingly.

"I'm partial to the Brisket Bomber," Shane said in a way that made him feel like he should maybe reconsider.

"Mmm. Tough choice." Iris perused the menu while their drinks were delivered.

"Do you want your usual, Ruby" Shane asked his niece as she carefully placed her paper straw into her plastic glass.

Ruby nodded. Grilled cheese and tater tots it would be.

"What's a Blackwell Belle?" Miles's question seemed to take all of them by surprise.

"Ah." Iris frowned for a moment, then seemed to catch herself. "It's a performing group my mother and Aunt Dandelion started a long time ago."

"Dandi—" Shane wasn't sure he'd heard her correctly until her lips curved.

"Yep, that was her name. Their parents started the whole flower name thing, and my mother— Flora—picked it up and ran with it. There's Jasmine, me, Magnolia, Violet and Willow."

"Is a willow a—"

"Don't go there," Iris said in an automatic tone that told Shane he wasn't the first to make that observation. "Mom considered the Blackwell Belles a family obligation of sorts, so she made us a second-generation troupe."

"What kind of performing?" It was the first time Eric showed any curiosity about Iris.

"Trick riding mostly." Iris took a healthy drink of her beer. "Wow. You weren't kidding. That is good."

Shane smiled in approval.

"What kind of tricks did you do?" Eric asked. "Like rope tricks and stuff?"

"We did rope tricks, sure. But there was a lot

of acrobatics and stunts, too. Flipping up and over the saddle, riding bareback a lot of the time. We shot arrows and even juggled rings of fire. Batons sometimes. Ever do an extended back-bend while riding a horse? Or dangle off the side of a saddle by one foot?"

"Nuh-uh." Eric's suspicious eyes had shifted to awe. "You can do that?"

"Well, I *could* do it. About a decade ago. We'd perform at rodeos and riding events. We had this one thing, a pyramid where three of us would ride horses and two would stand on our shoulders holding special event flags or sparklers."

"Bet sparklers spooked some of those horses," Shane observed.

"Sometimes," Iris agreed. "And then there was Ferdinand, of course. He was our bull and a bit of a diva when it came to performing."

Shane shook his head and sat back, amused by the wide-eyed wonder on Ruby Rose's face. "I'm afraid to ask, but what does a bull named Ferdinand do in a trick riding show?"

"Anything he wants," Iris retorted. "Seriously, though, he followed direction perfectly. A bit of comic relief at times, but he was a gentle giant. We were quite the hit for a lot of years."

"Why'd you quit?" Eric asked.

"That's none of our business, Eric," Shane said.

Eric didn't look convinced. "Just sounds pretty

awesome to me. Don't know why someone would stop."

"You're right," Iris said slowly. "Some of it was awesome. But it wasn't really what I wanted to do with my life. My mother and Willow, they thrived on performing and love being the center of attention. I'm happier in the background. I liked it for what it was and I enjoyed spending time with my sisters, I guess, but we're all so different from one another. I wanted to do my own thing."

"I can totally relate to that," Shane said and earned a glance of understanding. "That's one reason I started my consultation business. It was different, but kept in line with what the family does."

"I really wanted a career in design," Iris said. "Not architecture per se, just something… impactful. Something that made people happy."

"And so Saddle-Up was born," Shane observed, recalling the logo painted on the side of her trailer. He also might have, before jumping into the shower back at the ranch, done a quick online search just to get the bare basics of Iris's business. "It's good branding."

"Thanks." Iris's smile seemed genuine now. "When the Belles broke up, I got our aunt Dandelion's trick riding saddle. It's acted as inspiration. She was always very encouraging for us to do something we loved."

"Even if it meant leaving the troupe?"

Iris shrugged. "I like to think so. She passed away before things went awry."

"Seems boring to me," Eric grumbled. "Going from riding horses all day to fixing up old stuff."

"That's okay," Iris said with a pointed look at Shane before he could chide his surly nephew. "It probably does sound boring to some people, but me? I like puzzles. I like challenges. And I like turning things that are worn down and almost forgotten into something amazing and useful again. You'll see what I mean," she said, noting Eric's furrowed brow, "when I get done with Cassidy."

"When did you stop riding?" Miles asked.

"I stopped trick riding about twelve years ago." Iris drank more of her beer. "But I still love to ride in general. Don't get much cause to these days. I'm usually working or driving around."

Shane caught a longing in her eyes. "You're welcome to ride any of our horses while you're at the ranch," he offered. "In fact, you'd be doing us a favor, getting them out on the pastures and away from the stable and training pen."

Iris toasted him with her mug. "I might just take you up on that."

"Hey, guys." Shane reached into his back pocket for his wallet. "How about you hit the arcade while we wait for our food?"

"We usually have to wait until after dinner," Miles said and earned yet another elbow from his brother.

"They want to talk without us," Eric whispered loudly enough to be heard. "Come on."

"Ruby? Do you want to go with them?"

Ruby shrugged, nodded and slipped under the table and crawled out to join her brothers.

"Keep an eye on her, please," Shane told the boys, who acknowledged his request with a predictable eye roll. "I'm sorry about the third degree," he said to Iris when they were alone. "I'm still getting used to everything I say being absorbed by those sponge-like ears."

"No harm done," she said, but her mood had definitely dipped. "It's part of who I am, the Belles. Can't get away from it even if I wanted to. My mother started a YouTube channel to upload our performances. And, as they say, the internet is forever."

"Really?" He might have to check out the channel for himself.

"Oh, really. Mom's always been about promotion and fame and…well, that's about it, really." There was no mistaking the bitterness he heard in her tone.

"Doesn't sound like they're happy memories for you."

"Some of them are. We didn't end on the best

of terms. My youngest sister, Willow, she accidentally shot our other sister Maggie in the arm with an arrow during our last performance, and let's just say you can't get the band back together after something like that."

"I imagine not," Shane said. "Was Maggie okay?"

"She was. But that was the beginning of the end for the Belles. And the family, pretty much. We all took off in different directions and haven't looked back."

"That's rough. Losing family's never easy."

"Not as rough as what you all have been through." Compassion flickered across her face. She reached out, touched her hand to his. "I'm sorry about your brother."

"Yeah, thanks." He should have known the conversation would loop around to Wayne and Chelle. "Sometimes it feels like we lost them yesterday, other times it feels like forever." He was still in that phase where when he awoke every morning, for the briefest of moments, he forgot they were gone.

"Do you mind me asking what happened?"

"Freak accident. They'd gone to San Antonio for a second honeymoon over New Year's. Well, technically, it was their first honeymoon. They never got a real one when they married. A driver lost control of his car and hit them as they were crossing the street. I was in Oklahoma at the time helping a ranch pull out of a financial spiral when I got the call. I'd just talked to them the week before, had an earful from Chelle about how I didn't come home for the holidays often enough. She wouldn't hang up until I promised..." he broke off, shook his head. "I promised to come home for Dad's birthday. Guess I kept that promise even though we didn't do much to celebrate." They couldn't fathom doing that in the weeks following the accident. "Wayne had taken over ranch operations right after he and Chelle got married. Dad wanted to take a back seat, let Wayne run with things. I struck out on my own."

"Now you're back and running things."

"I'm trying to." His father wasn't making it easy, though. While Butch wasn't willing to get back on a horse and participate in the management of the ranch, he certainly had his ideas about how Shane was running it.

The brothers, while devoted to each other, had been different in a lot of ways. Most importantly, their ideas for making certain the Holloway Ranch remained viable and sustainable for future generations. Wayne's magic touch when it came to dealing with their father hadn't been an issue. Shane, on the other hand, could say the sky was blue and Butch would argue it was gray.

Shane swallowed the sigh lodged in his throat. "It was the right thing to do. Come back and take over. Dad claimed he wasn't up to it anymore, and the kids…"

"They need you."

"Taking them on the road with me wasn't an option, and, like you, that's where my business keeps me. They were born on the ranch, same as me and Wayne. Same as Dad. It's the only home they've known. They already lost their parents. I wasn't going to turn the rest of their lives upside down by making them nomads. Now I deal with two day school schedules, home schooling, ranch work and keeping the house running." Remembering what she'd said earlier had him flinching. "Sorry. Nothing wrong with being nomads, of course. I loved it and clearly you do, too, but—"

"It's not always great for kids. Believe me," she said quietly. "I understand. And I agree. Are you still doing your consulting business?"

"On the side." Some days he missed it more than others. "I'll get back to it. Eventually. Probably when Ruby Rose graduates high school."

"Not every brother would do what you have," Iris said softly. "Giving up your life to come back home, take care of your family."

"It never occurred to me to do anything else." He hadn't been thrilled about it. How could he be when it meant the reason for coming home was that his brother was gone? "They need me and that's all that matters. We're all still struggling, Eric, especially, it seems. He's so angry. He thinks he's hiding it, but he's more like me than his dad. I can see it. Feel it. It's lurking, simmering, and if I try to talk to him, he just walks away or tells me everything's fine. Miles on the other hand is a complete open book, which also makes him an easy target when it comes to life's ups and downs."

"He does strike me as a bit on the impulsive side," Iris laughed. "And Ruby Rose?"

"She just turned six last month. She knows her parents aren't coming back, but I don't think she's processed the why or what it really means. How can she at that age? She has dreams about them. Sometimes wakes up at night crying. Breaks my heart all over again."

"And then there's your dad."

"And then there's my dad." Shane blew out a small breath. "Butch 'never show emotion or weakness' Holloway. The ironic thing is one of the main reasons I left home was to salvage our relationship. We couldn't be in the same room together for long before we started going at it. Sometimes I think we took opposite sides of an argument just because it was easier than trying to have a normal conversation. When I was on the road, things got easier for both of us. We got more…cordial with one another."

"I get that." Iris pulled her hand back and into her lap. "Sometimes you just have to break away to find out who you really are. What's important to you. And maybe even to appreciate your family."

"I'd give anything to have Wayne and Chelle back," he said. "Not a day goes by that I don't wish for that, but that's not how things go."

"Trust me, when your family is involved it's hard to work around things that have festered for years." The regret in her voice mirrored his own in so many ways. The fact neither of them had any answers to the questions they were left with spoke more loudly than any admission of their remorse. Or even guilt.

"No chance of reconciliation then with your family?"

"You've never met my mother." Iris's smirk conveyed volumes. "Suffice it to say she's never seen me as anything more than a means to an end, if she saw me at all. But that's not important. Let's change the subject, yeah? Or maybe eat?" She glanced over as the server carried a tray of plates their way.

"Sure." He couldn't help but think she'd given him the best out possible. "I'll go find the kids," he said as their dinner was served.

CARVER WITTINGHAM, proprietor of Lone Star Ranch Depot looked, to Iris at least, like a haggard extra from an old TV Western. A prospector maybe. Or a cattle trail cook. Short, stocky, he wore a full beard that matched his gray hair and wrinkled tanned skin that illustrated decades of North Texas sun.

"Butch gave me a heads-up you'd be coming by." Carver's voice was as gravelly as the Holloway driveway. "Welcome to Cottonwood Creek, Ms. Blackwell."

"Call me Iris, please." She took a deep breath, inhaled the familiar scents of fresh-cut wood, even fresher manure and refrigeration coolant. Fall decorations—from makeshift scarecrows to stacked plastic pumpkins, fall-themed banners and yard flag—were everywhere she looked. "And thanks."

The store took up nearly an entire block in the small town and reminded Iris of a certain warehouse store known for carrying everything a human being could need or want and a whole lot more they didn't. Lone Star Ranch Depot was firmly dedicated to ranch and farm life out here in Northern Texas. Oh, there was fresh produce and pantry grocery items lining a multitude of aisles and refrigerators and freezers, but there was also a selection of equipment, supplies, power tools and prefabricated shed kits that came with free delivery. Her remodeling heart was instantly happy.

"I like to touch base with the local stores when I start on a project," Iris told him. "See if they can handle any orders I need to make. I can get most anything online, but I prefer to buy local."

"I sure appreciate that, Iris."

"You say that now," she teased. "I can come up with some pretty unique asks." That was one of the downsides to not coming in with a preconceived design idea until she saw what she was working with.

"Lucky for you, I appreciate a challenge. We're a one-stop shop for people within a two-hundred-mile radius," Carver assured her. "If you don't see it, I can find it somewhere."

"Sounds ideal to me." She checked behind her to where Shane and the boys were checking out a selection of belts and buckles. Ruby Rose stood somewhat away from them, looking occasionally in Iris's direction as she twisted her tiny hands together. "I've got some general ideas for a plan of action, but I'll know more once I get the guts pulled out of the trailer. I tend to work a lot with fiberglass siding for the exterior, but also will be needing fiberglass and spray foam insulation."

"Got plenty in stock," Carver said.

"What about wood? For custom countertops, say?"

Carver's busy brows went up. "Come on back and I'll show you." He waved her behind the counter and through an open doorway. Whatever she'd been expecting to find, it wasn't the Shangri-la of exterior building materials. "Now, of course I've got the brand-new stuff," Carver said. "Pre-varnished or stained and sealed, but I'm guessing you'd think that a shortcut."

"You're guessing correctly," Iris confirmed. "I'll use premade cabinetry work for kitchen and bathrooms, but other than that, I try to give my clients what they're paying for."

"Like I said, I can order anything that strikes your fancy, but come look at this. Bo Perkins over in the next county had new stables built earlier this year, ended up reconfiguring and downsizing his original plans. I bought the surplus off him dirt cheap." He tapped a hand against a thick stack of siding. "Along with a good bunch of the wood from the original building. If you and Butch decide it works for you, I can let you have it at a steep discount. It's just taking up room here."

She checked the dimensions of the metal siding, the amount he had, and did a bend test just to make sure it wasn't substandard. High quality. Would take paint well with that finish. And hold up a good long while. "That might just work." She nodded and tried not to drool over the stack of wood nearby. One thing she'd learned early on was to temper her excitement around any materials that caught her eye. She gestured to the large open panel door leading outside. "What's that?" Even as she moved toward it she could feel her pulse kick up.

"Oh, that there's what we call The Dump. I always tell my customers if they can't use it, leave it with me or I'll haul it. Someone'll be able to find a purpose for it." Carver whipped back a blue tarp. "I keep most everything for at least a year then shift it over to Lubbock for recycling. I've got everything from discarded kitchen cabinets, sinks and shower stalls to wood from old barns and farmhouses around here. Some of it's not in that great of shape but some—"

"Some are diamonds in the rough." She ran her hand along the thick grain and tried to tamp down her excitement. "This is maple, isn't it? They stopped using this type of wood for barn building years ago." Her fingers itched to grab a sander and start restoring. Even if she couldn't convince Butch it would be perfect for his Cassidy, she couldn't let it just rot away. "How much?"

"Hmm, I don't rightly have a price for all this off the top of my head."

Uh-huh. "I bet you can come up with one, though." Oh, the countertops she could make with this beautiful wood.

"Might be I could," Carver hedged. "You, ah, you do a lot of RV remodels then? Enough to make a living on?"

"I do, I make a very good living." She wasn't surprised at the question. She got it often enough. It seemed like unstable work, and being a woman brought in a whole load of other doubts. "I do motor homes, trailers, horse trailers. If it's on wheels, I'll have a go. Even built a couple of tiny houses last year. Having an online channel helps me find customers. I document all my jobs, do instructional videos on everything from wiring to plumbing to engine rebuilding." Not that Cassidy had an engine, but Iris would have to rebuild its hitch and get new tires, and she had her eye already on some fun new custom rims from an online artist. "I have a number of sponsors that help keep me moving around to the next job. Here." She pulled out her cell phone, quickly connected to the store's Wi-Fi and pulled up her website, SaddleUpDesigns.com. She clicked on her teaser promo trailer, a three-minute fast-forward mashup of various projects she'd completed over the years, everything from renovated RVs and campers to Western-themed playground equipment and porch railings. "Take a look."

"Well, I'll be." Carver shook his head as he watched the video. "That's some quality work."

"Thanks." She never met a power tool she didn't

like. "I enjoy what I do, plus it's a good workout," she said, sharing easily. One thing her training as a Belle had given her was superior upper body strength. Hauling her sisters around had been better than any rowing machine in a gym.

"You ever take on, I don't know, smaller projects?"

"Depends." That tingle of anticipation that always accompanied a promising venture worked its way up and down her spine. She'd learned early on, after striking out on her own, to never say no to a job offer. "You have a project in mind?"

"Something special for my wife," Carver said. "She's been asking me since last fall to find her a custom dining room table before Thanksgiving. We've got the whole family coming out this year, and darned if I can find one big enough premade." He eyed Iris as if still carrying a bit of doubt that she could handle a job that large. "If I came up with the materials, how about a trade? Say, supplies for your time?"

"That's a lot of labor, and it'll compete with my work for Butch." Iris did her best to tamp down her excitement. She loved haggling over a new business proposition. "How about…" She scrunched her mouth and pretended to think hard. "You let me come by and fill up my truck from The Dump stash three times and we'll call it a deal."

"Three?" Carver's eyes narrowed. "I wouldn't be surprised if you drive a long-distance eighteen wheeler. I'll agree to two truckloads."

"With a first look agreement on anything new you get in as long as I'm here in Cottonwood Creek," she countered.

"Shrewd." His smile was slow and sly. "All right." He held out his hand and she shook it gladly. "You come back any day next week after ten and have a chat with Edith about the table. She can tell you what she wants. I can't risk getting anything wrong."

Iris locked her hand around Carver's. "You've got a deal."

CHAPTER FOUR

SHANE LED OUTLAW back into his stall and, after giving the eight-year-old Morgan an approving pat and nuzzle for a successful morning work-out, set the bucket of feed within reach and slid the paddock door closed. The chestnut-colored horse had become a favorite of Shane's since he'd come home. Not just because Outlaw had been his brother's horse, but because Outlaw and Shane understood each other. Sometimes it took a while for a horse and rider to get used to one another, but not in this case.

The first time Shane had climbed into the saddle and headed toward the horizon felt a bit like an emotional breakthrough for both of them, sharing their uncertainty and grief about the future as they galloped along.

Shane quickly addressed the half dozen other horses in the stables, filled their feed buckets, offered a handful of carrots to Miss Kitty, Ruby Rose's favorite horse, and made a mental note to send Eric out with apples for all of them after breakfast.

Shane had been up long before the sun, heading out to the west pasture to feed the majority of their cattle that continued to graze. The nearby water levels seemed to be holding steady, so it would be a couple of days before he'd need to move them to the next batch of acreage. The feed he'd dropped would last until this time tomorrow and, with temperatures remaining the same, should make for an easy few days. That didn't mean he didn't have plenty of other work to do. He'd sent Roy and Hank, two of the ranch hands who had stayed on after Wayne's death, to check the fence line on the other side of the property.

They'd headed out well-fed, as Hank's wife was a masterful cook and was always up with her husband. The ranch hands each had a home on the far side of the northern pasture. Barring any issues, he'd have time to get the stalls cleaned, catch up on paperwork and reach out to the usual business folks to make sure they were on track for a full buyout of the stock next spring. Once he locked that into place, he could start looking at how best to expand their herd and hopefully bring their production up the 30 percent Wayne had been banking on.

But first things first. He didn't have to check the clock to know it was just gone seven. He'd spent enough time working ranches that the sun's location told him what time it was. His stomach was growling, and he was definitely looking forward to one of his father's special breakfasts before he drove the kids to their first of a two-day in-person school week.

He had to give his sister-in-law credit; Chelle had been a whiz at keeping the three kids on target with their homework and homeschooling along with getting them into town on Wednesdays and Thursdays for in-person lessons. With fewer than sixty students in the elementary and high school combined, a full week of in-person classes wasn't cost efficient for either the town or families.

But it was necessary to continue to give his niece and nephews the chance to socialize with other kids, which was what Shane reminded himself of when he dreaded making the drive in and out of town twice a week. Something else his father could be helping with, but darned if Shane could get him off the ranch. The closest he'd gotten was that Butch spent a good portion of his days outside with Iris as she worked on Cassidy. He doubted Butch realized how much livelier he'd become since Iris had turned up. Watching—from a distance, of course—the way Iris and his father interacted had lifted a good amount of the worry weighing on his heart.

Shane was about to click off the lights, then stopped himself, tempted to give in to the curiosity that had plagued him since Iris's arrival almost a week ago.

She'd been true to her word, staying under the radar and out from underfoot. He, on the other hand, had been unable to quell his curiosity about both her and the work she did. He'd made it a bit of a habit to check in with her, see what progress she'd made with Cassidy. They'd chatted frequently and each time he'd found himself walking away from their encounters with a smile on his face and a bit of a spring in his step.

She was, for want of a better term, fascinating.

He imagined the groceries she'd picked up after their dinner in town had to be running low by now. He also shouldn't have been surprised that she'd managed to wrangle herself another job given her easy manner with folks. It had become clear Iris was the kind of person who looked at things not only as challenges, but as opportunities. Something he could definitely appreciate.

Yet again, he found himself curious as to the latest developments, not only with Cassidy, but with Iris. To say the thought of her hadn't been lingering in his mind would be a lie. She had definitely moved into the zone of distraction.

Iris Blackwell was the kind of woman who

made a lasting impression. Every conversation he had had resulted in him spending a little more time watching her renovation videos.

The woman not only had talent when it came to seeing the hidden beauty beneath long-forgotten recreational vehicles, but her natural way in front of the camera spoke of her training as a Belle. He found himself grinning like a goofy teenager. Whatever else she thought about her upbringing, it had definitely given her poise and presentation to spare.

He was about to fail in talking himself out of finding an excuse to go to her. He... Oh, heck. He liked spending time with her. He'd told himself it was just that he'd been lacking in female company of late, but, yeah, that wasn't it.

His inclination had everything to do with Iris herself.

He'd just check on her. It would be polite after all this time. He clicked off the overhead light and, tugging the collar of his jacket tighter against his throat, walked around the stables to where her truck and trailer were parked near the no-longer-severely-listing Cassidy.

With an industrial-size jack, she'd wedged a stack of cement blocks under the sagging monstrosity to help with the stabilizing. A heap of trash and discarded innards from the trailer were piled high behind the trailer and, near as he could tell, had been growing by the day. Old windows, what was left of that door and segments of the rotted floor were all included. The scrub down she'd given the exterior, no doubt to check the siding to see if it had held up, had left Cassidy all but glowing in the sun and ready for a fresh coat of paint. In less than a week Iris had already made a marked improvement.

Today was the first morning he hadn't heard her banging around inside Cassidy when he got back from feeding the cattle. The glow of a light from inside of her own trailer had him shaking his head as he knocked gently on her door.

In the few moments it took her to answer, Shane stepped back and cast an appreciative eye on the side of her twenty-eight-and-a-half-foot trailer. The cursive Saddle-Up was painted in a kind of rope font that looped around a dark red saddle decorated with various flowers. "Morning. I didn't wake you, did I?" He tried not to gulp at the sight of her tank top and hip-hugging shorts illustrated with comical, sleepy owls. Her hair was knotted on top of her head and round glasses perched on her nose. She looked like a distracted, sultry librarian. Cosmo poked his nose out and earned a quick pet for a greeting. "Hey, boy."

"Nah. The interior's been gutted and all cleaned out. It's now ready for installation, so I'm spending today mapping out the electrical wiring for Cassidy." She stepped back, waved him in. "Got an early start. I'm on my second pot of coffee, if you want some?"

He stomped his boots before stepping up, removed his hat so it wasn't knocked off his head when he ducked inside. The trailer was instantly warm, immediately comfortable and incredibly impressive. Cosmo circled around him once, gave him a good sniff, then immediately went to his oversize fluffy bed wedged against one wall of the trailer.

"I was just headed in for breakfast." But that didn't mean the aroma coming from her machine wasn't enticing him. "But, sure. I'll take a cup."

"Would you like the grand tour? You don't have to move to take it," she teased.

"Yeah." He was already awed. There wasn't an inch of space that hadn't been put to practical use. She'd used a selection of muted earth tones with splashes of greens and blues to balance out the brown, tan and gray. Behind him sat a double bed on which a swirling circular patterned bedspread was stretched to wrinkle-free perfection.

"So, bed." She pointed behind him. "Obviously. Those two cabinets on either side? Clothes closets. And the bed lifts up. That's where I keep my shoes and other outdoor equipment. All my tools and equipment are stashed in the compartments with outside access."

"Nice." He looked down. "Hardwood floor?"

"Laminate. It's lighter weight. I debated on that, actually. The laminate can get dented more easily, but it was easier to install. Plus, it was a new product I was curious about. Over here in the kitchen." She did a Vanna White move with her arms that had his mouth curving. "My favorite part of the renovation. I've got butcher block countertop. That way I don't need cutting boards when I cook." She indicated the commercial-grade organized knife magnet attached to the sink side of one of the cabinets.

"You cook?" He hadn't meant to sound so shocked.

"Cooking's cheaper than eating out. I'm self-taught, but not half bad." She laid a hand on the double stainless steel sink. "I've got a two-burner propane stove and oven, microwave and an eight-cubic-foot refrigerator. The latter runs either off solar power or, since I'm plugged in regular amp wattage, with electrical." She reached behind her, pulled on a handle and revealed a roll-out pantry stuffed to the gills. "I can get two, maybe three weeks of food stashed in here. And this…" She spun around and lifted the table off its pedestal. "I made a kind of banquette, if I had an overnight guest, turns into a bed. Just push this back." She lowered the table into a space under a long narrow window. "And voila. I typically leave the table up, though, for extra work space. TV's there." She pointed over his head. "It's on a swivel so I can watch it from anywhere. Hooks into Wi-Fi I can run through the solar system. Full bathroom with a standard shower stall in the corner. Couldn't figure out a way to fit in a soaking tub, but I haven't given up completely on that dream. And I've got an office right in this area here." She stepped toward the fridge and popped open an accordion door which exposed a narrow office space that consisted of a built-in desk, large computer monitor, laptop and a comfy looking chair. "That's my design studio. Oh, that reminds me." She snapped her fingers and ducked inside to pull out a plastic case from its cubby. "I've got some videos to make today. Updates after the preliminary 'here we go' video release."

"This is amazing." He pointed to the dedicated display space above her bed. The plexiglass case was attached to the wall and displayed a shiny, polished mahogany embossed saddle. "Your aunt Dandelion's saddle?"

"That's it." She looked at it with affection. "I keep it in plain sight for continued inspiration and to remind myself I'm following my bliss."

"You must miss her."

"I do." Iris's smile was quick. "That saddle has come to mean a lot to me for a number of reasons. Which is why it has a place of honor in my home."

"A home you did all the work in yourself." He didn't mean to sound as dismayed as he did.

"Thank you."

He blinked, frowned. "For what?"

"For not sounding surprised." The affection and appreciation he saw on her face warmed him from inside.

"I'm not. I haven't spent a lot of time with you." He didn't know why he felt compelled to explain. "But you have more than proven your skill and talent at this." He accepted the coffee she handed him. "So, you're an early bird, too." He sat in one of the cushioned seats he immediately noticed was memory foam. Comfy. Cosmo scooted forward on his stomach, knocked his head against Shane's leg. Shane reached down to provide another pet.

"I can sleep maybe four, five hours before I get antsy. Always been that way. Drove my sisters nuts, but I'm guessing it comes from spending so much time on ranches growing up. Someone was always working around us." She sipped her own coffee, walked past him to one of the closets by the bed. "I'm just going to get dressed while we chat." She pulled out a pair of jeans and a dark

T-shirt. "How about Butch? He get up with the chickens?"

"He used to," Shane confirmed. "Before his heart attack."

"Oh." She held her clothes against her chest and faced him. "I wondered about that. He mentioned something about being in the hospital. When was this?"

"Back in April. Doctor said it wasn't a massive one. Could have been. We caught it in time and got him to the hospital in Claxton."

"That's…" She frowned. "I passed Claxton on my way here. That's like fifty miles south, isn't it?"

"About." He drank more coffee, had to admit it was a lot better than his. Must be the fancy machine she had on that countertop of hers. "When I called the medical clinic in town they said to give him some aspirin and take him straight in. They gave him a stent, put him on the right meds and said he could get back to work." He shook his head. "He hasn't been interested, though. Other than an occasional ride, he's kept himself in the house mostly."

"Depression after a heart event is very common," she said.

"And it was right on the heels of losing Wayne and Chelle. No doubt the two are connected." He'd spoken to his father's doctor about how to address Butch's less than enthusiastic attitude about life, but the answer was always the same. It was up to Butch to change things. Wayne might have been able to get through to him, but Shane couldn't force it. "I feel like I owe you an apology. I wasn't exactly happy when you first showed up."

"Do tell." She scooted past him again, went into the tan and cream-colored bathroom and drew the door half-shut. "I kinda picked up on that."

"Yeah." He wasn't the best at making a good first impression. He focused on keeping his eyes averted from the back of the trailer. "I was wrong to be suspicious."

"Worried I was here to run some kind of con on your unsuspecting father?"

Shane grimaced. "You might be the only person to ever call him that in his entire life. But, yeah. The thought occurred."

"Good," she called. "That means you care."

And with that comment, his unease faded. "Seeing and hearing him talk since you've gotten here, seeing him excited about the work you're doing on Cassidy, it's the most animated and interested I've seen him in months." He hesitated. "Not that you're here to be some kind of babysitter or entertainment."

"I didn't take it that way," she said.

He hoped so. Still… "I'm afraid what it does probably mean is that he's going to continue to be involved in whatever you do."

"He has his say." She stuck her head out, beamed at him. "I bring him out every evening when I'm finished, show him what I've done, make sure what I plan to do next is still okay with him."

"People change their minds?"

"All the time!" Iris exclaimed as if it both annoyed and excited her. "And there are always little jobs I can have him do if he's so inclined, but so far he's been pretty hands-off." She leaned back enough to grin at him. "I'll draw the line with welding equipment, though. In case you were worried."

Oddly, he wasn't anymore. "Be careful what you wish for," he said under his breath. "He might just take you up on it."

"I'm always careful with my wishes." When she emerged, she'd donned those clingy jeans and smart T-shirt and was dragging a brush through her long blond hair. "Is that what you wanted to talk to me about this morning? To make sure your dad wasn't driving me to distraction?"

"Ah, actually." He embraced the impulse, something he seemed to be doing a lot where Iris was concerned. "I thought maybe you'd like a home-cooked meal for a change. Cooked by someone else, I mean." How was it possible he was bungling this? "Dad's probably got something on the stove by now and the kids'll be getting up and ready. It's a school day. It'll be chaotic so I'll understand if you'd rather not—"

"I thrive on chaos, and I'd love to have breakfast with you all." She shoved her bare feet into a pair of sturdy sneakers. "Give me two minutes to brush my teeth and we'll get going."

THE SOUNDS OF pounding footsteps, raised voices and slamming doors greeted Iris as she followed Shane in the front door of the house. She could smell bacon cooking and coffee brewing and a bit of muttering and stomping down the hall. Clearly Cosmo could smell breakfast as well, since he tootled straight down the hall and disappeared around the corner. She could hear Butch's enthusiastic welcome over the din of shouting.

"Give it back!"

Iris looked up the staircase to where Miles yelled and pounded on a door. "Eric, it's my turn in the bathroom!"

"I just love how they prove me right." Shane's sheepish grin was tempered by an affection that Iris suspected he wasn't aware he displayed. "Guys, settle down!" He hung his hat on the hook by the door, shrugged out of his thick denim jacket. "Hurry down for breakfast. We're leaving in forty-five minutes. And we have a guest."

Miles leaned over the second-story banister and scowled down at them. "Eric won't come out of the bathroom and I have to goooo!"

"Then use the bathroom in my room," Shane called up after him.

"I can't cuz Ruby Rose is in there, and she's crying and won't come out," Miles practically wailed.

"Of course, she won't." Shane's expression faltered. "Like I said, chaos. Just follow Cosmo to the kitchen." He pointed down the hallway. "Help yourself to more coffee if you'd like."

"I will do just that, thanks." Coffee was, after all, Iris's main source of hydration until noon.

She took her time, appreciating the collection of family photographs arranged on the walls, the cozy, homey touches like a cross-stitched sampler stating that a messy home is a happy home. As the noise continued upstairs, she looked at the various images of the kids as they'd grown, from babyhood to today. The family photographs of them with their parents, who were represented with pictures from their wedding and various family celebrations, made her heart clang in sympathy. She touched a finger to the frame showing them beaming at each other, rays of sun spilling down on them, and she could almost hear them laughing.

"They were happy." Butch's voice caught Iris's attention. She turned her head, saw the grief before he covered it up. "It's the one thing I'm grateful for. That Wayne and Chelle were happy together right to the end."

Iris nodded, throat tight with emotion.

"Come on in and have some coffee." Butch rolled his eyes to the staircase as the sentimental moment broke against the sound of slamming doors. "That'll probably take a while."

The sage green paint on the walls complimented the yellow exterior of the house and continued from the hall and living areas into the kitchen. A continuation of decor that could have come across as overwhelming but instead cast the entire residence in a comforting, welcoming atmosphere. She'd had her share of conversations with Butch and Shane, but those had been on her turf, not theirs and she had to admit, her curiosity about their home had increased. She just hadn't wanted to intrude or overstep.

She'd gotten used to and had begun looking forward to Shane's "just checking in" stop ins. His easygoing manner and apparent interest in her work made for both a nice break in the day and a boost to her rarely sagging confidence.

Now, as she got a good look at Butch and Shane's

home, new decorating ideas started swirling through her mind where Cassidy was concerned.

"I hear your family's lived on this land for quite a long time," Iris said as she joined Butch in the kitchen. A kitchen that was an interesting blend of old-school cast iron practicality and modern appliances. Butch moved around effortlessly enough as he set a plate of crispy bacon and fried eggs on the table.

"When I was born, this was only one story with one bedroom," Butch said. "My father started the renovation on my thirteenth birthday." Pride coated his words. "Said I was finally able to help him do what he wanted to do with the place."

"So you helped to add the second story?"

"Second story, mudroom and the added suite on the other side of the living room. Took us about a decade all said, but it paid off in spades. My mother might not have agreed, though. Wayne got the ball rolling on the main floor extension, added in a bedroom suite for me and an extra guest room and bath."

Building a home, over generations, over decades, while a completely foreign concept, also held appeal to Iris who, growing up, had always longed for a place with roots to live in. A home base. Someplace to come back to.

Oh, they'd rented homes, of course. But it was always someone else's house and they were always moving on. It took her until she was thirteen before she'd accepted it wasn't going to happen. It was easier to give in to that fact than keep hoping things would change. Now she took her home with her everywhere she went.

The polished hardwood floors, white baseboards and crown molding added an architectural interest to the Holloway house she didn't see often in homes of this age. Someone, Butch's father, Butch himself and clearly Wayne and his wife, had taken very good care of this place. It would be a wonderful legacy to pass on to Eric, Miles and Ruby Rose.

"Do you all eat like this every day?" Iris asked as she took over buttering the half dozen slices of toast sitting on the counter.

"School days, yes," Butch admitted. "It's one thing I can help with without an argument. My wife was an excellent cook. As was my daughter-in-law. I learned a few tricks from them."

"How about your boys?" Iris asked as she accepted a mug of coffee from Shane's father.

"Neither was ever going to starve," Butch said. "Shane's got more talent on the grill than Wayne did. That older boy of mine was a fire hazard on that front. Nearly set one of the barns on fire using lighter fluid on the charcoal."

The affection she heard in his voice sounded stronger than the grief, although that was there as well. "If you have some time today, I'd like to finalize the plans for the interior. You were still trying to decide how many you want the trailer to sleep, last we talked. I'd like to know what I'm working with before I finish mapping out the electrical."

"We can do that," Butch said.

She carried the plate of toast to the table, and Butch pointed to a chair for her to sit. "I'm also interested in what you and your wife used to do when you all went out on the road."

"Took my honeymoon in it, as a matter of fact," Butch said as if he just remembered the detail. Another trip to the counter had him retrieving a bowl of tater tots. Footsteps pounded down the stairs. "I've got some photographs of that trip, I think. And of the boys growing up. I can dig those out if you're interested."

"I'm definitely interested." One aspect of her design style that she always prided herself on was the personal touch. "As soon as we're good with the plans, I can head in and talk with Carver about special orders. Plus, I get to see what he's got in The Dump that we can use."

Butch didn't look impressed. "You really think there's treasure there?"

"Oh, I know there is." She held her mug to her lips and smiled at his dubious expression.

"I've even got my eye on some amazing maple that would be great for somebody's countertops."

"PaPa, Eric still won't come out of the bathroom and Uncle Shane's is locked. Can I use yours?" Miles speed raced into the kitchen and nearly bashed face first into Butch.

"Go on," Butch approved. "What do you say to Miss Blackwell?"

"Oh. Hi, Iris!" Miles shot her one of his cheeky grins and waved. "Sorry! I gotta go!" He raced out again.

"Iris is fine," she told Butch at his disapproving frown. "Miss Blackwell makes me look around for my mother." And that was something she definitely didn't want.

"Flora Blackwell." Butch clicked his tongue and shook his head. "There's a woman who commanded attention. I remember her as something of a firecracker."

"An apt description if ever I heard one." Iris arched a brow and silently wished she hadn't said anything. "Shane mentioned you guys saw us perform back in the day."

"Oh, we did more than see you perform." Butch took a seat at the head of the large dining table and scooped two eggs onto his plate. "Your mother and my Jesse were friends. Off and on, mind you, over the years, but anytime you all came through this way for a show they made it a point to get together."

Iris frowned. Strange. As far as she knew, her mother didn't have many friends outside the show circuit. "Really?"

"Sure. She and your dad stayed here a couple of times when they were traveling around. Barlow and me go back, too. When I went on buying trips, odds were I'd run into Big E. I bought a couple of our horses from his sister Denny once upon a time. Still have a couple of them, actually. She's your grandmother, isn't she?"

"She is indeed." Something uneasy shifted inside of her. She'd worked hard separating herself from the Belles and Flora and...well, all the Blackwells, really. She didn't particularly like her two worlds colliding.

Whatever else she might have said faded at the sight of Shane entering the kitchen, holding a still crying Ruby Rose in his arms. She had her head on his shoulder and her left hand was clutched in a tight fist.

"Hey, now? What's all the sniffling about?" Butch pushed to his feet and laid a hand on his granddaughter's back. "Ruby Rose, what's got you upset?"

"It broke." The sob of despair scraped against Iris's heart. "Eric broked it."

"What broke?" Butch asked Shane.

"Her bracelet." Something in Shane's voice had Iris realizing this wasn't just any bracelet. "I told her we can try to fix it."

"It won't be the same," Ruby Rose cried. "It's all Eric's fault!"

"How so?" Butch continued to rub her back, then caught her against him when she dived out of her uncle's arms.

"He grabbed my arm." Two fat tears plopped onto Ruby Rose's chubby cheeks. "They went everywhere and I couldn't get them all!"

"I think that might be why Eric's hiding in the bathroom," Shane explained before he headed back upstairs.

"Well, now, we can fix your bracelet, munchkin, don't worry." Butch sat back down and held her close. "Let's see what's in your hand."

Iris watched as Ruby opened her hand. The broken string hung loosely amidst a small smattering of beads, some of which had spelled out her name.

"They're all gone." She was crying harder now and was more difficult to understand. "I heard them fall on the floor and I couldn't find them."

Iris winced. The heating vents had probably gobbled up the beads.

"Ruby Rose—" Butch tried again.

"I made this with Mama," Ruby Rose wailed and cut him off. "I made this with Mama before she went away and now it's broken forever and I can't have it anymore."

"Oh." Iris swallowed the sudden emotion in her throat.

"It'll be okay, baby girl." Butch carefully shifted the beads and string to the table before he tightened his hold on her. "We'll make you another bracelet."

"I don't want another bracelet! I want Mama's bracelet. I want Mama!"

Iris blinked as Shane returned, holding Eric by the shoulder as he steered the older boy to the table. Miles came up behind them and slunk into the chair beside Iris.

"What do you have to say to your sister, Eric?" Shane prodded.

The boy's jaw tensed, and Iris could see by the way his eyes were narrowing that he was angry. No doubt this is what Shane had been talking about the other night at dinner.

"She was looking through my stuff," Eric said. "She wouldn't get out of my room. I asked her nicely. I wanted her to leave but she wouldn't."

"That doesn't give you the right to put your hands on her," Shane said. "Or to break something that means a great deal to her. In this family, we don't strike out when we don't get our way, understood?"

"Yes, sir," Eric grumbled.

"Ruby Rose?" Shane addressed his niece, who turned her tear-stained face up at him. "You went into Eric's room without permission."

"Yes," she whispered. "I wanted to see the picture."

Iris waited for someone to ask what picture, but the way Shane's face lost some of its color told her everyone else already knew.

Iris saw the shock on Eric's face before he looked up at his uncle. "I didn't know."

"You didn't ask." Ruby Rose scrubbed her hands on her cheeks. "You just said get out and grabbed me."

"I'm sorry," Eric whispered. "I…" He turned and ran out of the room and back up the stairs.

"I just wanted to see Mama and Daddy again," Ruby hiccupped as she slid out of Butch's lap. "From our picnic day. Eric has a picture and I don't."

Shane crouched and took hold of Ruby Rose's hands. The compassion on his face, compassion he was trying so hard to temper with sternness, sank through Iris and straight into her heart.

"We don't go into each other's rooms without permission, Ruby Rose. You know that." He touched a hand to her face. "Next time ask when you want to see something he has that you don't."

"It's okay." Eric returned and held out a small framed photograph. "She can have it." His lower lip trembled. "I shouldn't have grabbed your wrist, Ruby Rose. I'm sorry I broke your bracelet."

Ruby Rose accepted the picture, stared down at it for a moment before she clutched it against her chest. "Mama." Her broken whisper had Iris covering her mouth and looking away.

"Maybe we can keep the picture here, in the kitchen for a while," Shane said after he cleared his throat. "So we can all see it whenever we want to, yeah?"

Ruby Rose kissed the picture before she handed it over, then shocked everyone by throwing her arms around her brother. "I'm sorry, Eric. Don't be mad at me anymore."

"Okay." Eric awkwardly patted her on the back, much the way Butch had moments before. The little boy looked absolutely lost and miserable.

"Can we eat now?" Miles demanded with a heavy sigh. "I'm starving!"

"I think that sounds like a good idea." Shane set down the picture of his brother, sister-in-law and the three children all huddled together beneath a massive tree by the bank of a lake. "Thank you, Eric," he said quietly when Eric walked past him. "That was very kind of you."

"Yeah, well." Eric shrugged and sank into a chair across from Iris, while Ruby Rose climbed into hers.

Through a film of tears, Iris looked down at the abandoned beads and string before she carefully scooped them into her hand. "Do you have a small bag or container?" she asked Shane under her breath when she moved around the table.

"Yeah." He retrieved a sandwich baggie from a nearby drawer. "I guess I'll go on a bead hunt later today."

She set the now filled baggie beside the picture. "I'll help."

CHAPTER FIVE

MUCKING OUT THE horse stalls wasn't on the top of Shane's list of favorite things to do when he got back from dropping off the kids in town. Normally on school days it could wait until Eric got home, but after the morning he'd had with Ruby Rose and her bracelet and the way his father had disappeared into his bedroom after breakfast, Shane found the activity was doing wonders for burning off conflicting emotions and a truckload of frustration.

As he stabbed the hay and pitched it around the stall, he couldn't help but think that maybe they'd all been walking on some weird kind of eggshells around one another since Wayne and Chelle had died. After almost a year, finally, this morning, perhaps because of the emotional upheaval the bracelet incident caused, it felt as if the bubble of grief had burst. Maybe, just maybe, they'd turned some kind of corner.

The pain, the heartache, all of it had felt so real and normal instead of being buried in a foggy haze.

"Normal," he muttered. As if he had any concept of what that meant anymore.

"You digging for buried treasure in there?"

Shane looked over his shoulder and found Iris leaning against the stall door, arms folded across her chest, casting what he interpreted as an appraising look in his direction. He wondered if she had any idea how pretty she was, how perfectly she fit into whatever scene she stepped into. Until he'd met Iris Blackwell, he hadn't realized how heavy his heart felt at times. Now, when he saw her, it lightened like a holiday balloon.

"More like getting my aggressions out," he said as he did one final sweep. "It was a morning and a half."

"You handled it well," she said.

"Didn't know what else to do," he admitted. "Actually, that's not true. I just try to ask myself how Wayne would have handled it. He's my parental guiding star."

"Not Butch?" she teased.

"No," he said with a bit more finality than intended. "Not Butch. Although my father has developed real patience and understanding now that he's a grandfather." He certainly hadn't had a lot of it while he and Wayne had been growing up. He'd spent a fair amount of his early years waiting to be told what he'd done wrong, or how it was different from what was expected.

"Grandparents get that privilege of do-overs," she agreed. "They tend to try to make up for the mistakes they made the first time around."

Yeah, Shane hoped that was the case with Butch. "You taking a break from your electrical map?"

"Butch didn't seem in the right frame of mind after all, so I'm pushing things out a day." She looked back at the clock. "His heart wasn't really in it, and I think he's still trying to make up his mind about a few things, so I called it off. I told him I had plenty of other stuff to do in the meantime."

"I'm sorry he's messing with your schedule."

"I build in buffer days. Sometimes delays hit because of overdue orders, other times it's grieving fathers still trying to cope with losing their sons."

It unnerved him, how easily she understood their family dynamics.

"He did find me a box of old photo albums for me to look through," Iris said. "Pictures of Cassidy from when he and your mom first got her. I'll go through those and come back to him tomorrow."

"Yeah?"

"Yeah." Her smile seemed more tempered. "Also, in the meantime, I thought maybe we could go on that bead hunt."

"Right." He stabbed the pitchfork into the hay and rested a gloved hand on the handle. "I looked around upstairs. I found a few, but I think most of them—"

"Fell down the heating grate?" She sighed. "I kinda figured. I've got an idea that might help."

"Okay." He'd do just about anything to put a smile back on Ruby Rose's face. She'd still been a bit sobby when he'd dropped her off and frequently looked forlornly down at her bare wrist.

Iris held out her hand. "Come with me." With the sun streaming in behind her, she looked like a visiting angel.

He moved before he thought better of it. There was something about Iris that transfixed him, hypnotized him. Had since she'd first arrived on the ranch. She could have asked him to walk off the edge of the world and he'd probably have gone willingly, if only to be able to touch her.

He tugged off his gloves, shoved them into his pockets and grasped her hand gently, tried to ignore the shiver of attraction that raced from his fingertips all the way to his spine. She led him out the side door, to her own RV. Once inside, he spotted the box of photographs she'd mentioned, stashed safely beside her bed. On the dining table, however, was a collection of various plastic boxes.

"I dug these out of my storage spot earlier,"

she said. "I…" She seemed to struggle for the words. "I kept some of my costumes and things, from the Belles' performing days." She clicked open one of the boxes, turned it to face him. "We all learned to sew pretty early on. Rhinestones, sequins, baubles and beads. The Belles should have bought stock in craft supply companies," she added on a laugh. "I thought we could reconstruct Ruby Rose's bracelet before she gets home. Or at least come up with something that heals her heart a little."

He stared down at the box and felt his chest tighten. "That might just be the nicest thing anyone's ever offered to do for us."

"Well, that sounds a bit sad," she teased in a clear attempt to lighten the mood. "It's just a bracelet, Shane."

"It's not, though," he said quietly and picked up a bright pink bead. "It was the last thing she made with her mother, and in Ruby's mind she'd have it forever. I keep telling myself it would have broken eventually."

"Probably. But Eric rose to the occasion and tried to make things right. You nailed it, though," Iris said. "He's struggling."

"I do know." He sat down at the far side of the table. "I just don't know what to do about him. I'm not sure if I should…or… Maybe let's tackle

one problem at a time, okay? I'll go get the bag
with the—"

"I already did." Iris pulled it out of her pocket
and set it on the table. "You saw her bracelet
more than I did, so you choose what to include.
I've got a marker we can use to make letters on
some of these square ones, since I don't have
any alphabet ones to match the kind that spelled
out her name." She lowered herself into the seat
across from him. Their knees bumped when she
shifted.

"This will work just fine." He couldn't stop
himself. He reached out, caught her hand and
threaded their fingers together. "Thank you. It's
nice. Has been nice, having someone around to
talk to who's not related. I know it's not what you
signed up for when you came out here."

"I live for the unexpected." Her voice was
quiet, a bit dazed. "Ruby Rose reminded me of
something I lost a long time ago. To my sister,
J.R. Funny enough, it was a bracelet." She rubbed
her thumb across the pulse in his wrist. "I'd forgotten, or maybe I'd made myself forget. Aunt
Dandelion had this sterling silver charm bracelet she'd been adding to for years, ever since she
was a little girl. Tiny items, a miniature saddle,
a drum, a flag. Things that represented special
accomplishments by the Belles, or even personal
events. Flowers, of course." She laughed. "I'd

spend hours when I was little, just going through those charms and playing with that bracelet. It... I don't know." She frowned, as if trying to figure it out. "It felt like I was looking at her life, one charm at a time. When the Belles broke up, it happened so fast. We each took something, impulsively maybe, and just went off on our own, grabbing whatever had occurred to us."

"Like you taking the saddle," Shane said.

She nodded. "Like me taking the saddle. Or Violet taking Ferdinand. Although that made some sense, since she'd have been the one to be able to stable him. J.R. took the bracelet. That bracelet." She touched her other hand to her heart. "If someone had broken it, especially one of my sisters, I can imagine that's a wound that would have taken a very long time to heal."

"Even without it being broken," Shane said. "It seems to me as if someone else having it hurts you." He didn't like the idea of anyone, especially her sisters, causing her pain.

"Mmm." She nodded and pressed her lips into a tight line. "Probably why Ruby Rose losing hers struck so hard. I'm fixing something of hers that can't be fixed for me. It'll have to do, yeah?"

"Yeah," he said and lifted her hand to his mouth, pressed his lips against her knuckles. He felt it, her hitch of breath, the sudden trembling in her hand before she squeezed his fingers. "We'll make sure it does."

"Ruby Rose?" Shane knocked a knuckle against his niece's bedroom door and pushed it all the way open. "You ready for bed?"

"Yes." She was sitting on the edge of her bed, wearing her favorite pink rabbit nightgown, looking out her bedroom window at the old oak tree and its leaves rustling in the autumn wind. The night was so black that he could see the bedroom reflecting in the glass.

"Would you like me to read you a story?" It was a question he'd asked nearly every night since he'd moved back home. She had yet to say yes.

"No, thank you."

Her continued politeness concerned him. He kept waiting for the bombastic, energetic little girl he remembered from his last visit before the accident to emerge out of the cocoon she'd wrapped herself in. He'd read countless online articles and websites about helping children cope with grief and the loss of their parents, but everything he'd tried hadn't seemed to make a difference. He hadn't pushed, deciding that waiting was the only way to really move forward. They'd maneuvered through their grief in their own time and some days were better than others. Except it had been almost a year, and apart from the bracelet incident, he hadn't seen any more progress, either with Ruby Rose or Eric.

"I have something for you." He crouched beside her, pulled out the triple reinforced bracelet Iris had helped him construct. Well, she'd constructed it. He'd only picked out the beads. "Miss Iris and I tried to find as many beads from your original one as we could." He dangled the elasticized bracelet from a finger. "We know it isn't the one you made with your mama, but it can be a memory of that one. If you'd like to have it."

Ruby's eyes widened. She looked at the bracelet, then at him, then back at the beads.

"It's stronger than your other one. And see this here?" He rotated the bracelet to show her the latch. "Iris said we can make it bigger when you need it to be. We just have to add a couple of loops. She showed me how."

"It's pretty," Ruby whispered. She tucked a springy curl behind her ear before she held out her arm. "It looks too big."

"Well, let's see, shall we?" He gently snapped it on and tugged on the threads the way Iris had taught him. "There." He took Ruby's hand, turned it over so her name showed. "What do you think?"

"I like it." Her smile was timid. "Thank you, Uncle Shane."

"You're welcome, sweetheart." He touched a hand to her head. "That doesn't mean you have to stop feeling sad. I know losing your bracelet hurt your feelings."

She sighed and shrugged just as Eric did, Shane noticed.

"And it's okay to still be sad about your mom and dad. I am. I miss them a lot." He cleared his throat. "Every single day."

"You do?" Ruby looked surprised at this information.

"I do. Sometimes I'm so sad about it I just want to be by myself and be angry and wonder why it happened."

"I do that," she whispered.

"I know. But you know what else you can do when you feel sad? You can come talk to me about it. Or to PaPa."

"Eric said not to bother you." The confusion in her eyes clearly said she'd been trying to follow her older brother's wishes. "He said we should be very strong and careful not to make you angry or upset in case you sent us away. But we don't want to go anywhere, Uncle Shane. We like it here and don't want to live anyplace else."

"Of course, you don't." Shane got up and walked around to sit on the bed beside her. Where on earth had this come from? Where did Eric get the idea…? "Sweetheart, you never have to be scared to talk to me about anything. I came home to be with you guys. You're my family. You always have been, even when I didn't live here."

"Eric said we're just an…ana…bligation."

"A…" His mind raced for a moment. "An obligation? Is that what he said?" He wrapped an arm around her shoulders and gave her a gentle squeeze, his heart breaking at his nephew's accusation and misunderstanding. "Technically, I guess that's true, but that doesn't mean it's a bad thing. You three, well, four with PaPa, you're the best obligation I could ever ask for. Your mom and dad, they trusted me to take care of the most important things in their life and that's you. You all are the greatest gift I've ever been given. Why would I want to give you all away?"

She leaned against him, played with her bracelet as she snuggled closer. "I don't know."

"Okay, let's clear this up right now, then." He leaned down, pressed his lips to the top of her head and squeezed his eyes shut until he saw stars. "We're family, Ruby Rose. All of us together, in this house, we have to rely on one another and trust each other. I love you and I plan on keeping you with me for as long as you want to be here. I'm sorry if you didn't think that was the case."

"That's what Miles said," Ruby confirmed. "He said Eric was being dumb."

"You know we don't like to use that word

around here," Shane chided, but let it go at that. "I'm glad to know Miles didn't agree with Eric, though."

"Are you mad Eric said those things?"

"No," Shane shook his head, his thoughts racing in an entirely different direction now. "No, I'm not mad." But it was past time for him to have a long, serious talk with his nephew. Man to boy. "So, we're agreed? If anything ever is bothering you or making you sad, you'll come to me or PaPa?"

"Okay." She reached up and locked her tiny arms around his neck, squeezed so hard he almost lost his breath. "I love you, Uncle Shane. Thank you for not sending us away."

"I love you too, baby girl." He held her for a long time, rocking her back and forth, taking comfort in the knowledge that he'd been trusted with this special task. "I love you, too."

"Uncle Shane?" There was something different in her tone now, something…softer. Unexpected. Hopeful?

"Yes?"

"I know you said we can't get another dog."

"I'm working up to it," he assured her. With all the chaos over the past few months and trying to get his footing with this new life, adding a new dog to the mix just seemed like one thing too many. That said, Cosmo certainly had made an impression. And was a clear example of how effortless a new dog would probably be. It was just a matter of time before he gave in.

"Mama was going to get us chickens. Real chickens. Not like Oscar." She pointed to the maligned and well-loved stuffed chicken resting against her pillow. "She said I could help her with them." Ruby Rose sat back and blinked those dark, hope-filled eyes at him. "Can we maybe get a couple? I'll take care of them, I promise."

"Chickens, huh?" That explained the half-built pen out by the barn. "That is definitely something to consider. I'll think about it, okay?"

"You promise?" She didn't look convinced.

"I promise," he assured her with a smile.

CHAPTER SIX

"OKAY, BUTCH. Today is decision day." She didn't like using her stern voice, but she was out of time. "I need to get my orders in pronto so I have something to work with next week." She'd ended up giving the older man a couple of days to come around. With part of the job coming to a standstill, she'd spent the time sanding and refinishing the four kitchen cabinets she'd found at The Dump during her last trip into town. She'd also replaced the hinges and cut them down a bit to fit into the smaller space. It was time well spent, but she was anxious to get back on track.

Seated next to Butch at the Holloway kitchen table, Iris shifted her laptop so he could see the screen more clearly as she clicked through the animation. "So, option number one for sleeping arrangements." The illustrated Murphy bed lifted and lowered. "This is a bit like my trailer. Flipping up the double bed here can allow for room for a low back sofa underneath it." To be honest, option one wasn't her favorite for Cassidy's layout. It would be practical enough, but not as utilitarian as the newer ideas she'd come up with.

"That's clever," Butch said as he peered closer at the computer screen. His approval, however, was part of the problem. He liked things well enough to start with, but then, after he'd had time to think, he changed his mind.

Change was hard, she reminded herself. Already the trailer looked nothing like the one he used to use. The renovation was messing with Butch's past, a past he was clinging to perhaps a bit too tightly.

She reached down, sank her hand into Cosmo's thick fur to anchor herself once more in the here and now.

Part of her hadn't minded the extra planning work. Focusing on her project kept her from falling under the spell of Shane's family life. She was seeing long-forgotten dreams playing out all around her—how he was with his nephews and niece, how dedicated he was to the ranch and his father, even when they butted heads. There was something incredibly tempting about life on the Holloway Ranch and about Shane Holloway in particular, but she refused to let herself get too comfortable. Or attached.

The sooner she finished this job, the sooner she moved on, the better for all of them.

She'd long given up any hope of a normal, root-bound life. It simply wasn't the Blackwell way, at least on her branch of the family tree. No more breakfasts, no more dinners in town. She wasn't going to be here for long. She didn't need any-one—the kids, Butch, especially Shane—getting used to her presence. And she especially didn't need to feed her growing romantic fantasies about the single dad with the devastating twinkle-eye smile who made her hope for the impossible.

The back-and-forth with Butch had given Iris some insight into what Shane dealt with on a daily basis where his father was concerned. It was obvious the older man was struggling, just as they all were, but he wasn't a lost cause. Not by a long shot.

"And this here?" Butch pointed to the still-to-be-determined area she'd mapped out across from the kitchen.

Eric, who was trying hard not to look as if he was interested in their conversation, kept glanc-ing up from his science homework that he'd been noodling over for the past half hour.

"We've got a couple of new options to consider, Butch." Iris clicked to her second of three plans. "We can do recessed bunk beds for the boys on one side or do two narrow twin beds separate. They'd act as seating during the day, but that takes a lot of space." She wasn't over the moon about either of those solutions, which was where option three came in. "You said you wanted space for all your grandchildren to ride along with you."

Butch sipped his coffee and nodded. "I like the idea of a family camping trip. Like Jesse and I used to take the boys on. You'd like that, right, Eric?"

"Sure."

Iris could tell the boy was trying not to let his excitement show. The quiet young man had, over the past few days after the bracelet incident, wiggled his way into her heart with his frank observations and studious gaze. He was one of those kids where you could see the wheels constantly turning in his head. Shane had called the kids sponges at one point, and she definitely agreed with that assessment, especially where Eric was concerned. He didn't miss a single thing.

"A couple days here and there out and about," Butch went on. "Down by the lake or even taking Cassidy down to Amarillo for a few days, or checking out the rodeo in Lubbock? Could be quite an adventure."

Especially for a man who hadn't left his ranch in more than a few months, Iris thought. "Four people in a twenty-eight-foot trailer's going to be a tight fit," Iris reminded him. "Even if a couple of those people are pretty tiny." She paused, glanced over her shoulder when Shane entered the kitchen. It was midafternoon. They'd missed each other more often than not the last day or so, but she had to wonder how the man had gotten more handsome in that time.

She blinked, cleared her throat and tried to ignore the distraction that was Shane Holloway. "Remember, they won't remain tiny for long." If Butch and Shane were any indication, Miles and Eric were going to be six feet tall at the very least, and, given boys' tendencies for growth spurts, it wouldn't be long before they reached that height.

"You're giving everyone their own bed?" Shane walked around the counter to study the screen. "What happened to roughing it? You used to make me and Wayne sleep outside in sleeping bags."

"You had air mattresses," Butch said as if that made a difference.

"Sure, the last couple of years. Ask me how many times we hyperventilated blowing those things up," Shane asked a snickering Iris.

"Most air mattresses have inflatable attachments," she observed.

"Yeah, not ours," Shane grumbled. "And someone conveniently kept forgetting to bring an air pump."

"Kept you out of trouble," Butch reminded him.

"Did you have to deflate them every morning?" Iris asked.

Now it was Butch who grinned. "Took them

a while before they figured that out. Could have just shoved them under the trailer during the day."

"Someone told us to keep the space tidy." Shane leaned against the counter. "And, yes, we had a slow learning curve. Wayne almost passed out one night."

"Perked right up when we mentioned missing dinner, though," Butch recalled.

Iris's heart skipped a beat. It was the first time they'd shared memories of Wayne Holloway that made them smile, Eric included.

"Okay, so, Butch, as much fun as I'm having hanging out with you guys, I can't spend all my time reconfiguring plans." She tapped open a new window. "I've had another idea that is maybe going to solve those problems you're thinking of. It's a different direction, but hear me out. I think this might end up giving us back some of that personal space you want for when you travel on your own."

"Oh?" Butch's brow furrowed.

"Let's say we take the front part of the trailer here." She indicated the space to the right of the door, "And do a triple bunk, with built-in storage under each mattress for their clothes. That'll take care of your grandkids at least and give us the rest of the trailer to flesh out to your personal specifi-cations."

"Like sleeping compartments on a train," Shane said. "That's kind of cool. I like using that pipe work as a ladder to each level. Could you install curtains for some privacy?"

"Ain't no privacy in trailers or on family trips," Butch growled.

"Tell me about it," Shane agreed. "But it would give them their own personal space. Maybe make the wall at their feet out of corkboard so they could hang up pictures and things?"

"That's…" Iris frowned, wishing she'd thought of it herself. "That's a really good idea." Relieved she had someone on her side, Iris nodded enthusiastically and typed the ideas into the notes section. "Curtains. Yep, absolutely. Corkboard. I can make that work." She could even personalize each one once the kids decided which bunk they wanted.

"This way we've got their sleeping quarters up front, and then yours in the back, with the bathroom and kitchen and storage in the middle." She did the measuring in her head. "If we go that route, we can work in a dedicated eating area. It'll be tight." But workable. Definitely workable.

"Make the dining area a convertible space like yours," Shane suggested. "Or something with added storage."

"Always with added storage," Iris agreed. "Butch? What do you think?" She held her breath, wondering if Shane's "help" was going to work against her.

Butch pondered, pressed his lips together, looked at the screen for several tense seconds, then glanced at his grandson, whose eyes had gone wide with wonder. "I think I like it."

There was something different about this response, Iris thought. Something that finally had her breathing a bit easier. "Yeah?"

"Yeah. Let's do it. This design," Butch said as if confirming with himself. "It'll work. For all of us."

"Finally," Shane muttered in a way Iris longed to. She pretended to ignore him even as she gave silent thanks for his input.

"Okay, then." Iris continued typing some notes. "I'm going to get to work on my special order and head into town to see Carver." She'd never been so excited to finish up the electrical before.

"Anything we can do to help?" Shane offered.

"Well, there's one thing." She looked to Butch. "Since I'm headed into town, I'd appreciate it, Butch, if you'd come with me. If you're up for it."

"I don't think—"

"I plan on picking up the wood for your countertops. If it's okay to store it in one of the barns?" she asked Shane. "I know rain's coming in soon. I don't want to take the chance of someone else snatching it up, but I'm also not quite ready for it."

"I don't really—" Butch hesitated.

"Plus I don't want to choose something you

honestly don't like," Iris pushed. "And you might see something else you want to use that I don't."

"Doubtful," Shane muttered and only when she glanced at him did she see the conspiratorial spark in his eyes. "You know what you're doing, Iris. I don't think Dad can contribute—"

"I know what I like and what I don't," Butch countered exactly as expected. "I know my mind."

"Great. Okay, then," Iris said. "I'll pull the truck around front when I'm ready."

"And I've got to ride out and check on the west pasture." Shane finished his coffee and set his mug in the sink. "Eric? How about you come with me?"

"What?" Eric blinked, frowned, as if he'd misheard.

"I'm going to check on the herd, see where we are for a change of pasture. You want to come?"

"You mean it?" Eric wore the distinct expression of someone expecting the rug to be pulled out from under him.

"I mean it." Shane nodded and glanced away, but not before Iris saw something akin to guilt flashing across his face. "I'll check on your brother and sister first and meet you in the stable, okay? We'll saddle up Outlaw and Red."

"But…" Eric looked suddenly uncertain. "Red was Dad's horse."

"I know. Grab your boots." Shane walked out

of the kitchen and headed to the stairs. "I'll meet you out there."

"Yes, sir." Eric dived into the mudroom and grabbed for his boots on the shelf by the door. Sitting on the floor, he quickly dragged them on.

"Guess I'll go make myself presentable for a trip to town," Butch said with a hint of dread in his voice.

Iris thought it odd how he continually refused to go into town, but she was also determined to get to the bottom of it. She was hoping that maybe being with someone not in the family might get him to open up. Or at the very least ease up.

"Have a good time," Iris called to Eric when he jumped to his feet and pulled open the door. "Don't forget your hat!"

"Oh! Right." Eric shot her a smile that, for the first time, seemed to light up his face. "Thanks, Iris."

She heard muted voices echoing from upstairs as she clicked off her laptop, shut it and got to her feet.

"Thanks," Shane said as he returned to the kitchen. "For getting Dad out of the house."

"Fair's fair. You helped me," she said. "Just returning the favor." Her stomach jumped as she managed a shaky smile. "We make a good team."

"We do, actually." He looked out the window to where Eric was racing toward the stable door.

"I've messed up with them. With the kids. Maybe with Dad, too."

"How so?" It wouldn't do any good to argue with him. Not about something like this. From her perspective, they were doing okay. Not great, maybe, but they were getting by.

"I left them alone too long. I've spent the time since I got home waiting for them to come around, to come to me. I haven't wanted to push them or make them talk about stuff they don't want to. The other night with Ruby Rose, when I gave her the bracelet you made her—"

She reached out, touched his arm. "You made it, too."

His smile was dismissive. "I should have spent time with them, together, and one-on-one, so they knew where things stood. So they knew what to expect. It's what Wayne would have done." He paused and a cloud of grief passed across his face. "Ruby Rose told me that Eric said I consider them an obligation. And that's why I'm here. Because I have to be. That's why they were trying not to get in my way or be a problem."

"Oh." It took her a moment to understand why that was a bad thing.

"All this time I've been walking on eggshells because I don't want to upset their routine, but they've been worried I'm going to send them away."

"Shane." She trailed her hand down his arm, weaved her fingers through his. "You're as much in the dark about this situation as any of them. You're parenting them as best you can. You can't blame yourself for not seeing everything through their eyes."

"Sure, I can. Eric's been asking me if he can help on the ranch more. From the day I got here, he's wanted to join in. I always said no. I didn't want..." His laugh sounded sad. "I didn't want him to feel obligated, to feel responsible for this place simply because of family. That he had to follow in his father's footsteps like some kind of mandate. Like my father always expected me to."

"You're not your father," Iris reassured him.

"No, I'm not. And Eric isn't me. I don't know what he wants to do, but I need to stop standing in the way of what he wants to try." He flashed a smile, but it didn't come close to reaching his eyes.

"That sounds like a very fatherly way of dealing with things," Iris said.

"Yeah?" He seemed to brighten at her approval.

"Yeah." She reached up, touched her fingertips to his cheek. A tornado of emotions cycled through her, the desire to comfort, the need to touch him. She rose up on her toes, eyes wide as she pressed her lips against his. She'd meant it to be a moment of approval, but the instant she kissed him, something sweet and unexpected launched inside of her and warmed her from her hair to her toes.

She released his other hand, and it came to rest on her hip. The kiss she'd meant to be no more than a moment long shifted as he angled his head and gently deepened the connection. She heard, felt herself whimper as she held on to him. Reason screamed at her to step away, to run away.

But her heart…oh, her heart begged her to stay right where she was. Forever.

Something loud banged upstairs. The spell broke. Iris stepped back, blinked dazedly several times.

"I'm, um. Sorry." She tried to make light of what had just happened, but found she couldn't. Not with the way her heart was trying to soar out of her chest. "I don't think that was very smart." It may very well be the dumbest thing she'd ever done in her life. And she used to make a living hanging off the side of a stampeding horse.

"No apology necessary."

"Oh." Of course, he'd say that. That cheeky grin of his was back on full display, and she was suddenly wondering if somehow her life was going to be divided into two parts now: before she'd kissed Shane Holloway…

And after.

CHAPTER SEVEN

"ARE YOU GOING to move the cattle to the next pasture tomorrow?"

Shane looked over his shoulder at his nephew, who was sitting tall and proud not only on Red, Wayne's horse, but also in Wayne's saddle. It struck Shane, much like an October storm, how much Eric looked like his father. Sounded like his father. Except Eric wasn't Wayne.

"What do you think?" They'd brought their horses to a stop close to where the cattle had spent the past few days grazing. Where Shane had dropped a long line of feed only hours before. He knew what needed doing. He was interested in what Eric saw when he looked out over the land that had been in the Holloway family for generations.

Shane pulled on the reins, brought Outlaw, a five-year-old quarter a few steps back. "Looking at the pasture and the water levels in their vicinity," he said. "What would you do?"

Eric's brows knitted and his hand tightened around his reins. "I don't know."

Shane didn't believe him. Eric looked uncertain, but not about what he was seeing; he looked unsure of what to say around Shane.

"What does your gut tell you?" Shane pressed. "Given what you're seeing out there, given what you know about the other pastures in the area, when do you think we should move them?"

"Not tomorrow." Eric looked surprised at his own statement. "I mean, unless you think—"

"Right now it doesn't matter what I think. I'm asking you. It's okay to be wrong, Eric. That's how we learn."

Eric visibly swallowed and took another look beyond. "Day after tomorrow," he said with a bit of a tremble in his voice. He cleared his throat, tried again. "The water over there." He pointed to the far end of the pasture. "I can still see it, so there's enough for them to drink. And I see leftover feed from this morning." He moved his hand across the plain. "The grass is still pretty thick, so yeah. I think the day after tomorrow at the earliest."

"Exactly what I was thinking." Shane nodded, leaned an arm on his saddle horn. "You used to come out riding with your dad, didn't you?"

"Yes." Just like that, the uncertainty was back.

"He was teaching me everything so I know what to do when I take over."

"Is that what you want to do? Take over the Holloway Ranch?"

Eric shrugged, but before he dipped his head, Shane caught the spark in his eyes. The same spark Wayne held whenever he'd looked out over this legacy.

"I'm not going anywhere, Eric." It seemed best at this point to rip off the bandage. "You're right, by the way. You and your brother and sister, and your PaPa, you all are an obligation for me."

Eric glanced up, barely moving his head.

"But an obligation isn't necessarily a bad thing."

"It's not?" Eric didn't look convinced.

"I suppose it could be," Shane reasoned. "But you know what else I feel beyond obligation? I feel honored. That your dad and mom thought that I was the right person to raise you should something happen to them. Wayne had so much faith in me it makes me even sadder that I only found out after he was gone. I love this place, Eric. I always have, but I also always knew it was your father who would inherit it."

"Is that why you and PaPa always argue?" Eric asked. "Because you're mad at him for not making it yours, too?"

"Maybe I was." It was as good an explanation

as any, he supposed. "There's a lot your grand-father and I disagree about."

"Like the sheep," Eric said.

"Like the sheep." Shane almost laughed. "I think we've both been a little scared to talk to each other about the truth of what we're dealing with, Eric. I didn't want you to think I expected you to take over the place eventually. I want you to have a choice. Maybe I went about it wrong, so I'm trying to fix that now. You're barely ten years old. At your age I had my head in all kinds of things, trying to figure out what I wanted to do."

"Because you knew you couldn't have the ranch," Eric said. "Because it was going to be my dad's."

"That's right." It wasn't easy admitting the big-gest parenting decision he'd made, to keep Eric at arm's length so he could decide his own fu-ture, had been a mistake. "I'm not asking you to make that decision now," Shane said. "But I'm going to stop trying to keep you away from it. It's a lot of hard work. If you're willing and you still want to learn, I'll bring you in all the way. You and I can work together. I'll teach you what I know, and together we can see where you want to take things. It won't be easy," he said. "If you want in, then you're in. That means really early mornings and working every single day. Even when you have to go to school."

"I know." Eric nodded in a way that Shane could see a weight lift off his nephew's shoulders. "I want to learn. I want…" His eyes filled. "I want to make my dad proud."

Shane reached out and rested a hand on his nephew's shoulder. He squeezed until he felt the tightness in his own throat ease. "You already have, Eric. So you want in? All the way?"

"I want in," Eric said. "All the way. On one condition," he added at the last moment.

"What's that?" Shane's mind raced with possibilities.

"We want a new dog," Eric said.

"Well." Shane heaved a dramatic sigh as if he hadn't already decided to start looking. "I guess since your sister wants some chickens I'd best give in on the dog." He held out his hand, a man-to-man offer that had Eric grinning from ear to ear. "We have a deal then?"

Eric grabbed hold and shook it, a smile finally lighting up his entire face. "Deal."

TAKING BUTCH WITH her into town made Iris wonder if this was what escorting an elderly person always felt like. The older man was fidgety and much less chatty on the drive than he'd ever been at home. He seemed to become quieter the closer they got, or the farther away they drove from the ranch.

By the time she parked her truck in front of the Lone Star Ranch Depot, he'd lost some of the color in his cheeks.

"You okay, Butch?" She touched a hand to his arm.

"Fine."

It dawned on her that she might have over-stepped, pushing him to come into town when he clearly wasn't interested in the outing. She had a tendency to do that, push when she should walk away. But she also knew from personal experience that there were times when pushing was the only means to get through things. "You must have a lot of memories about this place. About Cottonwood Creek," she clarified.

"Lived here all my life," Butch confirmed as he stared straight ahead at the metal-sided warehouse.

"I bet it's changed a lot."

"Has." He nodded sharply. "I'm not addled, Iris. I know how I look. And I know how I... feel." He spoke as if each word was painful. "I'm not addled," he repeated. "And I'm not broken. I'm just—"

"Missing your son." It took her until this moment, until the grief swam in his eyes, to understand. "You must see Wayne everywhere you look in town."

"Seems stupid." Butch nodded again. "He's

gone. Chelle's gone. But every time I come into town, he's there. Or he should be. I can see him. Where he's supposed to be."

Iris squeezed her hand on his arm. "I'm so sorry, Butch. I can take you back home."

"You could," Butch agreed. "Or I can start facing up to things. I can't stop living just because they died."

"No," Iris whispered. "You can't. Your grandchildren need you. Shane needs you."

Butch's laugh exploded through the car. "Shane doesn't need me. He barely tolerates me."

It was on the tip of her tongue to say that Shane loved his father, but she wasn't sure that's what Butch needed to hear just then. "I think maybe you two just don't understand each other," she said finally. "Can I make an observation?"

"I don't think I can stop you," Butch said.

"You're angry. Not just because Wayne's gone, but because Shane's here instead." She'd seen it on his face back at the ranch, when he didn't think anyone was watching. There was grief, of course, and the continued refusal to completely accept and deal with the loss of his son and daughter-in-law. But she'd also seen amusement and pride when he watched Shane with the kids. A pride that faded almost instantly. As if he was ashamed of his feelings. "You lost the son you knew the best. The son who understood you. The one you thought you'd be leaving it all to."

There was that shame again. "It's not intentional," he managed.

"I know." Iris heaved a sigh of her own. "But it's the way things are. I know what it's like not to be the favorite, Butch. I know what it's like to feel like the spare."

He turned his head, confusion and disbelief marring his face. "I don't want to feel this way."

"It's okay," she assured him quickly. "It's taken me a lot of years of self-examination to come to terms with it. My mother doled out affection as a reward, or as an offering for a job well done. Except with Willow, my youngest sister. With Willow, it always seemed so effortless, as if Flora looked at her with completely different eyes. It doesn't take much for a child to understand they aren't the favorite. All in all, I say Shane's doing pretty well."

"I love my boy."

She took the vehemence in his voice as a positive sign. "I can see that you do." She only wished Shane saw it.

"We're just so different," Butch said. "He never had his eyes on the ranch. They were always looking somewhere else. It felt like he didn't want anything I had to offer."

"Then maybe it's time you talked to Shane

about it," Iris suggested. "He lost his brother, just as you lost your son. He needs you, Butch. And you need him. Imagine what you can do together if you stopped fighting each other."

Butch huffed out a breath. "Thought I hired myself a renovator, not a therapist."

"I come with many skills," Iris said. "You want to join me inside?" She motioned to the store.

"Last time I was here," Butch said, "I was with Wayne. A few days before he left for San Antonio." It was as if he'd brought ghosts with him.

"It's fine if you want to wait out here."

"No, it's not," Butch said as he shoved the door open. "I need to do this. Hiding at the ranch isn't teaching my grandkids anything other than how not to move on."

Wow, there he was, the gruff curmudgeon who had somehow wiggled his way into her heart. "Okay, then." She followed him out and around to the entrance. "Let's do this."

"You gonna sit out here all by your lonesome or are you going to do something about that young lady out there in her trailer?"

Shane closed his eyes against his father's voice, slowly counting to ten. It used to take the full ten to lasso his temper. These days it took about five. Tonight, however?

Seven.

"Kids in bed?" Shane had been pleasantly surprised when, upon returning from his trip to town, Butch had done a bit of a takeover in the house. Something had come over him, certainly. Shane couldn't recall the last time his father had cooked dinner and done the dishes and offered to play a board game with his grandkids.

"Took some doing, but yes, they are." Butch handed him a bottle of beer and, after Shane dropped his feet off the porch railing, walked past him to sit in his own rocker. "You should have seen Iris wheeling and dealing with Carver and Edith down at the Depot." Butch leaned back, took a long drink and stared in the same direction as Shane did. Straight into the setting sun. "Woman's some kind of magician."

"I saw you came back with a truckload," Shane commented.

"She keeps this up, we'll be way under budget for Cassidy's refurb."

"Good to hear." Shane couldn't help it. His heart was hovering in his chest as if waiting for an unexpected shoe to drop. "You had a good trip into town then."

"Did." Butch's voice sounded like an overfilled cloud ready to burst. "Iris and I had a chat. She, ah, doesn't seem to beat around the bush about anything."

Shane's lips twitched. "I'd agree with that."

Iris was a straight shooter, that was for sure. She'd definitely shot him out of his comfort zone with that kiss. A kiss he was spending entirely too much time trying to figure out how to replicate. "She's a special woman."

"Glad to know you see it. Don't suppose you and she—"

"Dad." Shane rocked his head to the side, hoped Butch could see the silent plea in his eyes.

"Okay, okay." Butch held up a hand and backed off, something that put Shane even further on alert. "I hear you."

Shane's eyebrows arched. "You do?" *Since when?*

"I need to get something off my chest, Shane. And it's going to come out wrong because you and I both know I don't do well with words. But Iris suggested we talk, and maybe it's time we did."

Shane braced himself, even as he focused on remaining still. "Go ahead." Stopping his father from doing whatever he had his mind set on—Cassidy, for instance—was useless.

"I made a lot of mistakes when you were growing up," Butch said. "I... Eric said you two had a talk out when you were riding. That you hadn't been taking his offered help because you didn't want him to feel backed into a corner with this place."

"That was the gist of things," Shane said carefully. "I didn't want him to feel as if his life was already planned out."

"Like you think I did with you," Butch said.

"No." Shane frowned, sat up straighter. "No, I never thought that, Dad. I was well aware there wasn't a place for me here on the ranch." He paused and watched his father take that in. "You always saw Wayne as your successor. And that made sense. He was older and he had a natural feel for the place. When he looked at this ranch, he saw whatever you did. For the most part."

"We're back to those blasted sheep again, aren't we?" Butch seemed to catch himself before he slid completely into the abrasive tone that frequently ended any conversation between them. "I mean, yes, he and I disagreed. But there was always—"

"Respect," Shane finished for him. "It's okay, Dad. I'm not Wayne. I never was." He hesitated before adding, "I never will be."

"I know." Butch nodded. "And it's time I accepted that. Time I apologized for…" Butch broke off, glanced away. "This won't come as a shock to you, Shane, but I'm not an affectionate man. I'm not the best at…" He flailed one hand in the air.

"Feelings?" Shane tipped his beer to hide his smirk. "Runs in the family."

"No," Butch protested. "No, it doesn't. You and your brother, you were always easier with that aspect of life than I was. That's not me saying for you to expect me to go changing now, however. It's too late for that."

Clearly not, Shane thought. Otherwise this uncomfortable conversation wouldn't be taking place. "Dad, whatever it is you think you need to say to me—"

"I wished it was you." Butch blurted it out so fast Shane wasn't certain he'd heard correctly. "Those first few days after the accident. I wished... And I'm so sorry, son. I am so, so sorry."

Shane's heart leaped into his throat. "Dad."

"I know." Butch held up a hand, cutting him off. "I know, it's horrible. Unforgiveable. I never should have—"

"Dad, I understand." And in that moment, he did. "And it's okay."

"It is not okay," Butch practically spat. "It's..."

"Human. I know it's hard to believe, Dad, but you are human. And you've lost a lot in your life. First Mom, then Wayne and Chelle. It isn't fair."

"What isn't fair is how I've treated you. I aim to do better, Shane. I aim to be better. You aren't your brother."

"No, I'm not." But for the first time, Butch didn't sound as if he resented that fact. "I'm me."

Butch dropped a hand on Shane's shoulder, squeezed hard. "Forgive me, son."

Shane's impulse was to say that his dad didn't need his forgiveness, but it was clear it was something his father needed to hear. "I forgive you, Dad." He gripped his father's hand in his. "Clean slate, yeah? From here on?"

"Clean slate." Butch pulled his hand free and straightened in his chair. "I'm determined to step things up around here. Help more." He glanced toward the stables. "Maybe take a ride or two this weekend. Get back on the horse, so to speak."

"I'd really like that," Shane said. "Thanks, Dad." A knot he suspected had tightened decades before loosened inside of him. His thoughts turned to the trailer parked out by the stable. And to the perceptive, caring, incredible woman living inside.

Thank you, Iris.

CHAPTER EIGHT

"AND THIS SHOULD go right here." Screwdriver clenched between her teeth, Iris tightened the wire caps and pushed the last of the electrical into its created cubby space. She stepped back, giving the interior of Cassidy one long assessing look before she located her tablet. A wave of accomplishment washed over her, and she smiled to herself. "Now we get to play a little. Cos, what do you think? Ready to start sanding those countertops?"

Cos lifted his head, quirked it to the side, then heaved a sigh and returned to his nap.

"Clearly not ready," Iris said. She fanned herself. Normally she tried to avoid working inside the trailer at this time of the day. Later afternoon meant the sun beat down and turned it into a bit of a sauna, but she'd been so close to finishing this phase of the project she hadn't wanted to stop.

She reached for her water. As she downed a large gulp, she heard a distinctive giggle erupting from the other side of the trailer. She stuck her head outside, listened again. Stepping out, she walked around the trailer. Miles and Ruby Rose were crouched beneath one of the window openings, taking turns stepping onto one of the cement blocks to peer inside.

It wasn't the first time they'd spied on her. But it was the first time she planned to call them on it. "Hey." She leaned a shoulder against Cassidy's new siding and folded her arms across her chest. "What's going on, guys?"

"Aaaak!" Miles spun around so fast he toppled right off the block and landed on his butt. A plume of dust rose up around him as Ruby Rose gasped and looked instantly contrite. "Awww, man. That hurt." Miles sat forward, rubbed a hand against the base of his spine. "Sorry, Iris."

"You could have just come in," she let them know.

"Uncle Shane said we shouldn't bother you when you're working," Miles said. "I told him you wouldn't mind."

"I'm always happy to let someone know when they're bothering me. Come on." She held out her hand to Ruby Rose. "You want to see inside?"

"Can we?" Miles leaped to his feet and darted in front of her. "Way cool!"

"Definitely cool," Iris agreed.

She'd done her best these past few days to steer clear of Shane. She was still mortified about her impulsive meant-to-be-of-comfort kiss. Thankfully it seemed as if they both had plenty to keep themselves occupied. They offered congenial waves and acknowledgment, of course, and exchanged pleasantries the few times she'd needed to check with Butch about something in the house. But for the most part, they'd kept themselves to themselves.

"It's still empty." Miles's disappointment wasn't a complete surprise to Iris as she and Ruby Rose followed him into the trailer.

"It will be for a while yet," Iris said. "I just finished installing the electrical and—" she tapped a hand on the weaving PVC pipe "—the water system. Which I can now connect together."

"Huh?" Miles's face scrunched.

"I need to make sure the water system can work if your PaPa doesn't hook in to regular power."

"Oh." Miles nodded slowly. "Okay." He pounded his feet on the newly installed plywood planks. "Is this the floor?"

"It's the first layer," she said. "I'm going to install a thin layer of insulation and then the actual flooring."

"That's a lot of work," Miles observed.

"Yes, it is." She heard the boy's stomach growl and bit back a smile. "Hey, are you guys hungry? I baked some cookies last night. You've got some time before dinner, right?"

"What kind of cookies?" Miles asked suspiciously.

"Well, I call them kitchen sink cookies. They've got chocolate and pretzels and potato chips—"

"In cookies?" Miles screeched. "That's—"

"Delicious," Iris countered. "Don't believe me, you've got to try them for yourselves. Come on."

She led the way to her own trailer and pulled open the door. "Take a seat at the table." She could hear the horses whinnying in the stable and Shane's deep voice as he talked on the phone. "You, too, Cos." She whistled for the dog, who came bounding out to join them. "Now." She stood in the middle of the kitchen, hands on her hips. "Where did I put those cookies?"

"There!" Ruby Rose pointed to the saddle-shaped cookie jar on the counter.

Feigning surprise, Iris pulled the top off and peered inside. "You're right!" She pulled out two cookies—they were bigger than her hand—and set them on a napkin in front of each of them. "Milk?"

"Yes, please," Ruby Rose said as she nibbled. Her eyes went wide, and she took a bigger bite. "Yum!"

Miles scoffed but clearly wasn't going to be outdone by his little sister. "Hey!" He chewed and swallowed as Iris got them their milk. "These are good!"

"I never lie about cookies," Iris assured them. She leaned back against the counter. "How was school this week?"

"Awesome!" Miles announced, apparently unable to shove the cookie into his face fast enough. "We're decorating for Halloween. We made papier-mâché pumpkins and these creepy ghosts that hang from the ceiling. I think I'm going to be a car for Halloween. Or maybe a baseball player. I haven't decided yet."

"Sounds pretty awesome," Iris said. "Ruby Rose? What do you want to be?"

Ruby Rose shrugged.

"She should be a ghost," Miles said. "They don't talk much, either."

Ruby Rose stuck her tongue out at her brother before drinking some of her milk.

"Maybe she just doesn't have a lot to say," Iris suggested.

"Can I be a ballerina?" Ruby Rose asked Iris.

"Don't see why not," Iris said.

"A ballerina?" Miles rolled his eyes in disgust. "That's boring!"

"Miles," Iris said in a tone she'd often heard Shane use. "That's not very nice."

"I know." Miles sighed. "PaPa says my mouth has a mind of its own. Sorry, Ruby. A ballerina sounds amazing!" His overexaggeration had him nearly toppling out of his seat.

Ruby shrugged again, clearly used to her brother's less than constructive comments.

"I thought I heard you all in here." Shane poked his head in the open door. "Everything okay?"

"Fine." Iris flashed a nervous smile. Every cell in her body leaped to attention at the sight of him. She shoved her hands in the back pockets of her jeans and rocked back on her heels. "We were just talking about Halloween costumes."

"And eating sink cookies!" Miles held up the last of his.

"Cookies?" Shane's eyes filled with expectation. "Don't suppose you have any more hanging around?"

Iris rolled her eyes, pulled out another cookie and handed it to him. "Be prepared. They'll spoil you for all other cookies for the rest of your life."

"Doubtful." He bit in, took another bite. "Okay, so maybe you're right. Salty and sweet and with chocolate chunks? These are great."

"Thanks." Her entire body warmed at the compliment. "Good way to use up all the chip and pretzel crumbs in the bottom of the bag."

"Funny," Shane teased. "I just eat them. Hey, you two, have you done your homework for today?"

"Awww, man!" Miles splayed himself across the table in typical dramatic fashion. "No."

"Then hop to and get it done before dinner. Ruby Rose?"

"I'm done." She slid out of her seat and held up her napkin. "Where is the trash?"

Always the little adult, Iris thought as she pulled open the cabinet under the sink. "Thank you, Ruby."

"You're welcome. Can I play with Cos for a little while?" She bent down to scratch his head and earned a big tongue slurp as a reward. She giggled, and the sound bounced around the trailer and lifted Iris's heart.

"That red ball is his favorite," Iris said.

"Okay." Ruby Rose picked up the ball and waggled it in front of him. "Wanna play, Cos?"

Cos shifted into sitting position, banged his tail against the wall then followed her outside.

"Miles, homework, please," Shane told his nephew. "Your brother's working on his in the kitchen."

"Fine." Miles hauled himself out from behind the table. "Thanks for the cookie, Iris."

"You're welcome, Miles." It dawned on Iris that every time she was around the kids she couldn't stop smiling. They just made her...happy.

"Haven't seen you very much lately," Shane said. "Was it something I said?" He leaned against the counter, finished his cookie.

"More like something I did," Iris muttered. "I'm just embarrassed about...you know."

"Kissing me when I was emotionally vulnerable?" Shane said, that teasing glint in his eye making her lips twitch. "Well, I think there might be a way to solve that problem." He stepped forward, rested his hands on her hips and dipped his mouth to hers.

The man could short-circuit a nuclear power plant. She could taste sugar and chocolate on his lips as he kissed her, and, as much as reason told her to push him away, desire and longing wrapped around her heart and she grabbed hold of him.

"Not a fluke," he murmured against her lips. "Hello, Iris."

"Hi." Her nervous laughter had her biting her lower lip. "This still isn't a good idea, Shane."

"Why not?" He looked genuinely perplexed at the comment.

"Because." She struggled for the right words, but the truth couldn't be softened. "Because I'm not staying. Because I have a life and a career, and they don't include staying put on a ranch in North Texas."

"Oh," Shane said thoughtfully. "That."

"Yes, that." She touched a hand to his face, wished harder than she'd wished for anything else that circumstances were different. "This is nice. You're nice. And kissing you is very nice—"

"Is it?" he teased.

She sighed. "I like you a lot." Too much. "But—"

"But you're just passing through," he finished with a slow, disappointed nod. "Yeah. I get that."

"Do you?"

"Yes. And if you want me to stop kissing you, I will."

She hesitated and caught the gleam in his eye.

"Or not," he added and kissed her again quickly. "I actually did have a reason for coming in here. Other than wanting to kiss you again."

"Do tell." She pulled herself free and wiped up imaginary crumbs off the counter.

"Well, Dad's inside getting dinner together and the kids are doing their homework."

"Or playing with my dog," she corrected.

"Right. I was wondering if maybe you were ready to take me up on my offer for a ride around the Holloway property. Let me show it off a bit to you?"

"A ride." The longing surged afresh. She wasn't going to let herself surrender to the promise of what she knew couldn't be hers, but she could enjoy the moment for what it was: perfection. "I had planned on getting to work on the... You know what?" She held up her hands in surrender. "I'm on schedule and I could use a break. I'd love to take a ride with you."

"Great." He grabbed her hand. "Let's go. Before you change your mind."

CHAPTER NINE

"IT'S GLORIOUS."

Iris's comment upon looking out across the expanse of the Holloway property had Shane shifting into a position of pride. The awe and wonder in her voice had him smiling and his heart tilting toward a future he couldn't let himself contemplate. She'd made her position known; she wasn't staying. Not here. Not anywhere. He was just going to have to accept that.

Unless he could find a way to change her mind. Step one was showing her what was possible.

"I can't believe you ever wanted to leave this place."

"I see it with different eyes now," Shane admitted. "Since Wayne's been gone. I used to think of this place as a kind of anchor around my neck. Now?"

"Now it feels like yours?"

"In a way." He appreciated how she understood him. He'd never had such a...connection with a woman before. As if she could read his mind. Not that he could read hers. She remained a bit of a mystery in a lot of ways, but the idea of trying was more appealing every day. "It'll be mine for a little while. I'll act as caretaker until, and if, Eric is ready to take over."

"I noticed he's a little less rough around the edges these past few days," Iris said with a knowing look. "Him and your father."

"Apparently talking can help some situations." Shane tried not to sound completely dumbfounded. "You have a real talent at nudging people into the right direction, don't you?"

"Like I told your father," she said as she turned her face into the autumn breeze. "I have many talents. Don't always get a chance to put them to use."

"Well, we appreciate it." The tension around the ranch had eased. He didn't feel quite so cautious or worried about saying or doing the wrong thing. Nothing was perfect, and it was going to take some work, especially between him and his father, but their mutual agreement to try to understand the other person's point of view was at least a start.

Butch had been true to his word and stepped up around the ranch, started taking part in things again. Granted, his father had yet to join Shane on his morning feeding rounds, but he had driven the kids to school this week and that was a big help time-wise Shane hadn't expected. "Seems like you don't just rehab trailers and RVs, but families, too."

"Some of them, at least." Iris's smile was tight as she tucked her hair behind her ear. "Is Tulsa a racer?" She leaned down, patted Tulsa's neck and earned a whinny in response.

"She's been known to cut loose."

"Good. 'Cause I feel like a run. How about you?" She gave him that smile that lit him from the inside, then kicked her heels and set off before he could blink the fog from his brain.

"Now, that's just not fair," he said as he kicked Duke into gear. "Let's get them, boy."

Sloping down the hills and up and around the various pastures, Shane found himself dropping back on purpose. There was something hypnotic about watching her ride, as if she belonged in that saddle. The effortless way her body moved with the horse, the gentle hold she kept on the reins, how she lifted her face to the sun as she let Tulsa take the lead.

In that moment, he could imagine how she'd been on the performing circuit. How much attention she'd have garnered from the audience. For some, finding a natural rhythm with a horse was a lifelong struggle. He'd been relieved to see Eric was like his father and slipped into the saddle as easily as a fish swam through water.

How was it possible this woman was magic in so many ways?

She looked back over her shoulder. "Come on, slowpoke!" she called into the wind as Tulsa picked up speed. "Race you to the top of that hill!"

"You heard her, Duke." But he didn't pick up the pace. He was more than content to sit back, take his time and admire her riding.

By the time he did catch up, he saw the challenge on her face, but he didn't rise to it.

"Took your time," she teased.

"I had a pretty good view." The truth could very well set him free where Iris Blackwell was concerned. The woman had tied him into knots. "You must have been incredible with the Belles."

The light in her eyes dimmed. "I had my moments."

He wished he could make her memories of the Belles easier to deal with. She'd already done so much to start his own family healing; if only he could return the favor.

"The kids have an overnight field trip tomorrow," he told her. "A fall festival kind of thing."

"So Eric said." Iris adjusted her reins. "They're going to Lubbock, aren't they? For some big corn maze and pumpkin patch scavenger hunt."

"That's right. The school does two a year. One in the fall, one in spring. I'm planning on using the time to get a surprise for them for when they get back."

"Oh?" He'd recaptured her interest. "What kind of surprise?"

"Well, I am finishing that chicken coop first thing," he told her. "Ruby Rose mentioned her and her mom had planned to get some chickens. Ruby Rose still wants them, so I figured we'd take the plunge."

"Chickens. Awesome," Iris said. "Every ranch needs chickens."

"And then, we should decorate for Halloween. There's a closet full of holiday and fall stuff. I thought maybe I'd go through it and see what to pull out for the season." Her teasing grin had him curious. "What?"

"You just don't strike me as the decorating sort." She laughed. "You're full of surprises, Shane Holloway."

He certainly hoped so. "There's one other thing. I was hoping I could borrow Cosmo tomorrow morning. And you, too, if you're up for it? There's a rescue shelter in Claxton. Prairie Paws. I thought I'd head down and see about a dog for the boys."

Her brow furrowed. "And you think Cos will help?"

"We've got a lot of animals around here. I want to make sure whatever dog I choose can handle that. Especially if we're getting chickens."

"And sheep," she reminded him. "Don't forget about the sheep."

"Can't forget about the sheep." Especially since he had a meeting next week with a possible supplier. His father hadn't exactly come around to the idea, but Butch had stopped shooting daggers in Shane's direction whenever he brought up the subject. Something had to be done with that old barn, otherwise it was just a waste.

"Could be dangerous," Iris said. "Taking me into an animal shelter. I tend to want to bring them all home."

"About that we can agree. Which is why we need a unified front," Shane confirmed. "I need someone with me to keep me strong and resist temptation. You've got to keep me on track. One dog." That's all he could handle at this point. He held up a finger. "One."

"I'll promise to try," she said. "What time are we heading out?"

"The bus is picking the kids up in town at eight. Figure we'll leave here about seven fifteen. We'll drop off the kids then head out to the shelter."

"All right." Her brows narrowed, and she nodded as if making a mental note. "Cos and I will be ready to go."

To OFFSET THE time she was going to lose by spending the day with Shane in Claxton, Iris spent the better part of the night working, reconfiguring her plan of action. She was getting ahead of things, locking in various measurements and a list of all the scroll cutting she needed to do. She'd already cut out the exterior panels for the trio of bunks meant for the kids. The slats for the bunks were cut and stored away until she could build them. Once the kids were back from their school trip, she could work with them on which bunks they wanted and the colors they preferred.

She was being practical and responsible. Rain was headed to the area over the next couple of weeks. The more outside jobs she could complete before it hit would keep her moving forward and prevent the project from stalling out.

Late-night hours were far more productive for her peace of mind. At least, that's what she told herself, as she tried to dislodge her nerves about spending an entire day with Shane Holloway.

Nerves that dangled a little too close to the precipice of fear.

Nerves that jangled to life whenever she closed her eyes and saw him standing there, his arms filled with giggling happy kids or holding the reins of a horse.

Working until she dropped meant stopping the tornado of uncertainty circling inside of her. She would not give in. Iris Blackwell did not scare easy. She hadn't when it came to flipping upside down on a galloping horse and not when she'd struck out on her own.

And not when she felt herself falling tail over teakettle for one impressive, kindhearted cowboy.

Finally, she did give in to the exhaustion and flopped into bed shortly after two. Four hours later, at the gentle nudging of Cosmo's cold nose on the center of her back, she rolled out of bed. Face plunged under the shower spray, she almost drowned until her mind cleared and the debate she'd had over the flooring for Cassidy's remodel was over.

Dripping, she grabbed a towel and darted out of the shower to scribble down her decision on one of the numerous notepads she kept around her trailer. "I need to call Carver sometime today," she said out loud to plant that reminder in her mind. The stone plastic composite vinyl was a great compromise over the more expensive hardwood floor. The composite was weather resistant enough to be fine wherever Butch might take his trailer. "That might constitute genuine progress, Cos."

Cos blinked up at her, clearly unimpressed.

"Right." She glanced at the clock and lamented postponing her morning coffee. "I'd better get dressed." Minutes later, she reached for her bag and pushed open the door. "Come on, Cos." Travel mug in hand, she patted her leg. "Let's go, boy. We're off on an adventure today."

Cosmo leaped free of the trailer and raced off toward the house. The chilly morning air blasted like ice over her still damp hair and made her shiver, but it helped erase the last of the brain fog.

"Ruby Rose, you can't bring Oscar." Eric's long-suffering big brother act never ceased to bring a smile to Iris's face. She rounded the corner of the house in time to see the siblings' standoff. "I mean it, Ruby. There's no room for him."

Ruby Rose pointed to the video game in Eric's hand and glared at him. "You aren't supposed to bring that."

"No video games allowed," Shane said as he hauled three small sleeping bags outside. "It was on your permission slip, Eric. Put it back in the house, please. Miles! Get a move on!"

Iris stood at the front of the truck, hands tucked into the pockets of her jeans, her purse slung over her shoulder. Cos took off after Eric, who'd gone back into the house. "Can I help?" she asked.

"You can try," Shane said under his breath. "I can't get her to leave the chicken behind."

"The…chicken." Iris frowned, not understanding until she saw the puffy stuffed chicken in Ruby Rose's arms. "Oscar, I presume?"

"Comfort animal," Shane said. "Oscar usually

stays in her room, but this is her first sleepover and she's nervous. About a lot of things."

"I know the feeling," Iris said. "Let me try something," she added, when Shane looked curious about her comment. She left him behind as she headed for Ruby Rose. "Good morning, Ruby."

Ruby gave a little wave. Her curls were as springy as usual, and the long-sleeve purple shirt she wore under her jacket had an appliqué of a butterfly.

"I hear you're going on a campout." Iris gently touched the little girl's soft curls. "Who's this you're bringing with you?" She pointed to the clearly well-loved chicken. "I haven't seen him before."

"Oscar." Ruby Rose hugged him tighter.

"Hello, Oscar. Looks like you two have been friends for a long time."

Ruby Rose nodded.

"Well, I think you're both very brave to go on this field trip. You're braver than me. I'd be worried he'd get lost."

Ruby frowned, looked down at her stuffed friend.

"You are going to have so much fun and so many things to do," Iris went on. "I heard there's a big cornfield maze and a scarecrow making contest. And you'll be having s'mores. They're one of my absolute favorite things to eat in the entire world."

"And face painting," Ruby Rose added quietly. "Does it hurt?"

"No, baby." Iris could barely resist the urge to pull her in for a hug. "Face painting doesn't hurt. Maybe Oscar wants his face painted, too?"

Ruby Rose shook her head hard. "He doesn't like getting dirty."

"Me neither. You just be really careful not to lose track of Oscar while you're having fun, okay? We want to make sure he makes it back home safe and sound."

Ruby Rose looked at Oscar, then at Iris. Then back at Oscar. "I don't want to lose him." She kissed him on the beak.

"Then I'm sure you won't," Iris said.

Ruby Rose chewed on her bottom lip before she pressed Oscar against Iris's chest. "Will you take care of him until I get back?"

"Oh." Iris clutched the chicken in her hands as Shane circled around, shooting her a look that had her blushing. "Well, sure. Of course, I will." She'd never anticipated being put on chicken duty. She'd assumed Ruby Rose would just take him back up to her room.

"He gets lonely without me." Ruby Rose stepped closer, whispered, "And scared. Especially around new people."

"I'll make sure he doesn't get scared or lonely," Iris promised and meant it with all her heart.

Shane loaded the last of their gear and closed up the back of the truck. Cosmo trailed after Eric as he slogged back to the truck, clearly annoyed at having to leave his video game behind.

"And you'll be with your brothers. And your friends from school. I bet you won't have time to get lonely or scared."

"You're going to have a wonderful time, Ruby Rose," Shane said. "Eric, go see where your brother is, please."

Eric heaved a heavy sigh. "Aw, man!" He stomped back to the house.

"Honestly, they're going for one night. You'd think it was a trip around the world." Shane stopped, hands planted on his hips, as Ruby Rose climbed into the back seat of the truck cab. The smile that broke across his mouth had her insides doing all kinds of jigs. "Morning." His gaze dropped to Oscar. "Nice chicken."

She laughed and knocked her arm against his. "Funny." Her cheeks went hot as his eyes skimmed her face. "I overslept this morning. How are you fixed for coffee in there?" She hefted her travel mug and gestured to the house.

"Fresh pot just finished brewing," Shane said. "Go help yourself."

Given her lack of caffeine intake so far today,

she nearly dropped to her knees in gratitude. When she stepped into the house, she definitely detected bacon and her stomach leaped to life. "Only coffee smells better. Morning, Butch."

"Morning, Iris." Butch barely glanced up from Shane's laptop. "Help yourself to coffee. Cosmo's already had his breakfast."

"Thanks." She eyed the empty dog food bowl near the back door. "You don't have to feed him in the morning, Butch. He eats in the trailer."

"He's a growing dog," Butch argued. "And I had extra chicken."

No wonder Cos was so anxious to join her this morning.

"One of those bags is for you," Butch told her. "Breakfast for the road."

She filled up her mug. "You didn't have to do that."

"Just as easy to add another to the pile," Butch said without looking away from the screen.

"What are you watching?" She wandered over, set Oscar down on the table, took her first sip of morning coffee and felt her system even out. Until she saw the video. Then her stomach flipped. "Oh, you've got to be kidding me."

"Don't go robbing an old man of his desire to walk down memory lane. Look at you go." He tapped the screen where the video showed Iris, standing on the back of a prancing horse, turning in circles. With her arms over her head, she looked like an equestrian ballerina. "You were a natural."

"If you say so." Even now her toes scrunched in her boots as if struggling for balance. "Keep that video to yourself, will you?" Iris pleaded.

"Oh." Butch glanced up, a sheepish expression on his face. "Might be a little too late for that. Me and the kids were watching some of these last night."

"For Pete's sake." Too late to put the toothpaste in the tube, she supposed. "Don't go expecting me to put on a show for you all. I'm too old for that now."

"And now look!" Butch's excitement almost made her smile. "You're riding standing up. And what's that your sisters are doing?"

"We called it leapfrogging," Iris said, as she watched Willow leap over J.R. so they could change horses. "Keep an eye on Magnolia, coming up from behind." Maggie, holding two pairs of reins in her hands had two horses under control, a foot on each saddle as she followed her sisters. For the life of her, Iris couldn't recall where Violet was in that part of the act. The shows were always a blur in her memory. The practice sessions, on the other hand, were all too vivid. Flora Blackwell had expected nothing but perfection.

Though Butch was clearly enjoying himself,

Iris had to resist the urge to slam the laptop closed. "You planning on doing anything while we're gone, Butch?"

"Ah, yeah." He shook his head, eyes filled with marvel and respect when he looked at her. "Told Shane I'd take over the chicken coop Chelle started for Ruby Rose." It was perhaps the first time he spoke his late daughter-in-law's name without too much of a grimace of pain. "Shane's got his hands full today, with the cattle and ranch, so figured I'd pitch in and give it a shot."

It would be interesting to see Shane's reaction to his father jumping in on a task he'd planned to take care of himself. "I look forward to seeing the finished product," she said. "Hey, boys!" she called when she heard Eric and Miles racing down the stairs. "Come get your breakfast, please."

It didn't dawn on her until she heard the words come out of her mouth how maternal she sounded. And felt. Something unexpected buzzed to life inside of her, but she pushed it aside before she could analyze it. Any concern that she might have overstepped was sidelined by the brothers racing into the kitchen and vanishing again, this time with a bag in hand.

"I think we are good to go." Shane had strolled in, grabbed his own travel mug and was filling it, glancing over his shoulder at the two of them. "What's going on with the laptop?"

"Nothing!" Iris said.

"More videos," Butch said as he turned the screen around. "There's an entire Blackwell Belles YouTube channel." He grinned at Iris. "I subscribed. Made myself an account and everything."

"Of course, you did." Iris rolled her eyes, but not before she saw the spark of sympathy in Shane's. "Apparently I've become family entertainment."

"Not for all of us." Shane touched her arm as he passed. "Dad, did you take a look at the coop?" He checked the door to make sure they were alone. "What number are you thinking for chickens?"

"Just one or two to start." He eyed Oscar. "Maybe add in something extra for this guy."

Iris hid her smile behind her mug. He was such a softie for his grandkids. "Don't forget a rooster." Her eyes widened in innocence when Shane frowned at her.

"You don't need a rooster for chickens to lay eggs," Shane said.

"I know." She shrugged. "But roosters are fun."

"Roosters are loud. No rooster," Shane warned his father.

"For now," Butch agreed. "Let's see how Ruby Rose does with the chickens first. Well, speak of the munchkin." Butch reached down as Ruby Rose raced over to him.

"PaPa, I'm leaving Oscar here." She pointed to the stuffed animal. "Will you help Iris watch him?"

Butch nodded as seriously as a mall Santa taking toy orders. "You bet I will."

"Thanks, PaPa." She ran back out before she could take one of the breakfast bags.

"I've got it," Iris said as she grabbed the remaining three. "Let's load up and move out! See you later, Butch."

"Have a good time!" he called after her.

"I'm sorry," Shane said as he caught up with her and closed the front door behind them. "I should have warned you he found the videos of the Belles."

Iris shook her head. "It's fine. Inevitable. At least it put a smile on his face. Speaking of smiles." She smacked one of the bags into his chest. "Here's your breakfast."

"Uncle Shane, I can't get Ruby Rose's belt hooked!" Eric yelled from the other side of the truck.

"Thanks." Shane accepted the bag as Cosmo let out a low bark.

"You don't get one," Iris told her dog. "You got kibble. And some chicken. No way you're starving."

Cosmo ran circles around her, stopped abruptly and woofed. Twice.

Clearly chicken and kibble didn't compete with breakfast sandwiches.

Iris bent low to talk only to Cosmo. "You ready to help find this family a dog?"

Two more woofs followed.

Cosmo leaped forward, and as Miles pulled open the back seat door, the dog hopped inside the truck without any further prodding and wiggled himself into the space between Eric and Ruby Rose's car seat.

THE DRIVE TO CLAXTON, located about fifty miles south from Cottonwood Creek, took a little less than an hour. In almost the same amount of time, they'd offloaded the kids and their stuff and waited for them to find spots on one of two rented school buses.

Ruby Rose, flanked by her brothers, showed more than a little unease about the entire trip. She clung to Miles's shirt as if it was a lifeline. For a tense few moments, Shane suspected she almost changed her mind about going. He'd been expecting it. This was, after all, her first time away from home. Truth be told, he almost made the decision for her but, at the last second, resisted the temptation to haul Ruby back to the car and keep her with them.

As if reading his mind, Iris caught his hand and squeezed, shaking her head ever so slightly but enough that he could see the slight movement out of the corner of his eye. How did she know?

Maybe because she felt the same way.

"She'll be okay," Iris whispered from where they sat inside the truck. Cosmo stuck his head out of the passenger door window and whimpered.

As soon as Ruby Rose had seen some of her school friends and how excited they all were to see her, she released her hold on her brother and managed a timid smile. The fact that Eric had foregone riding with his own friends in order to hop onto Ruby Rose's bus had Shane bursting with pride.

Eric was his father's son, no doubt about it. Wayne had always been a family first kind of man, and it seemed as if his oldest boy was following in his footsteps. "You miss them."

Iris's quiet observation slipped through the noise of his turning the engine back on. Behind him, Cos nudged his arm with his nose and sniffed.

"I do, actually." Odd. At first, he'd anticipated that some time without them would be a bit of a relief. "It's definitely quieter. Right, boy?" He reached back to pet Cos.

"Quiet is overrated."

"Maybe," Shane agreed. "You've definitely been quiet this morning. Everything okay?" She'd been noodling on her tablet for most of the drive and now she was back at it.

"Fine. Just finalizing the plans for Cassidy."

"Always working," Shane teased. "You're worse than me."

"Gotta keep up with the schedule," she said absently.

"Right. Gotta keep up with the schedule." The days she'd already been here had flown by so fast. He could only imagine that it would be the same for the rest of the month. "Have you booked your next job?"

"What?" She pulled her attention away from the tablet. "Uh, yeah, kinda."

Finally. He'd discovered something she wasn't good at: lying. Why she'd lie about that, however, was a mystery.

"You know, if you wanted to take a break, you're welcome to stay on with us through the holidays. If you don't have someplace important to be."

"Thanks." She shifted and looked out her window. "But I don't do holidays."

"Like in you don't celebrate them or you pretend they don't exist?"

"A little of both. Holidays are about family,

and honestly, they're just a reminder that I don't speak to mine."

"You don't speak to any of them? At all? I mean, I understand about your mom, but not your sisters? What about your dad?"

"I check in with him occasionally." Come to think of it, her dad hadn't answered the last few texts she'd sent. "He worries sometimes because I move around so much and I'm on my own. But he understands why I do it."

"You sure about that?"

"He says he does." She shrugged. "We're both choosing to believe it in any case." She glanced out the window but then looked back at him. "I know what you're thinking."

"Okay. I'll play," Shane challenged. "What am I thinking?"

"That I have an awful lot to say about how you and your family relate to one another but when it comes to my own—"

"When it comes to your own it's complicated," Shane finished for her. "It just strikes me as sad, Iris. I'd give anything to have Wayne back, for him to be here for me to call or text or even fight or argue with."

"Or take the pressure off dealing with your father."

He laughed a little. "Yeah, that, too. I guess it's just hard for me to understand why, when you have four sisters, none of you seem to be connected any longer."

"Like you said." Her voice was clipped, edgier than he'd ever heard it. "It's complicated."

And with that, he let the subject drop. For now. "I have a confession to make. Dad's not the only one who's been watching your videos."

She groaned. "Please don't tell me—"

"Not the Belles," he hurriedly assured her. As curious as he was about that part of her life, her current life interested him more. "Your renovation videos. Okay, like Dad, I subscribed to your channel."

"Oh." Now he had her attention. "And what do you think?"

He thought she was a master at communication and presentation. He didn't realize she filmed herself as she worked, then spliced segments together to show the progress. "You make renovating trailers look far easier than it actually is. Heck, you made me believe I could take something like that on."

"Don't underestimate yourself," Iris said. "It's just about following instructions and learning as you go."

"I like how you explain why you're doing what you're doing," he added. "What your options were and how you decided to take the path you did."

"There's always more than one way to attack

a project," she said. "Sometimes you have to come at the complicated ones from different directions."

"Yes," Shane said with a slow nod. Suddenly he wasn't so sure they were talking about renovating trailers any longer. "I imagine you do. Anyway, I'm enjoying watching the progress both live and online."

"Well, you did me a favor subscribing. I'm trying to get my followers up to a million and a half. Production companies like large followings for people they're considering giving shows to."

"Is that what you want? Your own TV show?"

"TV is the big dream," she said. "I'd be happy with more sponsors. Bigger sponsors. I'd love to start tackling larger projects. Home renovations, store remodels could be fun, too. I'm enjoying creating the table for Carver's wife, so now I'm playing with the idea of a custom furniture line. One of a kind things, you know? I try to stay open for anything."

"But RV and trailer remodels launched you."

"They did. It works well, keeps me moving around and something new is always on the horizon. Shakes things up, but it's all under my same brand. I'm one of those people that if I stand still or stay put for very long I start to wither. Or I get bored. Neither is very good."

"No," he mused. "I suppose not." He cleared

his throat as he took the turnoff toward Claxton. "Thanks again for coming with me today. I thought we could get lunch before visiting the shelter. There's an antique hardware store in town you might find interesting."

"Rustic Relics Hardware?" The excitement in her voice was equal to Ruby Rose's when she talked about chickens. "I've drooled over their website. I wanted to stop on my way to the ranch, but I ran out of time."

"No time like the present." Some women liked jewelry or fancy perfume. Iris Blackwell liked antique hardware. "You need me to keep you in line, like you're doing for me at the shelter?"

"Probably." She was back looking at her tablet. "I'll let you know after I check my budget."

"YOU KNOW IF you ever decide to trade in remodeling for Wall Street, you'd be very successful as a negotiator."

"Always good to have a backup plan." Iris looked down at the bag Shane carried for her, one of two loaded with purchases from Rusted Relics. The two hours they'd spent inside had been like a trip to an amusement park for her—from water faucets to cabinet pulls to hinges and doorknobs and… Oh, she couldn't begin to stop her mind from spinning. She'd haggled her way to an even better deal than expected. "That place is amazing! I mean, those antique cabinet pulls are going to be perfect for Cassidy." They were the precise mix of vintage and practicality she'd wanted.

"And a number of other projects, considering how many you bought," Shane observed.

"Everything I bought is smallish and can be easily packed. Remind me to show you my storage system on the bottom of Wander. You wouldn't believe how much I can fit under there."

Including my past with the Belles. Iris frowned. Where had that come from? Probably from Butch watching those ridiculous videos.

They stashed their bags in the truck. She sniffed the air, turned in a slow circle.

"I smell barbeque." Tangy, spicy, tempting barbeque. Her stomach growled.

"That'd be Smoky Trails." He pointed down the street. "I wasn't sure if you'd be hungry enough yet."

"For barbeque? Always. Oh." She looked at Cos, who heaved a sigh and looked at them over the back seat. "I can't leave him in here any longer."

"You don't have to. They've got dog-friendly patio seating. And even a menu for them. Come on, boy." Shane dropped the truck bed, and Cosmo jumped down.

Iris pulled his leash out of her purse. "Lunch." Cos rushed over to her.

"Guess I'm not the only one who likes barbeque," she joked.

The weekday lunch rush was in full swing, with most of the outside picnic tables filled. The chattering and good moods were no doubt enhanced by the amazing aroma of the food being placed in front of them.

"Hi, welcome to Smoky Trails." A young man with a spiky haircut and an armload of platters did a bit of a spin. "Grab a seat anywhere and we'll be right with you. Hey, there, pooch." Cos nudged his nose against the man's knee and stared longingly at the plates.

"Cos, behave," Iris warned. Cos immediately sat and looked at Iris as if to say, "Well? I'm behaving. Reward me already."

Shane touched a hand to the small of her back and guided her to an available table. Cos made a few friends along the way. When they sat down and Iris looped the leash around her bench, Cosmo sat on the ground between them and immediately settled in.

"So, what do you usually get?" Iris asked Shane as she plucked up a menu. "Where do you even start?"

"Ribs," Shane said without bothering to pick one up for himself. "And we'll get a pooch platter for Cos. Don't worry. Nothing spicy. It's a good selection of meat, sweet potatoes and melons."

"Well, Cos is definitely eating well today."

With their food ordered, Iris took a deep breath and released it, letting the tension she'd carried with her from the ranch melt away.

"Feeling better?" Shane asked as their drinks were delivered. They knocked their bottles of root beer against one another in a toast.

"Better than what?" She drank and swallowed a large amount of bubbles.

"I get the feeling talking about your family isn't your favorite topic of conversation."

"It's not." And she certainly didn't want to start all over again. "Look, Shane." How did she explain this in a way that made sense when, at times, it didn't make sense to her? "Complicated is just that. Complicated. And I get what you were saying about doing anything to have Wayne back. But that isn't how it works with this side of the Blackwell family. It…can't."

"Why not?"

She rolled her eyes, gnashed her teeth. "Boy, you just aren't going to let this go, are you?"

"I will, if you really want me to."

She eyed him. "Hmm, somehow I don't believe you. So let me just say this. I am perfectly happy and content with my life, Shane. I love what I do, and I'm really good at it. I'm achieving a lot of my goals, and I make people happy. I live on my own terms, and the only one I have to worry about is him." She pointed to Cos. "And obviously all that takes is food and love."

"But—"

"But nothing. Please, Shane." She paused. "Before the Belles broke up, I went to the doctor. I just wasn't feeling right, you know? I was barely twenty, and can you guess what the doctor told me? That I had high blood pressure, anxiety and the beginnings of an ulcer. At twenty."

"That's terrible." Shane looked shocked.

"No, that's my family. My mother in particular," she added. "Six months out on my own and I was healthy again. Physically and, just as importantly, emotionally. So I am begging you, please. Just let it drop."

"Can I make one last observation?"

Clearly she wasn't going to be able to stop him. "Fine." She held up her index finger in warning. "One."

"Did it ever occur to you that maybe you had all those things wrong with you because you never were honest with your mother about your feelings? That it all just manifested in a different way?"

Iris blinked. Of all the cowboys in all of Texas, she had to end up with one who could give a top-notch therapist a run for their money. "I guess that heart-to-heart with your father makes you think you have all the answers, huh?" She'd meant it to sound teasing, but even she heard the edge in her voice. She rubbed a hand against the sudden, familiar ache in her stomach. "Whether it's occurred to me or not, that part of my life is the past. I'm focused on today, now and the future. I don't need to tarnish it by reconnecting with my family. They don't…" She took a deep breath. "We don't understand each other. I'm not sure we ever did."

He nodded. "Okay. I just hope one day you don't wake up and wish things were different."

"That hasn't happened in twelve years, so I don't anticipate it happening anytime soon." She knocked her bottle against his once more. "End of discussion. That was your one. We're done," she added when he opened his mouth.

"All right."

"So." Her mind raced for a new topic. "How'd you get your dad to take over constructing the chicken coop?" Shane's sly grin had her laughing. "You tricked him again, didn't you?"

"I made sure he saw me working on trying to finish out Chelle's plan. I also made certain I was doing a terrible job. I feel like I've unlocked a secret trove of treasure where he's concerned."

He might not understand her familial issues, but he'd definitely figured out a constructive way to deal with his father. "Ruby Rose is going to be so excited."

"I hope so. I also hope she knows what all is entailed with handling and caring for chickens."

"Chickens are pretty self-sufficient," Iris said. "They eat, they poop, they lay eggs, they sleep. They aren't exactly the most complex species of the ranch."

"True enough." Shane laughed. "And it'll give her some responsibility, which I'm going to start increasing for all of them pretty soon."

When their food—a large platter of sticky, glistening ribs, potato salad, baked beans and two slices of homemade white bread—was delivered, Iris had the distinct feeling she wouldn't be eating again for days.

The pooch platter for Cos was a big hit. She'd never been entirely sure if Cos knew how to smile, but when he gobbled down his last mouthful of baked sweet potato, he beamed up at her as if she was the best human in the world.

Much the same way that Shane looked at her, she thought, when she caught his eye.

The same way she was afraid she was looking at him.

"Okay." Shane shut his door and walked around the truck just as Iris called out to Cos. "Here we go."

She clicked Cos's leash in place before climbing out of the car. "Could you maybe try to look a little less nauseous?" she asked Shane. "It's an animal rescue, not a skydiving competition."

Iris really shouldn't be one to talk. Her own stomach was doing a dance of unease as she followed him to the entrance of Prairie Paws Rescue.

From the outside, the facility looked like a normal house, with its dark painted wood and contrasting beige trim. But the giveaway was the large fence extending around the property and the sound of barking dogs emanating in the distance.

"Right. You're right." Shane slapped his hands together as if bolstering himself for a playoff football game. "We can do this."

"Yes, we can. Don't forget." She caught his arm and tugged him back. "You're here to find a dog for the boys, not for you. Keep your eye on the prize."

"Right." He raised both fists in the air. "For the boys."

He pushed open the door and stepped back for Iris and Cos to enter. Inside was a welcome area filled with wooden benches and chairs, and photographs of pets united with their new owners. Dogs, cats, rabbits and even… Iris blinked in disbelief. Was that a snake?

"People alert." *Squawk. Squawk!*

Iris and Cos both jumped before Cos barked

and took a step toward the parrot sitting on its perch atop a scarred Formica counter.

A swinging door burst open, and a short middle-aged woman with thick rimmed glasses stepped through. "Thanks, Sergeant Squawk. Hello!" She lifted the pass-through counter and approached them. "I'm Lilah Petrie. Welcome to Prairie Paws. Hi, hi, hi!" Lilah bypassed shaking Iris's or Shane's hand in favor of a drop-down greeting for Cosmo. "Aren't you a handsome fella?" Her hands went deep into his fur, and she gave him an affectionate scrub. "Please tell me you aren't dropping him off. Although—"

"Not dropping him off," Iris said immediately. "We brought him along to help choose a dog for *his* nephews." She pointed to Shane. "And as emotional support for both of us."

"Well, thank you for choosing us." Lilah stood up long enough to return behind the counter. She held up what looked like a treat, out of Cos's line of sight and silently asked Iris if it was okay. "It's handmade. No preservatives or junk."

"Sure," Iris said. She was going to have to take Cos out for a run after everything he'd eaten today.

Cos devoured the treat and clearly would have liked more.

"Just so you know," Lilah said, "we're a life shelter. An animal stays here until he or she is adopted. We're run by volunteers primarily." Lila smiled through her recitation. "We have a flat fee for all adoptions, and that money goes to the care of the animals. We also travel to shelters that have different policies and rescue as many of them as we can."

"Sounds like we came to the right place," Shane said. "My nephews are ten and eight. We live on a cattle ranch, lots of horses and about to be chickens. Other animals coming in the near future, so we need to make sure the one we choose can cope with all that."

"I like to think dogs will cope with anything so long as they're in a happy, safe home. Come on back and let's get started." Lilah led the way to a large, multi-windowed room filled with cages and pens. "Most of these animals have been around other ones, so you shouldn't have too much trouble on that front. That there is Rufus." She pointed to the shepherd mix sitting pretty in the back corner of his cage. "He was surrendered by a family who had to move and couldn't keep him. Good with kids, not so much with other dogs."

Cos peered around Iris's leg toward Rufus, then looked farther down the aisle.

"Moving on," Lilah said as she took them through each animal and offered a bit of background.

"Do you mind me asking," Shane said when they were about eight dogs in, "which animals have been here the longest?"

Lilah brightened at the question and waved them through a different door that lead outside. She headed straight to one of the largest cages where a beautiful golden Lab paced back and forth. He stopped moving when he saw Cos, then carefully walked over to the door.

Cos moved closer as well. They gave each other a good sniff.

"Sundance has been with us for two years," Lilah said. "He had an older owner who passed away. He's a bit timid, but he's also friendly when he gets used to you. He just needs to find the right home. And the right people."

"Sundance," Shane said in a way that had Iris glancing back at him. "His name is Sundance?" Shane crouched and held out a hand for the dog to sniff.

"Always has been."

Cos scraped his paw down Shane's leg. "Yeah, boy. I know." He rested a hand on Cos's head. "You want a playdate?"

Cos whimpered. Sundance pawed against the fence.

"We've got a get-to-know-you yard right over there." She lifted a lead off a wall and unlatched the gate. No sooner had she locked the leash in place and handed it to Shane than Sundance knocked into Cos and the two of them started to run, taking Iris and Shane with them.

Iris gave up trying to hold on and let Cos go. He frolicked with Sundance as the Lab clearly tried to remember how to play, barking as he leaped and hopped about.

"How old is he?" Iris asked Lilah.

"About five as far as we know."

A whimpering from behind them had Iris turning her attention back to the cages while Shane monitored the two new best friends.

"And who's this?" Iris walked over to the cage where a Chihuahua stared longingly in Sundance's direction.

"That's Titan. Poor little thing is a nervous wreck," Lilah said. "We found him in a shelter in Colorado a couple of months ago. Normally, we'd keep him inside, but Sundance is a calming presence for him."

"Oh, hello." Iris laughed as a third dog in the next cage over let out a bark and knocked his head against the fence. Titan immediately walked over to stand near the Siberian husky. The two dogs calmed almost instantly. "What's your name?"

"That one's Roxie," Lilah said. "She and Titan are best friends with Sundance. We call them the Three Musketeers. We rotate them all in and out of the inside cages, but we try to keep them to-gether."

"I see." It wasn't often Iris regretted living on the road. Her lifestyle wasn't set up for multiple pets. She'd found Cos abandoned. He was already a road dog. She wasn't in a position to take on another one. Or another two. That didn't stop her heart from twisting.

"And here he brought me to keep him in line," Iris mumbled to herself.

"Excuse me?" Lilah asked.

"Nothing. Whatever paperwork needs doing, consider Sundance chosen."

Shane had gotten in on the chasing and was currently laughing, rolling around on the ground with both Cos and Sundance.

"You're sure?" Lilah asked.

"We were sure the second we heard his name," Iris said without hesitation. They already had Butch and Cassidy. Sundance completed the movie trifecta.

Once the paperwork was done—Iris took care of the few forms to fill out and the medical release—she returned to the backyard to gather up Shane and the dogs. Someone had to be strong. "Playtime's over!" she called.

Cos immediately raced over to her, and she reclaimed his lead. She waved the papers at Shane. "I made a donation to the shelter in both our names," she told him as he brought Sundance over to her. "Trust me, we were grateful and generous."

"Excellent." The joy on Shane's face was as bright and warm as the afternoon sun. "Thanks. I didn't even have to ask you."

"No." She loved the unbridled happiness and was grateful to witness it. "No, you didn't. Shall we head home?" Before her heart broke over Titan and Roxie who whimpered on the other side of their fences.

"You bet."

She walked away, and when she looked back, she saw Sundance stop in front of the cages where his two best friends remained. The dogs inside looked sad. Titan stretched up and stuck his paw through the grate and patted Sundance's nose.

"What's the story with those other dogs?" Shane asked as soon as they were outside and headed to the car.

"Titan and Roxie. Sundance's best friends." Iris blinked back tears. "They've been insepara-ble apparently. Come on, Cos." She opened one of the back doors of the truck, Shane the other. The two dogs settled in next to each other as if they'd known each other forever. Once they were all inside and were driving away, Iris tried to breathe without hurting. "Those poor babies."

"You were supposed to keep me from losing it," Shane said in a way that told her he was trying to tease her out of her mood.

"I know." She swiped at the tears. "I'm not set up for more animals. Cos, I can handle. Those other two need stability and…" Iris blew out a breath. "I'll be okay. Someone'll take them eventually. I'm sorry, Sundance." Iris reached back and petted the Lab.

Sundance whimpered and turned around to stare out the back window.

They drove on in silence, the sadness pressing down on her. She hadn't realized she was still sniffling until Shane let out a curse and, after pulling over to the side of the road, made a U-turn.

"What's going on?" Iris looked around. Maybe they'd hit something and she'd missed it.

"Guilt," Shane muttered. "Guilt is going on." He floored it back to the shelter, parked, opened the windows before he climbed out. "Stay here," he said before he disappeared inside.

The longer he took to return, the bigger Iris's heart swelled as tears of joy, of sorrow, of relief and gratitude flowed. She didn't want to let herself hope. She'd spent most of her childhood hoping—for a normal life. Someone to love. To be seen, just once, for something other than being one of five. None of it had ever come true.

She pressed her lips together so hard they went numb until Shane reappeared. He trailed behind a delighted looking Roxie on a leash and a trembling Titan tucked under his arm like a purse.

Iris covered her mouth, caught between crying and laughing. Happier than she could ever remember being. She leaned out her window.

"You had one job," Shane said as he handed her Titan.

She half laughed, half sobbed as she accepted the tiny, shaking dog.

Settling Roxie in the back with Cos and Sundance was a comedy of errors as the dogs got used to one another. Finally, they settled, Sundance in the middle, Roxie on one side with his head resting on Sundance's hindquarters. Cos barked once, then lowered his head next to Sundance's.

"Everyone happy now?" Shane asked the entire truck, smiling.

Iris couldn't stop herself. She leaned over and kissed him, despite her arms being filled with a trembling Titan. "Very happy," she said when she pulled back. She beamed at him, giving in, just this once, to the absolute certainty that Shane Holloway may very well be the best man she had ever known.

CHAPTER TEN

"WHAT. IS. THAT?" Butch asked.

Shane had spent a good portion of the drive home wondering how he was going to explain his canine haul to his father. Exceeding his expectations, however, was the mix of absolute confusion and horror on Butch's face when Iris climbed out of the passenger side with Titan in her arms.

To counteract the shock of the so not a ranch dog becoming part of the family, Shane opened the back and let Cos, Sundance and Roxie out.

"This is Titan." Iris cuddled him as Butch stepped closer. "He's part of a trio." Her smile was enough to erase any doubt or regret Shane might have had. He didn't think he could ever tire of making this woman happy.

"Don't ask." Shane held up both hands at his father's accusing flummoxed glare. "I caved, okay? And I doubt even you could have made it out of there without them. And she didn't help." He cast a playful accusatory look at Iris. "Not one bit, so if you want to blame someone, blame her."

Iris laughed, and as Titan was getting fidgety and anxious to be on solid ground with his friends, she set him down.

"One good breeze he'll blow away like a tumbleweed," Butch said in disbelief. "That's no ranch dog."

"Well, he'll just have to learn to become one. This is Roxie." Iris crouched and held out her arms. Roxie came over immediately, sat and offered a paw to Butch.

"That's better." Butch accepted the greeting, then allowed a sniff before petting the dog's head. "You're a beauty, aren't you, Roxie?"

Roxie barked once. Clearly she agreed.

Cos nudged Sundance over as Titan yipped and jumped around.

"And this one is Sundance, Dad." Shane had spent a good portion of his life attempting to decipher his father's expression and moods. He'd never been particularly successful. Until today. He suspected Butch had never been caught so off guard before.

"Sundance." Butch leaned forward, both hands extended out.

Sundance moved forward and placed his face into Butch's hands. "My goodness, you're a pretty boy." Butch sank his hands into the dog's fur. "Is that really his name?"

"Always has been, apparently," Iris said. "As

soon as Shane heard it he knew he'd found the one."

"One came with two more," Shane added.

"The kids are going to be thrilled, and you can't tell me that's not what really matters," Iris said. "And when he gets around to thinking about it," she murmured in a quieter tone so Butch couldn't hear, "so will your father."

Shane had to give Iris credit. She had an effortless way of dealing with Butch Holloway that left everyone else in the dust. All the more reason to love her.

Love? It took all his focus to remain where he was, still, attentive, present. But his mind spun in a way that pulled him from the moment and straight into what could be.

What he suddenly, and without doubt, realized he wanted.

"Didn't think I'd say this, Shane," Butch said. "But you did good." He stood and Sundance moved closer to nudge him with his nose. "You did real good. Even with that little spark of a dog."

Shane laughed as Titan yipped and jumped around him in a circle. "Going to take some training, I think. Roxie, too, maybe." Shane bent down, picked up Titan and grinned. "Wow, we must make a picture."

Iris came over and tipped his hat down. "Yes, you do." He straightened, and she rested a hand on his chest, then seemed to realize how intimate the gesture was and immediately shifted her focus to Titan.

"What's that sound?" Shane hadn't stopped long enough to listen, but there was no mistaking it now. "Dad?" He paused. "Are those... I thought you were just going to finish the chicken coop." Suddenly, he felt as off-kilter as his father. "Did you fill it as well? Did you go get birds on your own?"

Butch looked sheepish and stuffed his hands into his pockets. "Funny story. Today went a bit off the rails. I needed to get some extra wire and stuff from town and while I was there, Carver mentioned receiving an unexpected pallet of chicks. Guess there was a mix-up with an order, and he was practically giving them away. Anyway... I might've made an error of sorts." Butch shoved a restless hand through his hair. "I think you need to come and see."

"This can't be good," Shane murmured to Iris.

"Really?" She positively beamed. "'Cause I've got a feeling this is gonna be hilarious." They followed Butch—and the dogs—around the house, past the stable toward one of the two barns.

Shane passed Titan to Iris, who immediately set him back down, no doubt to get used to his surroundings.

Shane pulled off his hat, slapped it against his

thigh as the completed wired coop came into view. It was a bit larger than he expected. No wonder his father needed more wire. And the wood cubbies inside were anything but rudimentary and slapped together. He recognized the cubicles from Carver's stock. Four stacked on either side of the coop, each with removable tops for easy egg access and displaying ridged ramps into the openings for the chickens to pass through.

Shane had envisioned recycled items from the ranch being used to feed and water the birds, but nope. Clearly, Butch had had other ideas.

"I got everything we needed," Butch called over his shoulder. The dogs—all four of them—had their super sniffers exploring the area. "I had to add plywood around the base of the pen, at least for a while," Butch continued. "The little guys are better escape artists than I anticipated. I had to chase a couple of them into the barn."

Shane came to a halt at the latched door. He slipped his fingers through the wire, held on tight as he counted...eight, nine, ten... "Ten?" he gasped. "Dad, we decided on two. Two chickens. That was all."

"That's what I told Carver I'd take. I didn't realize he thought that I meant two cartons. And, so technically, it's twelve." He bent over, pointed beneath one of the cubbies. "Two of them are hiding. There they are."

Shane looked at Iris, who had a hand covering her mouth as she tried not to laugh. Once again, she was going to be a huge help.

"I know it'll be a lot more work," Butch said. "But I'll help Ruby Rose take care of them. It can be our special project."

"I was figuring on eggs for us, Dad." Shane shook his head. "Not enough to supply the entire town."

"Look on the bright side." Iris stood beside his father. "Forget sheep. You can branch out into chicken eggs. Are they all female, Butch? Just wondering," she said quickly at Shane's look of terror. "In case there's a couple of roosters in there."

"Should all be female," Butch said unconvincingly.

"*Should* be." Shane looked at the pen. And all the little yellow fluff balls bouncing around like pin balls. "Dad, they're going to need more room than this." He was going to end up needing an entire poultry hotel!

"I know. I figure we can work together on that as they grow. Maybe make a kind of chicken paradise, so to speak. We've got some time. Takes them a while to get big enough to lay."

The yellow birds bounced back and forth, flapping their little wings in a promise of what was to come. "They grow like weeds," Shane said. But it was obvious that Butch, despite his error in understanding, was rather proud of what had resulted. And that, he told himself, felt like a win. "Okay." Shane closed his eyes. "Given what we came home with, I guess I can't give you too bad a time about the chickens."

"Well, that's right nice to hear, Shane." Butch sounded so pleased. "I appreciate that. And I figured something else out. I like the idea of me and Ruby Rose going into the egg business. Plenty of people around here don't have any chickens."

"I can't imagine why that is," Shane said to no one in particular and earned a snort laugh from Iris. "So we've gone from no pets to three dogs and twelve chickens. In one day."

"More like two and a half dogs if you think about it," Iris said.

"Not helping," Shane muttered as inspiration struck like a lightning bolt. "Since you're of an open mind today, Dad, it's time we revisit the sheep conversation."

"Now, hold on." Butch shot straight up, his chest puffing out like a rooster.

"Uh-uh. You opened the door," Iris said as she backed away. "The least you can do is have a conversation and hear your son out, yeah?" Hands up in surrender, she whistled for Cos to follow. "Have a good night, boys. I'm going back to work."

It was, Shane thought, the smoothest exit he'd

ever seen from someone who was basically running away. There was no other description for how she scurried and quickly disappeared out of sight.

"So, about these sheep," Butch said, and Shane sighed.

This was where he was. This was his life now. Running a ranch with his ornery father, three dogs, a dozen chickens and three kids he loved as if they were his own.

Sobering. Exhilarating. Yet it still took Shane a moment to realize, standing there by the coop, watching his father head inside the ranch house, that he was, perhaps, for the first time in his life, utterly and completely content.

Except for one thing. He cast a look at Iris's trailer as she closed the door behind her and felt the longing pinch his heart. One very important thing.

IRIS WAITED UNTIL she and Cos were back in her trailer before she gave into the anxiety she'd been trying to push aside for most of the afternoon.

Her hands were shaking, her knees trembling as she leaned back against the door and pressed her hands against her chest. Her heart was racing so fast she couldn't catch her breath.

"This cannot be happening," she said as if she could change things. As if she didn't feel herself go all soft and warm whenever Shane Holloway looked at her. Touched her. Kissed her. Smiled at her.

"Two kisses," she said softly. "You've kissed the man twice. That doesn't mean anything." Except even as she thought it, she could feel her lips tingle. "Nope. Not doing it. I am not falling in love with him. I refuse to. Do you hear me, Cos?"

Cos looked up from where he'd curled up in his bed, brows raised and that "Whatever you say" expression on his face.

"You suffer from selective understanding," she told the dog. "You know exactly what I'm saying."

Cos huffed and rested his chin on his paws.

"Iris Blackwell does not fall in love." Not with a rancher. Not with his charges. Not even with his crotchety, grumpy father.

How could she? She didn't even know what love really meant. What it felt like. And even if she did, she was not a forever kind of woman. She was born with wheels on her feet. She was incapable of staying put.

She had no business even thinking about staying here with the Holloway family and sharing their life.

Her roots had been pruned the second she'd sat on the back of a horse and entered the spotlight. She didn't belong anywhere or to anyone. Other than to herself, of course. And that was the way she liked it. She'd learned early on not to rely on anyone else for her happiness, and she definitely didn't want anyone relying on her. The prospect of disappointing people scared her.

Doubt niggled along the edges of her heart. It had to be that way; she needed to be that way. To survive. To thrive.

Still, her heart pounded. "Only one way out of this."

She grabbed her laptop and, after pouring herself a glass of wine, settled in to make a new plan of action. An accelerated plan. If she stopped allowing herself to get distracted and instead focused solely on Cassidy, she could get the remodel done in seven, maybe eight days. It would mean earlier mornings and later nights, but it would get her what she wanted, what she needed: back on the road before Halloween and well ahead of schedule.

Yep. That was the answer.

She had to get off the ranch and away from Shane Holloway as soon as possible.

It was the only way to protect both their hearts.

"Knock, knock."

Iris pulled the trigger on the nail gun to lock one of the final pieces of wood paneling in place. Since their trip yesterday, she'd known it was only a matter of time before Shane poked his head in and reminded her of his existence. As if she could forget.

She'd prepared herself for his appearance. Or so she thought.

The second she set the nail gun down and faced him, she felt that hitch in her chest that both confused and excited her. "Hey. You headed out to pick up the kids from their overnighter?"

"I am." He stepped inside, walked around a little, shook his head. "Wow. I didn't think it could keep looking better, but I barely see the old Cassidy any longer."

"That's the point," she said with forced cheerfulness. "I got ahead of plan. Only thing holding me back now is waiting on the order for new bathroom components."

"Ahead of plan, huh?"

She heard it, the disappointment, but she chose to ignore it. "Butch said it was okay to set up a workshop in the second barn. I don't want to take a chance of losing my momentum when the weather turns."

"No, we wouldn't want you to lose momentum. But yeah." He seemed to catch himself. "Sure, it's fine for you to use the barn. It's a little small, one of the reasons we stopped using it for storing the extra hay for the season. Just be careful—"

"Not to do any welding and send off sparks?

Don't worry. I always weld outside, and I have no intention of burning anything down. So that's where the trio of beds is going to be." She plowed on before he tried to change the subject. Talking about the trailer, the design, her work was all safe. Being in close quarters with Shane? Not so much. "I just need to talk to the kids about what colors they want."

"Well, you're definitely making progress."

"I am, yeah."

"You feel like taking a break? Come with me to pick up the kids? I thought we'd stop—"

"No, thanks. I've got that—"

"Momentum. Yeah, so you said." He didn't move. He tilted his head much the way Cos tended to when he was curious. "Is everything okay?"

"Everything's fine. I just need to stop getting distracted and focus. I'm here to do a job, and the sooner I get it done, the faster I'll be back on the road." She brushed nervous hands against the back of her jeans. "Don't want to keep getting in your way."

"You're not in anyone's way." He approached, his boots landing heavy on the plywood floor still awaiting its final covering. "Iris—"

"You should probably get going," she told him. "The bus is supposed to be back pretty soon, right?"

"I've got time. Iris—"

He was behind her now. She could feel him, the warmth of his body radiating against her back. His fingers were rough against her skin as he touched her bare arm.

"Shane." His name escaped her lips before she could stop it. She squeezed her eyes shut. She needed to tell him the truth. She'd practiced it, rehearsed it until it followed her into her dreams. And yet now that the opportunity was here… "Shane, please don't."

"Don't what?" He stayed where he was as if he'd never move again. "Iris, what's going on? Why are you avoiding me?"

"I'm not," she lied as she kept her back to him. "We spent all day together yesterday. That's hardly avoiding you."

"Then you ran off almost as soon as we got home, and you've been hiding in your trailer or out here ever since. Talk to me. What's going on?"

She sagged, relinquished control just enough that she found herself facing him. Looking into those amazing, tempting eyes of his. Eyes that were filled with confusion and questions and oh-so-much promise.

"You know what's going on," she whispered. "I'm getting ahead of the curve. Ahead of *this*." She needed to just come out with it. "It's not going to work."

"What's not?"

She arched a brow, knowing a challenge when she heard it. "We like each other. We're attracted to each other."

"Yes. And?"

"And nothing." She shook her head. "Acting on it isn't professional and it's not what I do. This thing with you and me. It's not practical or rational or—"

"Maybe it's not meant to be any of those things." His gentle touch didn't faze her until his other hand came up and he took hold of her hands. He squeezed. "I have feelings for you, Iris. They came out of nowhere, much like you did. I've never—"

"Don't," she ordered and surprised them both with the strength in her voice. "Don't tell me you've never felt this way about someone before."

"Even if it's true?"

Especially if it's true. How many nights did she long to hear those words from someone? Even when she knew she wasn't emotionally ready to deal with them. But she'd let go of fairy tales a very long time ago. "I don't do family, Shane. You know this. I don't know how to…"

"To what?"

I don't know how to love you.

Instead, she said, "You know I can't stay."

"No." The patience in his voice had her wanting to hold on to him forever. "I don't know that, actually. What I do know is you're scared, and honestly, that gives me this weird feeling of hope. Because this…thing that's between us, it scares me, too."

She snorted her disbelief.

"Right down to my booted toes." He touched her face, shifted closer. Her hands clenched around his.

"Shane." She couldn't take the chance and believe, even as she tried to convince herself it didn't matter. "I don't know how—"

"Then learn," he urged. "Stop trying to outrun this. Outrun us. Stay and see if maybe there is a way to make this work."

She shook her head. "I need to leave."

"You want to leave. You need to finish the job you came to do," Shane said. "You said you'd be here until Halloween. That's two weeks away. Give me two weeks. Give us that time to show you what you're capable of being a part of."

"I don't—" The rest of her half-hearted protest was caught by his kiss.

A kiss that made her resistance dissolve, or at the very least abate. Her fingers were wrapped in the fabric of his flannel shirt. Now she did cling to him, returning his kiss as if it was her last action on earth. Everything about him made her system sing, her heart hum. Her blood surge.

"Give me these last two weeks, Iris, please." He murmured his plea against her mouth. "If you still want to go, if you're still determined to walk away, then fine." His fingers caressed her cheek. "I'll understand."

She wanted to believe him. She'd spent last night formulating a plan of escape that would keep her heart safe from falling any deeper for him. But standing here now, in his arms, she had to admit the truth. It was already too late.

"You don't have anything to risk by staying a little longer."

"You don't get it." How could he when she didn't? Another two weeks, another two days, she was on the precipice of giving in and she couldn't risk that. She couldn't risk them— Shane, the kids, Butch, even the chickens.

"If I give you the two weeks, work comes first."

"Absolutely." He nodded, looked around. "Work first. Starting tomorrow." His lips curved. "Come with me to get the kids. Be in on the surprise for them, Iris. It's partly because of you, after all."

She rolled her eyes, tightened her grip on his shirt and pulled him down for another kiss. "You do not play fair."

"I probably should have warned you about that." His smile was easy and stretched from ear to ear. "You ready?"

"Fine." She pretended to huff. "Let's go get the kids."

CHAPTER ELEVEN

"TELL US WHAT the surprise is, Uncle Shane. Pleeeeeeeease?" Miles threw himself forward in the back seat, arms outstretched while Eric and Ruby Rose looked out their respective windows.

"You shouldn't have told them," Iris chided from her seat beside him.

"Good thing we're almost home." Shane wasn't sure he could have taken much more of Miles's pleading. They took the second to last turnoff before the ranch. "Miles, you're just going to have to wait a while longer. And FYI, you all need to be on your best behavior because your PaPa is having some friends over for dinner. I need you all to help me unpack the car, then get changed and presentable." The three of them looked as if they'd been sleeping in dirt. Which he supposed, technically, they had been.

"That explains why I saw Butch hauling what looked like half a cow to the grill when we left," Iris said. "I've never seen him look so serious. And that's saying something."

"Dad loves to put on a show with those grills of his. Hope you're all hungry." Shane glanced in the rearview mirror. "Eric? Did you have a good time at the campout? You haven't said much."

"It was fun." As always, his oldest nephew was the master of understatement.

"He won the pumpkin carving contest," Miles announced. "They gave him a ribbon and everything."

"That's pretty cool." Iris turned around. "Congratulations."

"You'll have to give me some pointers when we carve ours for Halloween," Shane said. "I don't think I've carved a pumpkin since I was your age."

"It was way gross scooping out all those pumpkin guts," Miles said. "So squishy and gooey." He wiggled his fingers in front of Ruby's face.

"Ruby Rose, did you get to help with the pumpkins?" Shane looked at her in the rearview mirror.

"Yes."

"She carved a chicken." Miles rolled his eyes. "Who makes a pumpkin chicken?"

Ruby Rose gave him such an irritated look Shane choked back a laugh.

"Oh, that reminds me." Iris snapped her fingers and reached under her seat. "Oscar wanted to come along." She held out the stuffed chicken, and immediately Ruby Rose's expression brightened. "I took good care of him, just like I promised."

"Thank you." Her eyes sparkled. On the side of her face was a painted butterfly with gold and orange glitter. "I missed him." She hugged the chicken tight and offered up a smile to Iris.

"Thank you for trusting me with him. So, Miles. What else did you all do?"

As Miles's recitation filled the car, Shane found himself smiling. His instincts about Iris had been right. She'd been running scared and had even amped up her plans to disappear altogether.

He could always rely on her being honorable. No way was she going to bolt before she was done with the job she'd been hired to do. He had two weeks. Two weeks to change her mind about leaving.

He was realistic. It wasn't going to be easy. He was going to need help. He watched her animated way of interacting with Miles, the easy manner she had with all the children.

Otherwise known as his reinforcements.

Shane prided himself on being a man of his word. When he gave it, he meant it. But that didn't mean he wasn't hoping not to have to let her go.

He smiled to himself and must have chuckled because Iris glanced at him.

"What?"

"Just something I remembered Wayne telling me a while back." After Wayne had finally proposed to Chelle. They'd first met at a town hall gathering where she was protesting the decreased library hours. Wayne said he knew from the second he'd seen her spark he was done for. Convincing Chelle had taken some doing, but if his brother had managed it, so would Shane. He was nothing if not competitive, even if Wayne wasn't here to cheer him on.

Now Shane had experienced his own spark. And he was darned if he was going to let it die out.

"I'll tell you another time." He didn't think she could handle another confession of the heart today.

He took the final curve to the ranch, hit Send on the text he'd already typed out to his father.

"Man, I really wanted pizza tonight," Miles said as he finished regaling the car about the best way to eat a s'more.

"Maybe tomorrow. PaPa's in charge tonight," Shane said. "Or so I was informed before we left." He cleared his throat and kicked up the volume. "Speaking of PaPa. We made some new friends while you all were gone." He pointed out the windshield as Butch, Cosmo and the newly added dogs all came into sight.

"Oh." Eric's gasp of happiness and surprise filled Shane's heart. "You did it! You got us dogs!

You got two dogs! Really?" He was unbuckling his seat belt before the truck came to a stop.

"There's three, in fact," Shane said with more than a bit of irony in his voice. "The third might be a little hard to see."

"Oh, wow! Wow, wow, wow!"

Miles scampered out behind his brother as Ruby Rose struggled to unlock her seat belt. "Out! Out, please!"

"Hang on, sweetheart." Shane released his own seat belt and got her out as fast as he could. She squirmed, and it reminded him of Titan. Clutching Oscar to her chest, she hopped down and raced toward the others who were already out of the car.

"Oh, my gosh! Hi." Eric dropped to his knees in front of Sundance, Roxie and Titan who, true to form, was already dancing around the brothers in barking glee. "PaPa, what are their names?"

"This one here is Sundance." Butch placed a hand on the top of the Lab's golden head.

"Hi, Sundance." Miles joined his brother, reached out for a sniff and pat before Sundance gave them each a sloppy lick. "This is so cool! They're awesome!"

"This pretty girl is Roxie," Shane said as he came over and earned an eager expression from the husky. "She and Titan there were good friends with Sundance at the shelter, so Iris suggested we bring them all home."

"Really? Thanks, Iris!" Eric said. "Hi, Titan."

Ruby Rose stood off to the side. Instead of approaching the dogs, she seemed to be inching over to the house.

"You don't have to be scared, munchkin," Butch told his granddaughter. "They just have to get to know you."

She didn't look convinced. Before Shane could think what to do, Roxie walked away from the boys and came over to Ruby Rose. His niece stood there, eyes wide, as if frozen. Cos, always the peacemaker, toddled over and pushed his head under Ruby Rose's free hand. She grabbed hold and steadied.

Roxie dropped down to the ground and scooted forward on her belly, then rolled over onto her back and stuck her paws in the air. Cos barked and broke away from Ruby Rose, walked around his new canine friend.

"That means she trusts you," Iris told the little girl. "Come on. We'll pet her together." Iris joined Ruby, took her hand and touched the dog. "She's very gentle and sweet. And she likes you. See?"

Ruby Rose giggled when Roxie licked her hand. Roxie, sensing she had a new fan, did a bit of a somersault before jumping to her feet and asking for more pets.

"Okay, hi, Roxie." Ruby Rose's hand slipped into Roxie's silver-gray fur, the other hand still clutching her stuffed chicken. She beamed at Iris, and something tugged at Shane's heart. "She looks like a wolf."

"She does a little," Iris agreed. "I bet you'll always feel safe with her around."

"PaPa has another surprise. This one's just for you, Ruby. Come on." Shane held out his hand as Butch led the way over to the chicken coop.

They were barely there when Ruby cheered and broke away from Shane, racing over to the coop that was alive—and lively—with chicks. "For me?"

"For us." Butch picked her up and held her on his hip as she looked on eagerly at the coop. "You and I are going to take good care of them and maybe give eggs to people who don't have them."

"Like Mama said?" Ruby asked, clinging to her grandfather. "Can I name them?"

"Absolutely," Butch told her. "But you might want to wait a little while until they're bigger."

"So we can tell them apart," Shane added. "We got some time to clean up before your friends get here, Dad?"

"That you do." Butch set Ruby Rose back on her feet. "Reminds me, I'd best get back to the grill. Hurry on up, you lot. We've got some eatin' to do."

IRIS WAS HUMMING to herself as she cleaned up Cassidy's interior and got ready for the next day. Cleaning herself up took a little extra work, but when Iris climbed out of the shower and was blow-drying her hair, she caught a look at herself in the mirror.

There was a light in her eyes she couldn't quite decipher. A pink tint in her cheeks that added color she never knew she was lacking. Her mouth seemed curved in a perpetual smile she suspected hadn't dimmed since she'd first stepped foot on the ranch.

"Okay, you're being ridiculous." She was projecting of course. Or seeing things. One or the other. Instead of dwelling on those options, she let herself drift back to the kids seeing the dogs for the first time. It shouldn't have surprised her, the instant change she'd seen in Eric.

Something about having animals in your life always made the days a bit brighter and easier, and Eric, all three of those kids, deserved the absolute best. Iris's emotional truce with Shane was going to take some thinking. She felt a bit relieved he hadn't gone so far as to say the *L* word. She wasn't sure she'd have believed it if he had.

Heck, she couldn't even say it to herself without feeling like she was jinxing something.

She'd only been here a couple of weeks. Nothing lasting and genuine could come from so short a time together.

Iris might have agreed to stay through Halloween, but she wasn't under the misguided notion that she wasn't in a bubble of sorts, where the real world didn't quite intrude.

Here, with her work and the kids on their best behavior, and Shane trying to convince her she might belong here, it was easy to forget just how jaded she was about emotional connections and family relations. She'd said she'd give it a go, though, and honestly? She was looking forward to trying.

She clicked off the dryer, ran a brush through her hair and quickly changed into a clean T-shirt and jeans. For the next couple of weeks she was going to focus on looking for the good and believing anything was possible. It couldn't hurt. Could it?

A sharp bark was the response she got.

"You think so, too, Cos?" She crouched and grabbed his furry face in her hands and nuzzled his nose. "You're such a good boy, helping those dogs get acclimated."

A quiet knock on the door had her quickly straightening to answer it. "Ruby Rose." She stepped back, and the little girl climbed in. Iris was about to close the door when Titan followed, hopping up the steps and giving Cos a nose-to-nose welcome. Ruby had had a bath and was wearing an adorable pair of overalls. The yellow shirt she wore underneath had lace-topped ruffle sleeves. Her little boots completed the sweet outfit. "What brings you by, young lady?"

Ruby stuck out her hand, palm closed. Only when Iris placed her own hand below the girl's did Ruby Rose release what she was holding. "I made it at camp."

"For me?" Iris looked down at the beaded bracelet similar to the one she'd helped Shane reconstruct for Ruby. "It's beautiful!" She ran her finger over the blue and purple beads before she slid it onto her wrist. "I love it. Thank you. And look!" She tugged at her purple shirt. "It matches."

"Uncle Shane said you made mine." She held up her own arm. "You gave me back my Mama."

"Your uncle helped me." Iris sank into the table seat, determined not to get weepy. "We gave you back something you and your Mama made together, sweet girl. But I can't give you her back."

"I know." Ruby frowned, nodded in a way that made her look like the oldest six-year-old Iris had ever seen. "She's not coming back, is she?"

"No, she's not." She touched Ruby's hair. "I'm sorry."

Ruby moved in and locked her arms around Iris's neck. She squeezed hard. "I miss her."

"I'm sure you do." Iris swallowed hard, unable to do anything other than simply hold her. She caught movement out of the corner of her eye and laughed. "Uh-oh. I think Titan is making himself at home." The skinny little Chihuahua had curled up in the center of Cos's bed, and Cos, ever the gracious host, laid down beside the bed and sighed.

"Dogs are silly," Ruby Rose said. "Uncle Shane said it's almost time for dinner. Come on." She put her hand in Iris's and gave it a tug. Something told Iris there was nothing coincidental about Ruby Rose's appearance at her trailer. Clearly Shane was determined to pull no punches when it came to showing her just what she'd be walking away from.

Ruby Rose didn't stop tugging her forward until they walked all the way around the house. A massive propane grill was fired up and smoking as it cooked a significant amount of steaks and foil-wrapped potatoes. Ears of corn and whole bell peppers were being added.

Shane and the boys were setting the extra-large picnic table. The early evening breeze had kicked up and ruffled the edges of the gingham table cloth.

"Drinks are over there." Shane pointed to the pair of coolers against the house. "Dad got a bit inspired while we were gone. He even made dessert."

"One of my Jesse's cake recipes," Butch said. "Nothing fancy, but it'll feed a crowd."

"You had me at cake," Iris said. Ruby Rose finally let go of her hand and raced back to chase after Titan who, along with Cos, went off to frolic with Roxie and Sundance.

"Ah, the life of a dog." Shane came over, slipped an arm around her waist and tugged her close. "See? Nothing scary about family here on the ranch." Before she could respond, he planted a kiss on her lips. "You're staring."

"You're embarrassing both of us." Her face went barbeque hot. "Shane…" But when she looked to Miles and Eric and even his father, none of them seemed to notice the affectionate exchange. "You prepared them, didn't you?"

"Well, I…uh…" His laugh was contagious. "I plead the fifth."

"These rib eyes won't take long." Butch held up a huge slab of meat and dangled it over the heat. "Who's hungry?"

"Me!" both boys said, their hands shooting up in the air.

Iris looked for something around her, something inside of her to grab hold of, to cling to the belief that something like this wasn't possible for her. But there wasn't anything. There was only Shane and his family and an abundance of laughter. A longing she'd locked away ages ago unfolded inside of her, but she tamped it down, not wanting to give in. Not yet at least.

"We should probably wait to put those on until your friends get here," Shane said. He moved to join his father at the grill.

Iris joined in with the kids and dogs, throwing balls in various directions and watching the animals scamper after them. In the distance, she caught sight of a large vehicle making its way down the road to the house. She stood there, one hand shielding her eyes, another on her hip as the RV drew closer.

"I believe your company's here, Butch," Iris called.

"Looks like," Butch said. He lowered the hood of the grill and joined her.

Dust plumed up from beneath spinning tires, and slowly, the well-used, almost ancient RV rolled to a stop. "You're sure I'm not intruding being here?" she asked Shane's father. "I don't want to be in the way of—"

"Family's never an intrusion," Butch said in such a sweet manner she blinked in surprise. "Besides, they aren't just here to see me."

Iris frowned and glanced up, wondering why he seemed particularly determined not to meet her gaze. That unexpected longing that had been circling inside of her suddenly pulled back and was replaced with something she couldn't quite define.

Butch stepped forward, hand up to the RV as he approached.

Instantly, Iris's mind went into fix-it mode. The vehicle could definitely use some work. New paint, new brake pads considering the whining she heard as it stopped. The curtains looked as if they'd been dragged out of the 1970s, and she immediately imagined that the floor might be shag carpeting.

"Stop remodeling it." Shane's gentle accusation had her laughing. "You've already got a project in the works."

"Two," Iris reminded him. "Don't forget the dining room table. And stop reading my mind." She didn't need any more proof that he was the first person who truly understood her.

Shane shook his head. "You are such a workaholic."

"Maybe." The setting sun hit the windshield in just the right spot so she couldn't see who was behind the wheel. "But it's not really work when you love what you do."

The RV's door bounced open.

"Sorry we're late!" The big, booming voice had Iris taking a step back. She blinked, but the shock zapped any coherent thought out of her brain. "Had to detour back to Wyoming and pick up a tagalong."

There was no mistaking the boisterous, commanding presence of this man. From his over-size polished belt buckle to the dark hat perched on his head. She might not have met him many times over the years, but Elias Blackwell always made a lasting impression.

"You're only a day or two behind," Butch said as he slapped his hand into the other man's. "Good to see you, Big E. Welcome to Cottonwood Creek."

"Appreciate it." Elias let out a long breath, put a hand on Butch's shoulder. "We finally made it."

"Just in time for dinner," Butch said. "I've thrown the meat on the grill."

"Excellent, excellent. You must be Shane." Big E took a step toward them, shook hands with Shane.

It was all Iris could do not to try to sink into the dirt. Maybe he didn't recognize her. It had been years since she'd seen her great-uncle. Maybe—

"And there she is." Big E faced her, a wide smile on his round face, something akin to satisfaction in his eyes. "Iris Blackwell. Look at you, all grown up."

"Hi, Uncle Elias." Her smile was quick, still uncertain. "I, um, didn't know you were coming." She accepted the one-armed hug Big E offered. Because it was the safest topic of conversation she could think of, she added, "Nice wheels."

Big E laughed, squeezed her hard. "I wondered if you would approve. You know, I'm a fan of your videos. Been watching them the last couple of months. Got me to thinking I could probably do with some—"

"Don't go getting into business mode yet." A stern, don't-mess-with-me voice echoed from the RV's doorway. The older woman stepped down using a polished cane for assistance. Her silver hair was long and braided down her back, her skin a rich tone and wrinkled from years beneath the Wyoming sun. She was thin but not frail and, like a woman who alone had carried an entire business on her back for many years, had a spine of steel.

"Grandma." Whatever shock she'd felt at seeing Big E after all these years vanished beneath the sight of her Grandma Denny. "Oh, my gosh." She stepped forward and, ignoring the fact Denny Blackwell wasn't exactly a hugger, wrapped her arms around the older woman. "It's so good to see you." She held on tight. All the regret she'd had over not seeing her grandmother for years evaporated. "How are you? How are you feeling?" She stepped back, still holding on to her grandmother's shoulders. "What are you doing here?"

"We came to see you! And I'm fine, just fine." Denny waved off any concern she heard in Iris's voice. "Had to spend time back on the Flying Spur to see to your cousin's new baby, get my bearings again after a couple of weeks in that spine rattler, but I'm back in the saddle, so to speak."

"I can't believe you're here." Iris looked back at Butch and Shane, then at Big E, then at her grandmother who patted Iris's arm. "Talk about lucky. What are the chances of you showing up where I'm on a job."

"Yes," Shane said slowly as he looked at his father. "What are the chances?"

"Hi!" Miles popped up behind Big E and tilted his head back, held out his hand. "I'm Miles Holloway."

"Well, how do, Miles Holloway." Big E accepted the handshake warmly. "I'm Elias Blackwell, but most people call me Big E."

"'Cause you're so big, right?" Miles said in a far more serious tone than Iris could recall hearing of late.

"Let's just say that's true," Big E agreed with a solemn nod. "And you are?" He looked to Eric.

"Eric, sir." Sundance stood on one side of him, Roxie on the other.

"Sir, huh?" Big E nodded in approval. "Pleasure to meet you, son. Which would make this little lady Ruby Rose." Big E bent down, planted his hands on his thighs. "That's a mighty fine chicken you have there."

"His name's Oscar." Ruby Rose played with Oscar's wing. "I have twelve more chickens now. Real ones! We're gonna sell their eggs."

"Is that so?" Big E looked impressed. "Well, I'd be interested in seeing those while I'm here. You know, the last time I saw your grandpa was when you were born, Ruby Rose. And you two weren't any taller than those weeds over there."

"So you haven't seen each other in six years, and yet here you are," Shane said carefully. "Out of the blue. At the same time Iris has arrived." He eyed his father. "How incredibly fortunate and lucky."

"Isn't it?" Iris checked her phone, but didn't see any return calls from her father. Her father, who, for the past two weeks, had been dodging her calls. "Okay, let's have it."

"Let's have what, Iris?" Denny feigned innocence, but Iris wasn't buying it. Her grandmother was far too cagey to ever get away with something this obvious.

"Let me guess." Iris looked on the bright side, feeling as if a giant shoe was about to drop on her head. "You need a remodel of this thing, Uncle?" She pointed to the RV. "Looking for a consult?"

"Oh, now that you mention it." Big E scrubbed a hand across his whiskered chin. "I wouldn't be adverse to a consultation. The plumbing's been giving us some trouble as of late—"

"That's not why we're here, Iris," Denny said. "And before you start worrying yourself into a state—"

"Is it Dad?" Iris felt the color drain from her cheeks. "Oh, no. I should have thought… I should have realized, did something happen? Is that why he hadn't called me—"

"Your father's fine." Denny patted her hand. "My son's fit as a fiddle. He sends his love. As do Maggie and Violet."

Iris's mind raced. "Maggie and…"

"Oh, just get it over with, Denny." The third voice had Iris closing her eyes, but not before she saw the flash of apology on Shane's face. Iris turned, stepped out from her grandmother's aura and looked up at the woman now standing in the RV's doorway. "Surprise!"

Flora Blackwell held both hands over her head, posing as if flashbulbs were exploding all around her. Wearing pristine jeans with rhinestones down the side seams, her sparkly pink collared shirt was bedazzled just short of a disco ball. As usual, her boots—silver this time—matched the hat she reached for and plunked on her head. Her dark brown hair had been brushed until it shined, much like an award-winning show horse.

In that instant, whatever threadbare hope Iris

had had that her mother might have changed in the past twelve years vanished.

Regardless of how many years had gone by, Iris was twenty again, having been pulled right back into the past she'd been determined to outrun. A past that, until this moment, she'd thought she'd escaped.

Flora, always the performing professional, waited a solid five-count beat before she stepped down from the RV. She locked her hands around Iris's upper arms and pulled her into a fierce hug that Iris couldn't bring herself to return.

She stood stiffly until Flora's hold eased.

"Oh, it's so good to see you, Iris." Flora cupped Iris's face in her hands and beamed as if she'd been welcomed with joy. "Look at you. Just as pretty as always. Although I think I see some lines here." She touched a finger to Iris's eyes. "And here. We'll have to work on that. I've got an amazing cream that'll work wonders. What a success you're making of things with your little remodeling business. Those videos have stellar production value. It's just so cute what you do! You always were a go get 'em girl."

Her little remodeling business. Her *cute* remodeling business.

"Yep." Iris had long stopped arguing with her mother. "That's me all right. A go get 'em girl.

What are you doing here, Mom?" She already felt exhausted.

"What else was I going to do when you hung up on me after I called you two weeks ago?" Flora looked as if that explained everything.

"I didn't hang up on you." Iris hadn't answered the call. There was a big difference. Not that her mother saw it. Iris squirmed. Internally, all she could do was silently scream for someone to save her as she stared helplessly at the ground and her mother's silver-toed boots.

"I'm Shane Holloway, Ms. Blackwell." Shane stepped forward and introduced himself to Denny first, then turned to Flora, and Iris's heart lifted. He never failed to disappoint, did he? "And Mrs. Blackwell."

"Oh, it's Flora, please." Flora kept one arm locked around Iris's shoulders. "Aren't you a handsome one? He's very handsome, Iris." She squeezed and teased. "I don't know why I should be surprised that you've picked a good one. You know, I remember when you were sixteen and there was that boy in Dallas at the Four Stars show? You and he ran off behind the stadium seats—"

"That was J.R., Mom." And that boy had been far more interested in J.R.'s music collection than making his way around the bases.

"Was it?" Flora frowned, then waved off her comment. "Well, anyway—"

Iris had had enough already. "How long are you staying?"

"Oh, we've got an open schedule," Denny announced in a way that told Iris her grandmother knew precisely why Iris was asking.

"For the most part," Flora continued. "Didn't you hear? They're inducting me into the Cowgirl Hall of Fame!"

"Are they?" Iris nodded. "Wow. Congratulations. You must be thrilled."

"Beyond," Flora gushed. "It's a dream come true, and of course you have to come."

"Do I?" Yeah, that wasn't going to happen.

"Don't worry, we can talk about all that later," Flora went on. "And don't worry about us, either, while we're here. You just keep doing what you're doing. We won't distract you. We know you've got work to do. We'll have lots of girl time to chat. We just couldn't miss the opportunity to see you when Big E told us you were here! We've got so much to fill you in on. It's been so long, and you missed the family reunion this summer."

"I was working," Iris said as her mother raised an eyebrow and tossed her brown, highlighted hair behind her shoulder.

"From what I hear, you're always working," her mother chided. "We need to do something about that. And those lines. Ha! See what I did there?"

Oh, Iris saw all right. "So, you're just here to visit." The skepticism rang louder than one of Shane's feared roosters. "Unless there's another reason. One you're waiting to spring on me once my defenses are down, which I'm going to assume is the case, since Dad could have texted me with this Hall of Fame news."

"Now, Iris, I don't think—" Butch stepped forward, uncharacteristically attempting to play peacemaker.

"Hey, it's far too early for us to go dredging up the family drama just yet." Big E cut him off. "And if we aren't careful, those steaks of yours are going to be charcoal pretty soon, Butch. Let's say we get to paying attention to those." Big E slapped his hands together and motioned for Butch to head back to the table.

"My, what a cute dog!" Flora finally released Iris long enough to bend down and greet Titan, who yipped and reached up to plant his tiny paws on Flora's sparkles. "You're just like my Zinni, only bald. Zinni!" Flora called.

Iris and Shane turned in tandem as a ball of brown and white whizzed into sight, took one look at Titan and let out a sound that couldn't quite be described.

"Zinni doesn't bark well," Flora explained as

she scooped up the dog. "And we're still getting used to having her run around on the loose. She has a tendency to get the zoomies and scamper off." She bent down and held Zinni up to Titan. The dogs sniffed each other, and Titan, seemingly realizing that not all dogs were bigger than him, immediately yipped and stood up on his back legs, hopped in a circle. "Oh, my gosh!" Flora gasped. "Look at that, Iris! He could be part of the show! Go on, Zinni. Make friends."

"Zinni?" Shane muttered in Iris's ear.

"Zinnia, no doubt," Iris muttered back.

"No whispering, Iris. It's rude." Flora shot her an all too familiar look that soured Iris's stomach. "And yes, her name is Zinnia. What's for dinner? I'm starving." When she strode off, Ruby Rose, Miles and Eric trailed along behind her with the dogs, while Iris stood frozen to the spot.

She studied the RV and wondered how far and how fast she could go before anyone noticed.

"You wouldn't get half a mile in that thing."

"I'd be willing to try," Iris grumbled.

"So." Shane shoved his hands into his pockets, rocked back on his heels. "That's your mother."

That was her mother. "You know how you get that recurring dream, like you go to work naked, or you arrive at school totally unprepared for a test?" For two seconds, she reverted to Belle status and swooped her arm in her mother's direction as if to say, "See, I told you so." "Welcome to my nightmare. In full, sparkling denim-clad Technicolor."

"She's not that bad." Shane tried to reassure her. "This could be a good thing."

"You wanna bet?" She stood directly in front of him, inched up her nose and stared right into his eyes. "Seriously. She's, *they're* here for a reason. That induction thing is only the tip of a very cold iceberg. Twelve years have gone by and barely a peep." Unless Flora wanted or needed something, which was why Iris rarely answered her phone. "Now I've got three Blackwells turning up on the doorstep out of the blue. They're up to something." Hands on her hips, her anger and irritation finally broke through the shock.

"Maybe." Shane tried again. "Or maybe they missed you and wanted to see you."

Iris snorted. Her mother never, ever, came to Iris without a reason.

"Give them the benefit of the doubt, Iris." When he took hold of her arms and squeezed, she felt instantly better. He bent forward, pressed his lips to her forehead. "Maybe they'll surprise you."

"Oh, they'll surprise me," Iris said without hesitation as her recently stabilized world tilted. "The question is how."

CHAPTER TWELVE

THE LAST THING Shane expected to find in his kitchen at 4:00 a.m. the next morning was his father, Big E and Denny mulling, arguing and commenting on his sheep herd plans. It had been a night of adjustments as the new dogs and extra Blackwells settled in on the Holloway Ranch.

Currently, their new canine companions were lined up in front of the kitchen sink clearly waiting for their breakfast. Roxie's tail wagged so hard it thudded against the cabinet. The three of them together looked like nesting dolls.

"Your boy's got the right idea," Big E was saying as Shane sidled up to the coffee machine to fill his travel tumbler before he headed out. "Adding in another kind of herd is good for the land and can increase production for the cattle."

"Still don't see that we need it," Butch said stubbornly. "Everything's working fine as is. Income's steady, expenses, too. No need to change anything up."

Shane shook his head, silently wishing Big

E luck persuading Butch Holloway. Still, he'd take their good-natured bickering over what had transpired over dinner last night any day of the week.

One thing he'd learned since Iris had arrived on the ranch was that he had a lot of blessings to count. Here he thought he knew what family tension was all about, but that was before he'd sat at a dinner table with Iris and Flora.

It was evident to Shane that Flora was trying to connect with her daughter, yet it was even more obvious Iris wasn't having it. She'd shut down and locked herself down as tight as an Old West bank vault.

Still, Shane couldn't help but feel some sympathy for Flora despite her obviously trying too hard. Near as Shane could tell, she hadn't made a dent in Iris's resolve. By the time dessert was served, Iris had begged off for the night, saying she had an early start in the morning before retreating to her trailer.

Shane would have gone after her, but the look she shot him as she'd gotten up from the table said she wanted to be alone. He knew that feeling, probably better than most, and, after nudging Cos to go with her, he watched her disappear.

Shane had to give Flora credit. Iris's mother did her best to conceal her disappointment, but anyone who looked at her could tell she was at a complete loss as to what to do when it came to connecting with her daughter.

Flora had brightened considerably, however, when, after lamenting the rigid and unforgiving sleeping arrangements in Big E's RV, Butch offered Flora the use of their first-floor guest room.

From what Shane understood, Flora wasn't an early riser, so it worked out well for everyone, especially Big E and Denny who wouldn't have to worry about disturbing Zinni or Flora in the RV.

"You're wasting your breath trying to convince my father about the sheep, Big E," Shane said as Butch continued to waffle on the idea. "I've yet to find the right argument that works, and I've been trying for months." Not even reminding Butch the entire idea had been Wayne's made him budge.

"Then stop looking for one." Denny got up from the table, carried a mug to the counter and refilled her own coffee. "From what I hear tell, you're running this place now. It's your decision to make."

Big E guffawed. "Like that's stopped you from sticking your nose into how Corliss runs The Circle E."

"I get my say where my granddaughter's concerned," Denny countered. "But in the end Corliss makes the decisions."

Big E shook his head. "Delusional."

"Practical," Denny countered. "Talk don't mean anything. It may be you need to show him you're right, Shane."

"And what if I'm not? Right, that is?" As on the fence as he was about Flora Blackwell, he'd liked Denny straight from the jump. Big E, too, but Denny was a no-nonsense, in your face, tell the truth kind of person. Her older brother was a charmer. Near as Shane could tell, Denny saw charm as a waste of time. Roxie came over, knocked her head against Shane's knee and earned herself a pet.

"Then you own up to it and move on." Denny waved off his concern. "You don't gain anything from arguing about it and waiting for someone to change their mind. Act already. Poop or vacate the outhouse."

"Huh." Indelicate yet right on target. He toasted Denny with his coffee mug. "I think you may be on to something, Denny."

"Course I am. Built my own quarter horse ranch on my own while pregnant with twins. I know a good bet when I see one." She eyed Shane with approval. "You might be one."

"Why, thank you." Shane had been wrong. Denny did have a spark of charm as well.

"You two are up early," Shane said.

"Lifelong habits die hard," Denny said. "Be prepared. You won't see Flora 'til close to noon."

"Heard you say you were moving your herd this morning," Big E announced. "Thought I might go out with you. It's been a while since I sat in a saddle. If you're amenable to some company, that is."

"I'd be happy for the help." Shane checked his watch. "I'm meeting Hank and Roy in about a half hour."

"You taking the dogs?" Butch asked.

"Not this morning," Shane said. And not for a while. He needed to work with Sundance and Roxie individually before he could trust them around the herd. Titan was just going to have to get used to staying around the house and stable. He was a little too hyper to be near cattle, and one good accidental kick from a hoof could have him flying all the way to Aberdeen. "Too much going on this morning to get them acclimated."

"Well, in that case," Big E said with a sharp nod. "I'm ready to head out when you are."

"Before we go, I've got a question." Butch paused, looking at each of them. "Are we going to come clean about setting Iris up, or are we going to continue to pretend this visit is one big coincidence?"

"Don't know what you're talking about," Big E grumbled into what was left of his coffee.

"What he said," Denny pointed her thumb at her big brother.

"Now, Shane—" Butch chimed in.

"Iris isn't here, Dad. Neither is Flora. You blindsided Iris, probably because you knew it was the only way to get her and Flora in the same room. Ripped all the control right out of her hands. You hurt her." Shane shook his head as if he was lecturing a table full of toddlers. "You had to have seen it last night. What's worse is that I can't believe you were in on this, Dad. After everything that Iris has done for you. For our family." For Shane.

"Family's important." Butch had the decency to look slightly ashamed. "We didn't mean to cause Iris any pain. Sometimes you just have to do what's necessary to start the healing."

This familial epiphany must be a recent one. Shane recalled going years without hearing one word from his father when Shane was out on his own. "So what Iris wants doesn't matter, is that it?" Shane knew Iris didn't need him to defend her, but he felt obligated all the same. It's what a man did for the woman he loved. "She has her reasons for not wanting Flora in her life, yet none of you seem able to respect that."

"We can respect it, but we still want to change her mind," Big E said. "We need her to change her mind."

"Need." That one word set off a whole new

chorus of alarm bells. "Why would any of you *need* Iris to mend fences with her mother?"

Denny glanced at Big E. "Elias, we should tell him."

"Not now," Big E growled under his breath.

"He could help. Maybe he's right," Denny suddenly looked uneasy. "We don't know the particulars. Flora's certainly never been forthcoming about the issues between them. Maybe we've handled this one wrong."

"Aha. Iris was right," Shane mused as his mind raced. "She told me last night Flora had to be here for something else. Let me guess. This has something to do with that Hall of Fame ceremony?"

"Mostly," Denny said. "He mostly guessed, didn't he?" She leaned back when Big E tried to nudge her silent. "The rest of it is that Flora is hoping to convince the girls to reunite as the Belles and perform at her and Dandelion's induction ceremony. So far we've managed to get Magnolia and Violet on board. It's taken some coaxing and…" Denny winced. "And some deal making. It hasn't been easy, to be honest."

"Wow." Shane couldn't help it. His laugh wasn't one that brought tears to his eyes, but an ache to his heart. "Just…wow. So, Iris is what? Stop number three on Flora's apology tour? And the grand finale takes place at the Hall of Fame?"

Denny and Big E didn't deny it.

"Ceremony aside," Denny said. "I'd like to see my son's family back together, or at the very least, communicating again. We had serious doubts about even being able to find Iris. She moves around so fast and so often, we needed extra help in pinning her down long enough to get out here in time to catch up with her."

"Extra…help." Shane looked at Butch. "That must be where you came in, right, Dad?" Disappointment crashed through him. "This is why you hired her? To set her up for a family reunion she has no interest in? All that bluster about finally wanting to remodel Cassidy was just smoke so you could pin her down long enough for them to pounce."

"Now, hang on, there, Shane," Big E countered. "You're acting as if you haven't gotten anything out of this. From what we hear—"

"We saw how you were watching her last night," Denny tossed in. "I saw how you looked at her. You care about her."

"I do care about her. I love her." Finally, he had the chance to say the words that had been trapped in his heart. "But you all lied to her. Dad, you lied to her. How could you do that?"

"I did not lie," Butch protested. "Exactly. I may have left certain important details out of the conversation, but I did watch her videos online before I contacted her about hiring her to re-model Cassidy. I just never mentioned who sent me the link to her channel in the first place." He cast a glance at Big E.

"I don't see what the big deal is," Big E said. "Iris might have gotten an emotional sting out of Flora's arrival, but Butch here is getting a new trailer, Iris is getting a new video to feature on her channel and is being paid, Shane—you've gotten yourself twisted into the best kind of emotional knots possible, and we've got a chance to reconnect a mother and daughter and further heal the family tree."

The emotional fallout wasn't even a consideration for them. "But you went about this wrong. All of you." Especially his father. "Iris already doesn't trust Flora. Knowing you manipulated this entire situation makes you all guilty by association." He swore, his stomach pitching as a new thought shot through his mind. "You're not giving her a chance to heal. You're giving her another excuse to run."

"You knew nothing about what we were doing, Shane," Butch said. "She won't paint you guilty by association."

Wouldn't she? Shane wasn't so sure. She was already looking for any excuse to walk away. His father, her family may have just given her the biggest one yet.

Shane was about to reply, when Eric trudged in. "Morning," the boy grumbled as he rubbed his fists in his eyes. "Am I late?"

"You're right on time, Eric." Big E got to his feet and ended the conversation. "Let's get saddled up, yeah?"

"Drink some water, Eric," Shane suggested and turned him to the sink. "It'll help knock out the cobwebs. I just need to feed the dogs."

"We'll meet you in the stable," Big E said. "Let's get to it, Butch."

Shane watched as Butch shook his head, returned his attention to his coffee. "I'll pass."

"PaPa doesn't ride anymore," Eric said after glugging a glass of water.

"What do you mean, he doesn't ride anymore?" Big E looked aghast. An expression Shane suspected the man wasn't used to wearing. "What does he mean by that?"

"Dad gave up riding after his heart attack in April." Shane couldn't ignore the rush of pleasure it gave him to tattle on his father. "He lost his mettle."

"I didn't lose it," Butch shot back. "I'm just too old—"

"Nonsense," Big E said. "I've got more than a decade on you, and nothing's keeping me off a horse. It's where folks like you and me belong. End of story. Shane, hand me his jacket."

Big E held out his hand and stood there, jacket in hand, while Butch glared. "I can wait here all day, young'un. Get a move on. We're racing the sunrise." Big E eyed him with a warning. "Don't make me get ornery about it."

Eric looked up at Shane, his eyes wide with surprise and confusion as Shane produced the chipped bowls he'd dug out of the back of the cabinet for the new members of the family.

"Fine." Butch snatched his jacket out of Big E's hand and clomped out the door ahead of them.

"Guess that's something else good that's come of our visit," Denny said to Shane as he put the bowls on the floor and refilled the water dish. "We don't mean to do any harm, Shane. Especially to Iris."

"Intending to or not, you have." Shane added a second dish of water to the first. "Just giving you fair warning, Denny, because I feel safe in saying this entire plan of yours is about to blow up in your faces."

"Who would have thought a tape measure would bring reassurance and comfort." Pencil locked between her teeth, working beneath the bright-eyed glare of multiple lights, Iris reconfirmed that the bathroom pieces she'd ordered would fit in the dedicated space at the back of the trailer. Because the vinyl flooring she'd chosen was ideal for water-heavy areas, she'd saved a lot of time and frustration by planning to lay it throughout the trailer. Using blue chalk string, she'd snapped a line marking where the new dividing wall was going to be and where the envelope door would sit, then she did the same to indicate placement of the toilet, shower stall and sink.

It was a bit of a tricky fit where the door had to go, especially with installing the Murphy bed she'd convinced Butch to choose. She needed to leave enough walking space for him to get out of bed at night or for anyone else in the trailer to get to the bathroom.

"You wouldn't be a true Blackwell if you didn't use work to stop yourself from thinking."

Iris finished snapping out the last line, and, standing up, she finished pulling the last of the wiring through the cutouts in the wall. The trio of antique-looking sconces had to be planned for ahead of time. She moved carefully so as not to disturb the other chalk markings, but didn't stop working. After having installed all insulation and interior thick panel siding, she'd caulked around the newly installed windows throughout the trailer. Finally, she could see the end of the tunnel for this project. Better yet, she only had to worry about boarding up the empty door frame before the incoming storm hit. She hopped outside the RV and began her attack.

"Morning, Denny."

"Denny, is it?" Denny clomped over to grab a folding chair leaning against the side of the trailer. "Last night it was Grandma."

"Last night I was too shocked to be anything other than polite." Darn it! Iris gnashed her teeth. She'd been too efficient this morning and was caught up with all the indoor jobs that had needed doing. "Are you here to play peacemaker before my mother takes another shot at getting me to come back to the Belles for her big awards do?"

"I go where I'm needed," Denny said in a way that came across as more matriarchal than defensive.

"Where is Flora, by the way?" Iris checked her watch. "Since it's almost ten, she must still be asleep." Her mother had long become a creature of habit, working shows late into the night and sleeping far into the day. Yet another way they were absolute opposites from each other.

"Butch was kind enough to let her use the guest room in the house," Denny confirmed.

"Uh-huh." Somehow she doubted that had been Butch's idea. "Dad's finally returning my texts." She faced Denny, tried not to shoot an accusing look at her grandmother. "Guess what? Aunt Dandy is being inducted into the Hall of Fame, too!" She feigned excitement. "How great is that? Equal and top billing for the lineup, and yet Mom never mentioned that tidbit of information."

"Now, Iris—"

"Dad didn't even give me a heads-up about this, that you all was coming." That was a bit of a disappointment, yet not a shock. Her father had gone along with all of Flora's ideas—good and bad. "Guess he didn't want to ruin the surprise."

"We might have asked him to be careful with anything he might have said." Denny tapped her cane on the ground, cast an eye to the horizon. "We honestly thought surprising you was the best tactic to take. We didn't mean it to come off as an ambush." Denny paused. "I'm sorry if it did."

Iris shrugged and tried to pretend it didn't matter.

Denny's dark-eyed gaze shifted back to her and then to the trailer. "This is all your work, then?"

"It is. Cute, isn't it?" That word still stung like a bee.

"Your mama didn't mean that the way it sounded."

Flora never meant things the way they sounded. Iris shook her head. "It's funny hearing you defend her. My recollection's always been you didn't like her."

Denny turned, her gaze falling on the still to

be replaced door, and she heaved a sigh. "Had myself a bit of an awakening a couple years ago. Nearly died, actually. But don't you ever tell Corliss I said that," Denny warned. "I've still got her thinking I didn't realize just how close I came with all my health issues."

Iris didn't have any problem keeping that vow. She'd only met Corliss Blackwell, Corliss Blackwell Talbot now that she was married, a handful of times and all of them had been more than a decade before.

Denny went on. "It gave me a lot of thinking time. And, to be honest, reconciling with my brother might have made me see just how important family really is. That includes your mama."

"Denny... Gran." She said it because it seemed to make Denny smile, and while she was irritated with her mother, she didn't want to upset Denny any further. "I do appreciate what you're trying to do, thinking that Flora and I need to mend fences... What?"

Denny chuckled. "Those are the exact words Shane used this morning when he called us out on our peacemaking shenanigans."

"Did he?" Of course, he would have. He was the kind of man who would step in front of a runaway stagecoach for a stranger. He'd definitely try to deflect and defend in her name given their previous conversations about her mother. It helped, knowing she had someone on her side.

"None of my business," Denny continued. "But you've got a good one there. Good man. Good father. Good husband material."

"Okay, stop." Iris applied every mental brake she possessed. "No one's marrying anyone. Good man aside, I'm not the settling down kind. I've got a future ahead of me and it requires wheels, not roots."

"Been giving that some thought, have you?" Denny nodded with approval. "Interesting. Your mother—"

"Needs something from me." Iris was beyond feeling guilty over being rude. "Beyond me agreeing to perform. Doesn't she?"

Denny inclined her head, but refrained from speaking.

Iris wanted to be wrong. She'd hoped she was, but in truth, she'd never been wrong about Flora Blackwell for years.

Obviously, Flora wanted something, and it must be something big if her mother couldn't just come straight out with it. Growing up, the only time her mother ever paid any attention to her, ever noticed her, ever commented or made mention of her, was when Flora needed Iris to do something for her.

Otherwise, Iris may as well have been part of

the background players for all the spotlight Flora Blackwell ever cast on her. Standing in the background had always given Iris a bird's-eye view of who Flora really was.

"If you're here to soften me up for the big blow, it's not going to work. If Flora has something to ask of me, she can darn well do it herself." She headed over to her grandmother, held out her hand. "I don't want to fight with you, Gran. Come on. You don't look comfortable, and I bet you could use some coffee."

Denny eyed her. "Already had my allotment for the day."

Iris waggled her hand. "Then we'll find you something else in Wander."

"Wander?" Denny stood and surprised Iris by accepting her help. "That your trailer's name?"

"Wander Woman, yep." She shouldn't have been surprised at Denny's speed. Once the older woman was on more solid ground, she seemed fine. "Sun's just about up. Butch is probably almost finished fixing breakfast."

"He won't be doing that 'til he's back," Denny said as they made their way around to Iris's trailer. "He went out with Shane, Eric and Big E to move the herd this morning."

"Did he?" Iris's mood brightened. Finally, some good news. "That's great to hear." Maybe her family turning up had done some good after all.

Even a day ago, Butch going out riding seemed a bit like moving water uphill.

"That brother of mine has a talent for goading people into doing things they know they should do but say they don't want to," Denny grumbled. "Nice to know he can use his power for good."

"I suppose so." She pulled open the door. Cos's head popped up from where he was sleeping in his bed. He jumped to his feet, tail wagging and banging against the wall as Denny climbed inside.

"Well, I'll be." Denny turned in a slow circle. "This is a sight to behold, Iris. You did all this?" The shock and awe in her grandmother's voice made it clear that while Butch and Big E had watched her online recordings, Denny hadn't. "By yourself?"

"All by myself." Iris set the electric kettle to boiling and retrieved the hickory coffee substitute she kept on hand for when she overdid it on the caffeine. When she faced her grandmother, she found Denny looking at the saddle display.

"It's shinier than I expected," Denny said.

"You know about Aunt Dandy's saddle?"

"Might've heard about it," Denny said absently. "It's beautiful, isn't it?"

"That leather inlaid work is spectacular," Iris agreed. "It's genius craftsmanship. One reason I keep it front and center is as a guide for my work.

If I can make something half as fabulous as that, then I know I've done a good job."

"You've done a very good job, Iris." Denny turned, grabbed her hand and squeezed. "What you do for people, it's from the heart. I'm proud of you." She squeezed harder. "Very proud."

Tears burned the back of Iris's eyes. How many years had she longed to hear those words, not just from her grandmother, but from anyone?

"Thanks, Grandma." Overwhelmed, Iris pulled free and returned to the kitchen. "I don't know about you, but I'm starving. The men can take care of themselves when they get back. How about you and I have breakfast?"

RARELY WAS SHANE anxious to return to the house while he was out working the ranch. Normally, it wasn't difficult to keep his mind on the job, especially when that job was getting hundreds of head of cattle moved a pretty fair distance from where they were obviously very content.

Whatever magic spell Big E had cast on his father, Shane would be eternally grateful. Having the extra help, especially given this was Eric's first time assisting, made the job of shifting the herd three miles west far easier than Shane had suspected it would be.

With gray clouds rumbling in overhead and the threat of rain turning into a promise for the day and possibly into the night, he was glad he'd trusted his instinct to move the herd closer to the area of trees that could provide them wind protection.

With the wind kicking up and the sun nearly over the horizon, they reached the stable just as the first raindrops hit. He was tempted by Hank's and Roy's offers to tend to the horses and get them resettled in their stalls, but today was a learning experience for Eric. Shane wanted his nephew well-versed on the habits he needed to develop as he did more and more around the ranch. Tending to the horses was at the top of the must-do list.

Big E and Butch, however, accepted the ranch hands' help in order to head inside and get breakfast on the table.

By the time Shane and Eric were done and stomping in through the mudroom door, they were soaked to the skin, shivering and exhausted.

"You did real well today, Eric."

"I let a couple get away." Eric sounded grumbly, Shane thought, much like his grandfather, who, contrary to his own doubts, had done just fine back in the saddle. Butch would probably be a little sore tomorrow, but there was a light back in the old man's eyes Shane was grateful to see. So maybe there was a bright side to the Blackwells visiting after all.

"Cattle get away from me all the time," Shane lied. "You have a good eye and good instincts. You'll get even better moving forward." He toed off his boots and left them by the door. "I'm proud of you."

"Yeah?" Eric looked surprised at the compliment. "Thanks. I had fun."

That pride, that sense of accomplishment that Eric displayed was why the Holloway Ranch was going to be in good hands for a very long time to come.

"Do I smell homemade biscuits?" Shane asked as he and Eric entered the kitchen.

"You do indeed." Denny waved a spatula in the air. "It's my great-grandson Mason's recipe. Best biscuits you're ever going to eat, believe me."

"You two head up and change and dry off," Butch told them from where he was manning a giant cast-iron skillet of bacon. "We've got this."

"No school today," Shane reminded the head chef. "We'll have a full table."

"I remember," Butch said.

Shane showered and changed and was heading back downstairs when Ruby Rose poked her head out of her bedroom.

"Morning, munchkin." Shane stopped, buttoned the cuff of his shirt. "You ready for breakfast?"

"Yes." She was already dressed in jeans and a blue ruffled T-shirt. She held out her hair brush. "Help, please."

Shane almost froze. It was the first time she'd gone to anyone but her brothers for help getting ready. He steered her back into her room and sat on her bed, gently running the soft brush through her bouncy curls. "Sorry." He winced when the brush caught. "I'm new at this."

"It's okay. Daddy sometimes tugged too hard."

Shane swallowed around the lump in his throat. He brushed a few more times, turned her around, then spun her faster and faster until she giggled and fell into his lap.

"I'm dizzy!" she squealed and almost fell back on her butt. Titan raced in, his toenails clattering on the hardwood floor as he barked and leaped on her. She hauled the dog close and hugged him, earning a lick of appreciation in return.

"I think your hair looks perfect, Ruby Rose."

She scrambled to her feet, rose up on tiptoe to check the mirror over her dresser and nodded. "Thank you." Titan barked once in agreement.

Shane sat there for a long moment after she'd headed downstairs, watched as Eric and Miles slammed out of their room and followed her. A full house, not only of family, but of friends. It amazed him at how right it all felt.

The cloud of grief that had blanketed all of

them for so long had finally begun to lift. The sunshine that had started to stream through was lightening all their hearts. And opening them to new possibilities. Speaking of possibilities...

"Has anyone seen Iris this morning?" he asked when he returned to the kitchen. The only person missing was Flora, which, honestly, he was relieved about. She tended to suck most of the energy out of the room the second she entered it.

"I had coffee and breakfast with her earlier in her trailer," Denny announced. "She's headed into town to pick up stuff for Cassidy."

Shane frowned. "In this weather?"

"That girl can take care of herself," Big E said easily. "Don't go frettin' over her 'til it's necessary."

Why Shane felt like muttering, "Yes, sir," was a bit of a mystery. He helped load up the table, filled the kids' plates and then did coffee refills for everyone as Flora made her way into the kitchen.

"Well, lookie here," Denny said from her seat at the table. "And before noon. Miracles do happen."

Zinni yipped—if one could call it a yip, and joined Titan, who was face down in his dog bowl slurping up water.

"I smelled biscuits." Flora yawned and stretched her arms over her head. She wore a pair of dark green silky pajamas and matching pom-pom slippers. Any A-list actor would have nothing on Flora Blackwell making an entrance. "Isn't it late for breakfast?"

"Consider it brunch," Denny suggested.

Flora flounced into one of the two empty chairs at the table beside Ruby Rose. "I thought it was still the middle of the night."

Ruby Rose wrinkled her nose, looked at Shane in confusion. "It isn't, is it?"

"No," Shane said effortlessly.

"Oh." Ruby Rose gasped when Flora tucked an arm around her shoulders and gave her a tight squeeze.

"You are adorable. You remind me of my little girls when they were your age," Flora gushed. "Do you ride?"

"Flora," Big E warned. "Don't start."

"I can ride a horse," Ruby Rose announced. "I ride Miss Kitty sometimes, but she's very big. I need help."

"Nonsense," Flora dismissed the idea. "When my girls were your age they could ride just about any horse we put in front of them. You know I taught them everything I knew. We used to do trick riding shows. I do quite a bit of teaching these days. I'm proud of my students."

"Buckle up, Shane." Big E elbowed him in

the ribs. "You're about to get an eyeful of Flora Blackwell."

"We saw a video of Iris riding her horses," Miles said. "We watched on PaPa's laptop. She was a Belle!"

"She was indeed." Flora filled her plate with scrambled eggs and a biscuit the size of her fist. "But you know I was a Belle first. My sister and I created the act, and when I had my girls, they joined."

Shane arched a brow. Joined? From what Iris had said the girls hadn't had much of a choice.

"We used to travel all over the country performing. We worked in stadiums and rodeo halls and, oh, goodness, every kind of arena you can think of. Oh!" She clapped her hands together. "I know what we can do today."

"The kids have homework," Shane said.

"There will be plenty of time to do their homework," Flora said, with growing enthusiasm. "I saw a big-screen TV in the living room. Maybe we can get a feed in and watch videos of the Belles performing and I can teach you some of their tricks!"

"Can we, Uncle Shane?" Ruby Rose's eager plea was impossible to ignore.

"If we can get a signal, sure." Shane winced. "But only after your homework." He could imagine Iris's reaction if she came home and found them all sitting around watching her as a Belle. Which was why he started hoping now that the storm would knock out their Wi-Fi.

"I need to work on my Halloween costume," Miles said. "Uncle Shane, I might need some help."

"I forgot Halloween's coming up pretty soon," Big E said. "What are you planning to do to celebrate?"

"Head into town, probably," Shane said. He needed to get the rest of the fall decorations pulled out of the closet. And maybe buy a few more pumpkins in town for the front porch.

"There's a big parade on Halloween night," Miles announced. "Everyone in costume gets to march in it, and they give prizes for who looks the best! And I want to win!"

"That'll take a pretty special costume," Butch said. "You decide what you want to go as yet?"

"A car!" Miles sat up straighter in his chair. "One of those kinds that turn into a robot."

Shane balked. This was the first he was hearing about it. "You want to make a car costume that turns into a robot?"

"Yeah." Miles shoveled biscuit into his mouth then sputtered crumbs as he said, "I thk itd be awethome. Sorry." He ducked his head sheepishly and brushed off his lips.

"How about you, Eric?" Butch asked.

"I'm too big to dress up," Eric said in a way that said he wasn't convinced this was entirely true. "I don't think Ruby Rose has decided yet."

Ruby Rose shook her head.

"We'll figure something out for you, won't we?" Flora offered. "I'm going to go get dressed and see about that video feed. Oh, this'll be fun!"

"After homework," Shane reminded her, but she was already out of the kitchen, Zinni trailing behind. "Did she not hear or does she not listen?"

"Depends on the day," Denny said. "Don't worry. I'll run herd on her until the kids are finished with their homework."

"I did mine last night after dinner," Eric said.

"Oh." Shane blinked. "Well, good job, Eric."

"I can clean out the stalls while you work," Eric went on.

"You don't want to watch the videos?" Shane asked.

"Nah. That's boring."

"Is not!" Ruby Rose shot back. "It's fun and pretty."

"And boring." Eric rolled his eyes and ate another piece of bacon.

"Okay, then. Stalls it is," Shane said and earned a nod of approval from his father. "Let's finish eating and we'll bundle up and get to work."

CHAPTER THIRTEEN

As INDEPENDENT AS Iris was, even she had to accept there were some things she couldn't do on her own. Today she would have had to surrender to that idea even if the weather hadn't been working against her. The struggle, however, tempered the frustration that had descended since her mother's arrival. It seemed fitting that the storm that blew in was bigger and windier than the one that had shown up yesterday.

As the wind howled and the rain pelted the truck, she struggled to keep the steering wheel steady. Her eyes pivoted to the rearview mirror to make sure the tarp she'd tied down over the supplies she'd picked up this morning didn't blow off. Thankfully, what she was carrying was somewhat waterproof. Served her right, though, for trying to avoid the inevitable. Now she was stuck unloading her truck in the rain.

Beside her, Cos sat at attention, whining occasionally as the rain sluiced across the windows. "Don't worry, boy." She would have reached out to give him a consoling pat if she felt safe taking one hand off the wheel. Cos wasn't great in storms and frequently ended up climbing into bed with her when the trailer found itself battered by the weather. Even now he kept shooting her accusatory looks as if wondering why she'd been determined to bring him out in this mess. "We're almost home. I mean back at the ranch."

She bit the inside of her cheek. Slip of the tongue. The Holloway Ranch wasn't home. Especially with her mother currently visiting. Even now her face warmed. How embarrassing was it to have her family drop in unexpectedly somewhere that wasn't even Iris's place?

"Whatever she wants, it's gonna be big." Iris tried to find her way back to the happy place she'd found herself in after her breakfast with Denny. It had felt so good to connect with the older woman and left Iris feeling as if she'd marked something off her to-do list. The legend that was Denny Blackwell had always been a bit intimidating from a distance, but now Iris saw the woman had a bit of squishy softness to her. Well. A little bit, anyway. At least when it came to her family.

That was what had brought Denny out here, apparently. Her desire to help put the broken branches of her son's family back together. The last thing Iris wanted was to disappoint her grandmother, or her uncle. But the truth was, as far as Iris was concerned, there was no healing the rift. Flora was oblivious to her actions and how they affected others, especially Iris.

Iris took the final turnoff for the ranch, mentally mapping out the next few days of work. Given the weather was supposed to remain on the wild side for a bit, she'd shift her attention back to the dining room table for Edith Wittingham. Carver had asked about the project when she'd been at the Depot, and she'd shown him pictures of the table's current status. He'd purposely picked a varnish that would allow the table to be used either indoors or out, but that had been another special order. Now that the varnish was in the back of her truck, she could finally put that project to bed.

The wind howled and set Cos to whimpering again.

Iris kept her foot easy on the gas, not wanting to push too hard against the storm. Before long, she pulled the truck to a stop in front of the second barn, or her temporary workshop. As soon as she opened her door, Cos was out like a shot and racing toward the house.

"Thanks for the assist." She dropped to the ground, her boots sinking ankle deep into mud. She ducked forward, keeping her head down against the wind as she fought her way to the stable. She passed the new chicken coop, saw the telltale hint of yellow and white feathers inside the tiny cubbies. Even the chicks were smart enough to stay out of this weather.

"Please be in the office," she pleaded, banking on Shane's keeping to his normal schedule. Or, if her luck held and she escaped to her trailer, she could push off any confrontation with Flora until tomorrow.

Seeing her mother again had brought back every bitter memory and insecurity Iris had spent years burying. Now they were resurfacing faster than the good memories could keep them at bay.

Iris hauled open the main stable door, dived inside and slammed it shut behind her. Her boots clomped on the cement. As she walked, clumps of hay clung to the soles.

When she turned and shoved her hood off her head, she saw Eric standing there with a pitchfork in his hand. Shane stuck his head out of the office door.

"Hi." He smiled instantly, all the way to his eyes, and it set her toes to tingling. "I was beginning to worry about you."

"Rough ride back," she said. "But I made it."

"And here I thought you were trying to avoid your mother."

He really, really needed to stop reading her so accurately.

"I hate to ask, but I could really use your help." She pointed outside. "I parked near the backup barn. Any chance you can help me unload my truck? I'm afraid everything'll get damaged if I leave it in the bed until the storm passes. And yes…" She held up her hand to stave off the same argument she'd heard from Carver in town. "I know I should have waited until the storm was over before picking it all up, but I didn't. So here we are." It was bad enough when she had to clean up her own mistakes; asking for help to do so was just another irritant.

"Okay," Shane said slowly when she was finished. "Happy to help."

"I can help, too!" Eric ditched the pitchfork and raced over.

Shane frowned. "I don't think—"

"Could you manage the door for us?" Iris shot Shane a look that hopefully conveyed her wanting to keep Eric as encouraged and involved as possible. "It's a little rickety and could slam shut on us with the wind."

"I can do that." Eric grabbed his rain slicker off the hook and shrugged into it while Shane retrieved his jacket from the office. They went out the side door, where Cassidy and her trailer were battened down. She'd temporarily pulled plywood up over the door opening to prevent the interior from getting wet, then tied a tarp down as added protection.

The three of them trudged over to her truck. Iris's feet sank into the mud yet again. Every step she took resulted in a loud suctioning sound as she pulled her foot free.

"Wait until I tell you to open the door, Eric!" Shane shouted over the wind.

Iris unknotted the rope keeping the tarp in place. "On three," she told Shane. They slid the box holding the large sheets of waterproof vinyl for the shower, and she stumbled a bit. But she caught her footing, scrunching her toes hard to keep her balance.

They made quick work of shifting the new sink and shower pan. The box containing the new toilet was almost soaked through, but once she pushed it to the edge of the truck bed, Shane was able to pick up the whole thing from the bottom and carry it inside the barn.

Iris stretched out across the bed and grabbed hold of the edge of the box of supplies, hauled it closer, feet dangling.

"You got it?" Shane flipped the last of the tarp away and she pulled it loose.

"Yep." Her hands slipped a bit. Her fingers were frozen. She scooted back, kicking a bit to get her body out of the truck. Still clutching the box, her feet hit the uneven ground, and she let out a yelp. As she fell back, the box in her hands, she realized her boots were wedged so deep in mud that it felt like she was caught in cement.

Splat! She felt the cold and wet soak through her jacket and into her jeans.

"Eric. Close the door!" Shane yelled as he raced closer and dropped down beside her. "You okay?" He started to reach out, but she stopped him, preferring to sit there for a long moment, rain pelting her, fingers squishing in the mud.

"If you see my dignity around here somewhere, grab it for me, would you?" She started to shove herself up and Shane took her hands and pulled. Their fingers meshed and the sensation brought some levity to the moment. "Thanks." She stepped back and almost fell over again.

She overcorrected and her right ankle gave way, and she went down hard after whacking her chin on the open truck bed, which caused her to see little cartoon birdies flitting around her head.

She heard Shane get behind her quickly and pick her up. How he managed to turn her around so she could sit on the edge of the truck bed she had no idea, but for a flash, she felt like she was back in the Belles, jumping and flying over teams of horses.

"I'm fine." She swallowed the sudden bile in her throat, felt that familiar yet long-forgotten nausea churn in her stomach. "Really." She waved him off and squeezed her eyes against the pain bouncing between her chin, her jaw and her foot. "Get all this inside, will you?" She motioned to the box. "Please, Shane."

He glared at her, reached down and, with Eric's help, carried the last of the supplies into the barn.

Iris took long deep breaths. She just needed a couple of minutes. She could shake this off. Just like she'd been taught to do during her performing years.

"You can do it," Iris told herself now as she rolled over and started to lower herself back down to the ground.

"Oh, no, you don't." Shane appeared out of nowhere, scooping her into his arms, leaving her no choice but to hold on to his neck. "No weight on that foot of yours until we see what's going on."

"Just get me back to my trailer," Iris pleaded. "Shane, please…" She could feel the panic mounting as he started toward the house. The rain began coming down harder and faster. "Don't take me inside."

"Eric!" Shane yelled as the barn door slammed shut.

"Right behind you!"

"Go on ahead. Open the door," Shane called

as he made quick work of the distance between the barn and house.

"Shane, I'm fine. It's just a twisted ankle." Frustrated, angry tears burned behind her eyes, but she blamed it on the rain. Rain that seemed to be getting worse. "I need to move my truck."

"Your truck is fine where it is." He hoisted her a bit higher as he approached the back porch steps. Eric stood clasping the edge of the door as Cos stood inside whimpering and waiting.

"Ah, geez. Shane, put me down. I can walk." This was mortifying, mainly because it was her own fault.

"And give up my chance to play knight in shining armor?" His grin was quick but came with a warning glance. "Humor me, Iris."

She scrunched her mouth to stop from arguing. The warm, highly fragrant air in the kitchen set her stomach to churning once more as Shane put her down in the closest chair at the table.

Eric slammed the door.

"Eric, can you towel Cos off, please?" Iris asked.

Butch left the stove, wooden spoon in hand. "What's happened?" He then set the spoon down, walked into the mudroom and came back with a stack of towels. "You two swim through the mud?"

"May as well have," Iris said as Shane shrugged

out of his coat and let it drop to the floor with a wet splat. "I just took a tumble out by the truck. It's fine," she assured Butch, whose brow had furrowed with concern as she touched a hand to her chin to check for blood. "Really, Butch. I'm— ow!" She recoiled as Shane pulled off her boot.

"Let's see."

Iris shivered, and she told herself it was from the cold. His hands were as frozen as hers felt as she gripped the edge of the chair and tried not to lift herself up out of it.

His pressed and prodded and moved her foot back and forth. Not a lot, but enough to make her wince. "I don't see any swelling, so I don't think it's broken."

"It's not," Iris said. "I know what broken bones feel like." And broken pride. "I just need an ice pack to be safe."

"I've got an ice pack in my bathroom," Butch said.

"Eric," Shane called to his nephew, who, when Iris looked over her shoulder, was laughing and struggling with Cos to dry off his muddied paws. "Go check the cabinet in my bathroom. I think I've got some bandages in there."

"Okay."

"We'll get it wrapped just to be safe," Shane said.

"I'm making a muddy mess," Iris grumbled.

"Floors and chairs clean up fine," Shane told her. "That's what mops are for."

"I need a shower. And a change of clothes." She had half the storm soaking through her jeans, coat and shirt. Cos padded over, Sundance at his heels. Cos shoved his head up under her hand, demanding a pet. "I'm okay, boy. I can take care of myself in the trailer," she tried again when she and Shane were alone.

"Are you so determined to avoid your mother you're willing to hurt yourself further?"

"Yes." What was the point in lying? Her current situation was entirely the result of her doing just that.

"Congratulations." Shane met her gaze with his own determined one. "You're now the most stubborn person in a house that includes my father."

"I heard that." Butch returned with an ice bag and filled it from the freezer. "You can relax for a little while, Iris. Flora is entertaining Ruby Rose and Miles with Belle videos and teaching them how to do cartwheels."

"What about—ouch! Okay, stop poking at my foot."

"I'll get you some aspirin," Butch suggested.

Shane's mouth twisted. "You should stay off this for a little while. Today for sure."

"Here!" Eric returned, a handful of beige fabric bandages in hand. "There were a couple so I grabbed them all." He dumped them on the table. Without being asked, he scooped up Shane's jacket and carried it into the mudroom.

"We can call the clinic in town, see if they have some crutches for you," Shane continued.

"I don't need crutches."

"You do need a first aid kit for that chin."

"I know where we keep it." Eric raced out of the kitchen again.

"I need to get back to work." She rubbed sore fingers across her forehead as her chin throbbed.

"It'll wait a bit. Let's see." Shane pulled her hand away, moved closer. Too close. She didn't want to like the way his body heat acted as a furnace and warmed her from the inside out. "Well, that'll be a nice bruise." He touched her chin, pressed his lips to hers and earned a dazed smile. "How's your head feel?"

"Like it would be more comfortable in my trailer." Her nose almost brushed his chest. She could smell the storm on him. Water and the slightest hint of ozone coming from the lightning strikes streaking across the sky. "You can carry me back right now." She looked out the window, tried to ignore the continuing rain. "Seriously, before anyone else knows. I'll just stay there until my family is gone." She felt like a cranky two-year-old whining for a cookie.

Shane sighed, dragged over another chair and sat down. Resting one hand on the back of her chair, he brought his face close to hers once more. So close. Kissing close.

She wet her lips and swallowed hard.

"You can't avoid her forever. Maybe you should think about trying to have a conversation with her."

Iris stared at him. "Did Big E put a whammy on you? I thought you were on my side."

"I am on your side," Shane insisted. "I'm suggesting maybe you stop fighting it and see where things go."

Her chin wobbled. Tears plopped out of her eyes and onto her cheeks. Every bit of hurt and pain she'd buried for twelve years threatened to surge free. "You don't understand."

"Then make me understand." He touched her cheek, brushed a finger across her lips. "I'm not completely ignorant of challenging parental relationships."

The past lurched up, locked around her chest and squeezed.

"Iris. I'm here. I'm listening." He gently cupped her face in his hand. "I want to help. I can see this hurts you. You're trying so hard to act as if it doesn't matter, but it does. I see it in your eyes when you look at your mother. If you won't tell her, then tell me."

Part of her wondered what good it would do, to purge her selfish insecurities that, even if spoken out loud, wouldn't change anything. But that was before she looked into this man's eyes. A man who was so convincing she wanted to believe he could fix anything. Even her broken heart. "I—"

"Iris, oh, my darling, what happened? Butch just told us!" Flora swept into the kitchen and came to a halt behind Shane. Today's outfit was midnight blue with teeny tiny yellow rhinestones scattered about like stars. She was in performance mode; Iris could see it by the light in her eyes.

Iris sighed, sat up straighter, and Shane leaned back, the disappointment on his face somewhat comforting.

"I'm fine," Iris said. "It's just a twisted ankle. Won't take more than a day to get back to normal."

"Ha. Nothing keeps a Belle down for long, right? Like that time you fell off Faustus when we were rehearsing in South Dakota. Do you remember that? We were afraid you hurt your tailbone, yet you bounced right back up—"

Iris felt her skin go clammy. "That was J.R., Mom."

"Was it?" Flora looked perplexed, hands on her hips. "No, that can't be right. I could have sworn—oh!" She snapped her fingers. "I must be thinking of the time you sprained your wrist learning that alley-oop spin in Oklahoma."

Iris looked straight into Shane's stormy eyes. "That was Maggie."

"The dislocated shoulder in—"

"Was Violet. Just…stop." Iris held up her hands, unable to take any more. "I fell and twisted my ankle because I wasn't paying attention." *Because I was desperate to avoid you! To avoid…this.* "I'll be fine. Just…stop."

"But I want to help," Flora insisted. "Tell me what I can do. Iris, please." She looked down at Iris in frustration. Butch and Eric reappeared, the little boy clutching a white metal box marked First Aid. Butch laid a hand on Eric's shoulder to stop him from getting closer. "Tell me what I can do to make things right between us," Flora pleaded.

Something broke open inside of Iris. An opportunity of sorts. Iris's mother had taught her well. While Iris might not be a Blackwell Belle anymore, she could still put on one heck of a show. Seeing Denny and Big E appear beside Butch, concern marring their faces, solidified her resolve.

She met her grandmother's eyes, and Denny nodded. It was now or never.

"There's nothing, Mom." Iris shrugged and realized she meant it. And in that moment, she felt the promise of relief, what she'd been waiting more than a decade for. "There's nothing you can do to fix any of it. I've spent the past twelve years trying to accept that, but you know what I just figured out? I never did. Not until right now." And that knowledge was freeing. "You are who you are. You're not going to change, and I have to stop expecting you to. If you could…" She should have stopped there, but she couldn't. It was like a stampede of horses had been set loose and there was no pulling them back. "If you could change, then you would have put your daughters first, ahead of our act, your act!"

"Oh, for—" Flora's hands flounced in the air and she rolled her eyes. "You girls loved the act. We had a show to do, contracts to honor."

"Heaven forbid we break a contract," Iris said on a bitter laugh. "Or wear old costumes. Or show any weakness. Or voice any opposition to what *you* wanted. We couldn't have dreams that took us anywhere other than where you wanted us to go. You know what? You're right. I am still mad about what happened. All that glitter and those fancy costumes made me run in the opposite direction. Fixing broken-down cars, replacing tires, repairing trailers and rigs. I learned and tried everything I could think of, getting grease under my nails for two years so I could do something just for me. Something I had to keep secret from you because I knew you'd try to stop me."

"Stop you? Why would I stop you from doing something you wanted to do? I thought you all wanted to do the act! As it turned out, all those jobs trained you for what you're doing now, and you seem happy. Aren't you?" Flora's tone had lost its ire. She sounded genuinely worried. "You are happy? Iris?"

Shane huffed out a breath, shook his head ever so slightly. When Iris looked at him, she saw the sympathy, the understanding. And she saw the love. She swallowed hard, forcing herself to dismiss the idea this man could love a mess like her.

"You couldn't have asked us that back then, Mom?"

"You never said anything, none of you did. I thought the sacrifices I made were for us. For the Belles!"

"Maybe. But it didn't seem that way to us. Not always. Sometimes it seemed like it was for you." Exhausted, Iris let out a slow breath. Tears burned the back of her throat.

"Iris." Denny attempted to step forward, but Big E reached out and put a hand on her arm. "Let her respond, Den."

Something unexpected bloomed to life inside of her. Shane had been right. Confession, admission, was good for the soul. Iris saw the truth shining in everyone else's eyes: in Shane's, in Butch's. Big E and Denny. Only Eric looked lost and confused, and for that, Iris was grateful.

"I don't believe you didn't like being a Belle," Flora said. "It's all very easy to say now, given the new life you've since made for yourself. You should have spoken up then." She stepped back, turned slightly and only then seemed to realize that their audience had expanded. "You expect me to believe you'd have given it all away considering how popular you were? How successful? Is this how you're getting back at me? By trying to embarrass me in front of people? In front of strangers? And family?"

"These so-called strangers have made me feel more wanted in two weeks than you ever did in twenty years!" She hated the sob in her voice. Hated the weakness it showed, but she needed it all out. Now. Once and for all. And she needed Shane and his family to know, in case she didn't get another chance to tell them, just how much they'd come to mean to her. "They welcomed me immediately and saw me for who I am. What I can do. As someone who's valued and respected. Cared for. Even lov—" She broke off, turned terrified eyes on Shane.

"You can say the word, Iris," he said quietly and grabbed hold of her hand and squeezed. "Love only make things better."

Her heart tilted.

"How happy this must make you, then," Flora said. "Pointing out all my flaws for everyone to see."

"This isn't about you, Mom." The fact that Flora still couldn't see it made the situation even sadder. "This is about me finally standing up for myself. Finally speaking up." Iris squeezed Shane's hand and pulled herself to her feet, ignored the slight twinge in her right ankle.

The fact that the color drained out of her mother's cheeks felt, sadly, like an accomplishment. And in that moment, she'd never felt more sorry for someone in her entire life.

Iris held on to Shane's shoulder for support. His other hand came up and rested on her hip, squeezed in comfort. "I'm surprised you bothered to come here, Mom." She paused, took a deep breath, looked to her family and Butch and Eric. "Do you know how I felt growing up, Mom? I felt invisible. Ignored. I was the backup daughter. The substitute. I wasn't a marketable twin like Maggie or J.R. I wasn't the talented one like Willow or the amenable, kind go-along like Violet. I was the one you kept in your back pocket when something went wrong or needed fixing." She shook her head, a bit dismayed. "I was always a spare.

"I feel so stupid now," Iris whispered in amazement. "Clinging to this for so long when in reality, it doesn't matter anymore. I spent so many years doing everything I could to make you see me, but even now you don't. You're only here because, once again, you need something from me."

"That's not true." Flora's voice wavered but she stopped and seemed to gather some strength.

Iris stepped clear of Shane's hold, mainly because what she needed most at this moment was to stand on her own two feet. Butch shot forward, the sympathy on his face almost painful to accept as he took the box from Eric's hands and gave it to her.

"Thanks, Butch," she murmured as she wedged it under her arms. She limped forward. "Whatever it is that you're hoping I'll give you, the answer is no. I'm done, Mom. With all of it. The Belles. The Hall of Fame. You. Everything. I'm just…done." She shifted back to Butch, surprised at how free she felt. "Is there somewhere I can try to clean up? I can't get back to my trailer until the rain's stopped, and the mud on my clothes is starting to harden."

"Use the bathroom just down the hall," Butch said in a strangled voice as he tugged Eric aside.

"Come on with me." Denny stepped forward and tucked an arm around her shoulders.

"We've still got some of Chelle's clothes upstairs, don't we, son?" Butch asked Shane.

"Yeah." Shane reached out for Eric. "Yeah, we'll go find you something, Iris."

"Good lads," Denny said. "Iris, I'll give you a hand. Might be a bit tricky hopping around with one foot."

"I'll manage, Grandma." Whatever else she resented about her family's visit, she was grateful for having reconnected with her grandmother. "I always have."

"We'll wrap your foot when you're done," Shane called after her. She just nodded.

Big E stepped to the side to let her pass. "Iris—"

"It was good to see you again, Uncle Elias." Iris gave him a watery smile. "I'm just sorry you've had a wasted trip."

CHAPTER FOURTEEN

AN UNEASINESS SETTLED over Shane as he and Eric went through a box of his late sister-in-law's clothes. They'd collected everything months ago, shortly after Shane had arrived back home with the intention of donating her items and Wayne's to charity. Instead, because they couldn't be certain the kids might want something, they'd stashed all of it in the room that, at one time, had been the nursery. Eric, Miles and Ruby Rose had each spent their first year or so in this room. Now it housed a lifetime of memories for everyone who still lived in the house.

"Did Miss Flora hurt Iris's feelings, Uncle Shane?" Eric asked. "Is that why Iris is so upset?"

"Yes, she did, Eric. A long time ago." There was no sugarcoating the situation between Iris and her mother, especially since Eric had witnessed the entire exchange. Shane's heart broke a little more with every word Iris had spoken. Her relationship with her mother and Iris's experiences growing up certainly explained her tendency and desire to remain emotionally apart from others.

As bad as things had gotten between Shane and his own father, and despite Shane's determination to keep a lot of distance between them, they'd never written each other off completely. He'd always known, deep down, that if he needed his father to be there for him, Butch would be. He wasn't sure Iris had ever felt that way.

"But Miss Flora didn't mean to hurt her, right?"

Treading carefully, Shane set a pair of sweats and a couple of T-shirts aside to take downstairs before he sat on the edge of the narrow twin bed. "Not on purpose, Eric. No, I don't think so." He struggled for the appropriate words. "But I think maybe Miss Flora is the kind of person who might not be able to see when she's hurting someone. That's why it's so important to be careful with our words and our actions. You can never be certain when something you say might take up a place inside and turn into something angry down the road."

Eric seemed to consider that. He frowned. "It sounded awful mean to me, what happened to Iris. I mean, I've never felt…invisible. Especially around here. Somebody's always telling me to do something. And Ruby Rose is always in my room playing. Invisible sounds really bad."

"Yes, it is." Shane refolded one of the T-shirts.

"People tend to justify things they do wrong, Eric. They find excuses for it. Doesn't make it right, though."

"Like her not asking Iris if she wanted to do the trick riding."

"Exactly. Iris has been carrying that hurt inside of her for a long time."

"Maybe we can make her feel better."

Shane nodded. "I think we can all agree to try to do that." He already had an idea of how to help Iris take that next step toward healing. "Let's start with these, okay?" He picked up the shirts and pants, and together they headed downstairs.

In the living room, he could hear the videos playing again. The tinny arena music that echoed through the large room. On his way to the first-floor bathroom, he stopped for a moment and watched Flora helping Ruby Rose tumble and somersault across the floor, then practice her pose when she was done.

"A bit more practice and you'll be perfect at it," Flora said cheerfully as she applauded. "Miles? How about you?"

"Watch this, Miss Flora!" Miles threw his arms over his head, pushed off one foot and kicked his feet over. He did a bit of a flip and crash-landed on the carpet flat on his back, but did so with a laugh. "Aw, man. I messed it up."

"Then let's try again," Flora encouraged. "This time try to keep your…"

Shane shook his head, walked away before he gave in to the impulse to pull his niece and nephew away from Flora Blackwell. Mother and daughter shared the tendency to hide their emotions by distracting themselves. Cos poked his head up from where he'd lain down in front of the bathroom, let out a pleading whimper as Shane approached.

"She'll be out in a bit, boy."

He knocked on the closed bathroom door. Denny popped it open an inch, and the sound of running water emerged. Cos shoved his nose through the door and tried to push it open. Denny opened it enough for the dog to slip through.

"These are for Iris," Shane said. "Is she okay?"

Denny nodded, accepted the clothes. "I figured it was bad." Denny's eyes dimmed with sadness. "Had to be for the girl to take off on her own like that and stay gone for more than ten years. I didn't come close to seeing the truth." She shook her head. "Breaks my heart. For all of them." She kept her voice low. "We'll be out in a bit."

"I'm heading in to help Dad get an early dinner on the table."

"See you there," Denny assured him and snapped the door shut again.

Feeling a bit untethered, Shane returned to the kitchen, where Big E and Butch were nursing a giant pot of beef barley soup that was simmering on the stove.

Big E dipped a big soup spoon into the pot, leaned over and slurped. "Needs more pepper."

Butch, with his own spoon, tested, shook his head. "Salt. More salt."

"Let's add both," Big E agreed.

"How long before we eat?" Shane asked. "I'm starving." Best to try to get things back on track as soon as possible.

"Couple minutes yet," Butch said. "Got some bread in the oven and leftover biscuits. Grab the butter out of the fridge, will you?"

"I'll get the kids," Big E said.

"Have them come in to set the table, please," Shane said. "It's their job."

"Will do." Big E gave him a bit of a salute as he left.

Butch looked over at Shane once they were alone, caught Shane watching him. "What?"

Shane smiled. "Nothing. Just…thanks." He shrugged, feeling the unexpected need to admit his own feelings. "We might not have always gotten along, but you were still my dad. I always knew I could trust you when it was important."

"Trust's a fragile thing," Butch agreed. "Your

mama used to say that. Once it's broken it's near impossible to put back together."

"Glad we never had to work on that part of our relationship."

"You're not about to go all confession-y on me like Iris, are you?" Butch half teased.

"Perish the thought," Shane teased back. But he rested a hand on his father's shoulder and took a moment to appreciate the stability Butch Holloway had always offered. Deep down Shane had always known he could come home. Iris had never felt as if she had one.

Which made it all the more important for the Holloways to convince her she'd found one now.

THE STORM BROKE shortly before sunset, while Big E, Denny and Flora had dinner in the kitchen with Shane and his family. Iris figured she'd make a break for her trailer in a bit. When she felt steadier on her feet. When she felt ready to be alone again.

Sitting on the front porch in the rocking chair farthest from the front door, she stretched out, pointing and flexing her bandaged foot and mentally willing it to heal faster.

Cos whined and rested his chin on her knee. She reached down and stroked the dog's head, finding more than a little comfort with him.

Breathing deep, she leaned her head back and closed her eyes.

There was nothing better than a post-storm breeze. It acted as a final cleansing of sorts, clearing out the bad, bringing in a bit of promise with the return of the sun's rays. The gentle wind brushed across her face, lifted her still damp hair. She waited for the replay of what had transpired in the kitchen, to regret what she'd said to her mother. Or how she'd said it.

But there was no regret.

She'd kept it all bottled up for so long, it had fooled her into thinking none of it mattered anymore. Now that it was gone and out of her system? It didn't have any hold on her. She felt... lighter. Unencumbered. Free.

"Hungry?"

She opened her eyes, found Shane standing beside her, a bowl of soup in one hand, a small plate of fresh baked bread in the other. He also had a large ice bag stuffed under one arm.

"I'm here on my father's orders to feed you." He set the bowl and plate down, added a couple of napkins. "Ruby Rose and Miles were asking about you. Dad told them you have a sad heart and needed some time alone."

Iris looked at him. Really looked at him. The concern on his face mingled with an expression she couldn't quite decipher, nor did she want to. She didn't want pity or sympathy. She just wanted to move on with her life. Except...

How did she do that when just looking at him convinced her that her heart belonged here? "Here." He bent down, rested the ice bag on her foot. "Twenty minutes on, twenty off."

She knew the drill. "Everything okay in there?"

"Well, your mother's acting as if nothing unusual happened, and Denny's staring daggers at her, so I'm guessing it'll be a tense ride home tomorrow."

"That's when they're leaving?"

"According to Big E," Shane said. "They could change their minds. Who knows? Appreciate you giving me the excuse to come out and find you. Things were a little weird in there."

She smiled. "At least now you understand," she said. "I didn't really mean for it to all come steamrolling out like that." She picked up the bowl and spoon, took a mouthful, if only to distract herself from the conversation and the chill on her bandaged foot. "I spent twenty years of my life growing up with that woman, in that family, and yet I have no clear concept of how to even be a part of one. I never felt like I fit. Maybe that was my fault." Maybe she hadn't tried hard enough. Maybe she should have put some of the effort she'd put into her relationship with Flora into one with her sisters.

"Every family's different," Shane said. "There's nothing saying you can't try again with your sisters. And maybe even with Flora, if the timing is ever right."

There he went again, reading her mind. It wasn't the response she wanted to hear, but maybe it was the one she needed. She ate more soup, bit into the tender chunks of beef and fall-apart potato. "This is really good."

"Storm soup," Shane said. "My mother made it every time a storm blew through. Sometimes we ate it for days."

"It's a fine tradition and one I heartily approve of. So does my stomach."

"Iris—"

"Don't, Shane."

"Don't what?" He was challenging her again, she could hear it in his tone. Challenging her to read his mind.

"Don't ask me to stay. With you. With the kids."

"Been thinking about that, have you?" His attempt at teasing didn't quite come across.

"After that display you saw in the kitchen, I'm shocked you haven't discounted the possibility all together. I'm not mother material." She couldn't quite believe she'd said it out loud. "This...family thing. It's not for me. I know Flora tried. She did her best at the time, what she was capable of doing, with me, I guess." That was part of what really hurt. As opposed to her sisters, when it came to Iris, her mom's affection always felt forced and far from genuine. Was that Flora's failing? Or was it hers? "I'm okay alone, Shane. It's best to accept that rather than consider I might be unlovable."

"That isn't remotely true," Shane argued rather irritably.

"You are an incredibly kind man, Shane Holloway." She smiled, but she only felt sad. "But you've seen me around other Blackwells. I completely fail as one of them. You also have three beautiful children to raise. They need to continue to be the center of your world. That can't be when I'm in the picture."

"Loving someone new doesn't mean you stop loving someone else, Iris." The patience in his voice tugged at something inside of her. "I like to believe my capacity to love is limitless."

"It's too much of a risk for you all to take, I think." No, she wasn't thinking. She was afraid. "There's more of Flora in me than I ever wanted to admit. How she can compartmentalize things. Shove them away as if they never happened. I do that. It's how I've gotten by these past ten years. I won't bring that into your lives. I won't bring that to your kids."

"Because you care about us too much to take the chance." He reached out, grabbed hold of her hand. "That right there tells me you're nothing like your mother."

"You're just determined to prove me wrong." She squeezed back. There was no harm in admitting it now. She loved him. Loved him right down to her curling toes. She ached at the thought of not seeing him every day, not watching him saddle up and ride off into the sunrise. She couldn't argue why or when or even how it had happened because it simply was. Knowing that would have to be enough. "You made me a promise, Shane. That when I was done with your father's trailer you'd accept me going. I need you to keep that promise." If only so she had something solid to cling to. A return to her life. Before she'd met Shane Holloway.

"I never make promises I can't keep," Shane said. "But that doesn't mean I'm going to stop trying to change your mind, though." The front screen door banged open and Ruby Rose came out, dragging Oscar the chicken behind her. Titan nipped out before the door shut again.

"I'm done eating, Uncle Shane." She came over and stood beside him, looked at Iris. "Uncle Shane and PaPa said your mama hurt your heart."

"It's feeling better now," Iris told her.

When Ruby Rose moved toward her, Iris set her bowl down just in time for the little girl to climb into her lap. Ruby Rose curled into her, hugged her arms around her neck. Turning her nose into Iris's borrowed shirt, she smiled. "You smell like Mama." She cuddled closer.

"Well, this was your mama's shirt," Iris tried to explain around another bout of tears. She shot Shane a helpless look, silently pleading with him to run interference, but he simply sat there and shook his head. "I hope you don't mind I borrowed it." She pressed a kiss to the top of Ruby Rose's head.

Ruby Rose shook her head and snuggled into her shoulder. Iris's hold tightened, and she squeezed her eyes tight, committing the moment to memory. Something to take with her when she left.

"Just so you know," Shane said as he got to his feet. "Those worries you have about not knowing how to be a mother?" He looked down at Ruby Rose, then back to Iris. "You're doing a lot better than you think."

SHANE NOTICED SOMETHING when he returned to the kitchen. Everyone save Iris and Ruby Rose were still eating, some with far more relish than others. Sundance, Roxie and Zinni had made a kind of pooch puddle in the corner, half snoozing, half on alert for either dropping food or the promise of a game of catch. The chatter among Denny, Big E and his father was at full volume, but Flora had shrunk into the background and gone silent.

While he dug cookies out of the jar and placed them on a platter, he watched Iris's mother more closely than he previously had, as if one long examination might clue him in to what made her tick. She was the kind of woman who changed masks in the blink of an eye. If she was the center of attention, she looked one way. If she wasn't, there was a haunted expression that came over her. Not regret, exactly, or maybe he was trying to project what he wanted her to feel. What he thought she should be feeling.

Performers rarely turned off, and Flora Blackwell was one of the best. But even the best had their ghosts.

She'd put on a good show, but Shane could see where Iris's words had hurt. They'd struck hard, maybe hard enough to make her think, to make a difference. One could only hope.

He had one goal in mind right now. Convincing Iris to stay. But in order to do that he was going to have to use every ounce of charm and logic at his disposal, and in that sense, Flora may very well be his ace in the hole.

When Miles and Eric excused themselves to go up and work on Miles's Halloween costume, Flora excused herself also and headed out the back door.

"Something on your mind, son?" Big E pinned Shane with a look that yesterday might have left Shane squirming in discomfort. Today, however, he accepted the silent challenge he saw in the older man's eyes.

"Lots of things, actually."

"You plan on keeping them to yourself or are you going to share?"

"I'm going to share." Shane set the platter of cookies on the table. "But not with you." He grabbed his jacket and hat and followed Flora outside.

He caught sight of her just as she disappeared into the stables.

Something about the way she walked, with determination, as if she was chasing solitude, made Shane think mother and daughter were more alike than either of them would be comfortable with.

He closed the distance quickly, stepping inside the stable as Flora lifted a hand to Miss Kitty.

"This one's Ruby Rose's horse, isn't she?" Flora asked without looking at him.

"She is."

"I remember Iris at that age." Flora pressed a kiss to Miss Kitty's nose. "She was fearless. Never met a challenge she couldn't take on. Always striving to make things better. Easier. Happier. She won't believe me, of course." She glanced at Shane. "She doesn't think I remember anything about her life."

Shane remained silent.

"She was amazing on a horse," Flora whispered. "I'd never seen anything like it. None of my girls, not even Willow, had the natural instincts it took to be a Belle like Iris did. But she never seemed to need me as much as the others did." Flora glanced at him. "I guess I got that one wrong, didn't I?"

"It's not my place to say."

"Isn't it?" Flora's smile was strained. "You're in love with my daughter. I'd say that puts you in the perfect place."

"I didn't come out here to rehash it all, Flora." Shane stepped over the line he suspected wasn't his to cross. "She needs help, and I think you might be the only person who can give it to her."

"Iris doesn't want anything from me," Flora said. "Especially my help."

"So you're just going to hide yourself away until it's time to leave. Before you run away." Maybe Iris was right. Maybe there was a bit of Flora in her. "Whether she wants your help or not, she needs it. She needs to know you heard her. She needs you to tell her that her feelings matter. That she matters."

Her eyes flashed. "I love—"

"Words don't mean anything, Flora. And even

if they did, it's not me you have to convince."
Shane struggled to connect with how she was
feeling, but the truth was, he couldn't imagine
not loving Iris. At this point, he could barely remember a time when he didn't. "I love Iris. In
a way I never thought possible, but there's too
much standing between us right now for there
to even be a discussion of a future together. This
emotional baggage she's been lugging around is
partly yours. She's convinced herself she's not
worth taking a chance on. That she's unlovable."

Anger burned in Flora's eyes. "And you think
I can fix all that?"

"I think you're Flora Blackwell and you can do
anything you set your mind to. You came to the
ranch because you're driving around the country
trying to convince your daughters to come together for something you want. You're having a
pretty rough go of it, from what I hear. Iris isn't
the only one you've had issues with."

Flora scowled. "Big E and Denny have big
mouths."

"And bigger hearts," Shane countered. "Whether
Iris stays with me or not, I want her to be happy.
I want her to be able to move onward with a clear
head and heart. So I am begging you, Flora. Try
one more time. Be the mother she needs. Not her
stage manager or coach or talent agent. Be the
woman I'm looking at right now. Show up as the

mother who can admit she messed up. Please."
He didn't have any other card to play. Desperation
was it. "She's already spent all these years believing she doesn't deserve love. You may be the only
one who can convince her she does."

There was nothing else to say, which was why
he turned around and left the stable, so Flora
Blackwell could be alone with her conscience.

CHAPTER FIFTEEN

"STOP IT, ERIC! You're messing it up!" Miles's shout startled Iris out of a light snooze. She shivered, blinked into the darkness that had descended. Ruby Rose was gone, but Cos and Titan immediately leaped to their feet when she sat forward. The porch light blinked on, casting shadows across the stack of pumpkins and the bargain store scarecrow leaning against them.

Melted ice bag in hand, she stood up, tested her foot and breathed a sigh of relief when there was barely a twinge. "I think I lucked out, boys."

Cos barked once in agreement, and Titan, with his head tilted, did a little dance on his front feet.

"Now look at it!" Miles wailed. "It ripped! Go away!"

Iris's curiosity got the better of her, and she headed inside, made her way into the living room where Miles and Eric had spread out various pieces of paper, poster board and card stock, along with three rolls of duct tape, markers and two staplers.

"What's going on?" Iris bent down, picked up a ripped piece of paper and tried to decipher what they'd been working on. Ruby Rose sat on her knees in front of the television, hugging Oscar the chicken and watching one of the Belle videos. One of their better shows, if Iris was remembering correctly. Sometimes everything just came together perfectly, and this one had been the debut of their pyramid. But at that moment, she saw herself flipping around in her saddle to the roar of the crowd, the sparkling rhinestones of her cowgirl costume reflecting against the spotlight.

"I printed the instructions from online," Miles said and dragged Iris out of the memory. "I thought it would be really easy, but it's not working. Look." He held up two large sections of poster board. "I know it says to use cardboard, but I couldn't find any."

"Looks like you robbed a school supply store," Iris teased as she sat down and crossed her legs. Cos bumped up behind her, and Titan walked over to sit beside Ruby Rose. The little girl lifted an arm to tuck the little dog to her and scooted closer. "I'm sure your brother was just trying to help, Miles. Weren't you, Eric?"

"Yes." Eric looked just as discouraged as Miles. "I'm not very good at this, either."

"Hey, you can't expect to be perfect at something right off the bat." Iris reached out and plucked up the wrinkled printed instructions sheet. "Do you know how long it took me to be able to do that?" She pointed at the screen just as she completed a perfect leg extension. "Or how many times I had to fall off the horse before I could stay on?"

"A long time?" Miles guessed.

"A very long time," she confirmed as she scanned the sheet.

"But we don't have a long time," Miles moaned. "Halloween's almost here, and we need costumes now!"

"They have to sign up for the parade and costume contest this week," Shane said softly from behind her. She looked back. He was leaning against the door frame, arms crossed over his chest.

"I'm not going to enter." Miles pushed back and crossed his own arms in a huff. "It's just too hard."

"You're a Holloway," Shane said easily. "We don't give up when things get difficult." He met Iris's gaze. "We just come at it from a different angle. Or we ask for help."

Iris blinked and, feeling as if Shane saw far too much in her expression, looked again at the instructions. "Hmm, you're right, Miles, part of the problem is you need to make this out of something sturdier than this." She picked up a piece of poster board and wobbled it. "This isn't going to be strong enough. Come on." She got to her feet. "I've been breaking down all the boxes from the Depot. We can find plenty of cardboard to make this work."

"See." Eric elbowed his brother. "I told you she'd help."

Miles elbowed him back. "We—"

"You," Eric corrected. Miles rolled his eyes.

"Fine. I thought you were too busy with PaPa's trailer."

"I am an expert multitasker." She shoved to her feet. "We've got room in the barn to get a jump start on this. You, too, Eric. If you still want to help?"

Ruby Rose watched them gather up all the craft supplies. The little girl stopped beside Shane, crooked her finger for him to come down to her level and whispered in his ear.

"Really?" Shane looked surprised. "You're sure?" Ruby Rose nodded, looked up at Iris. "Ruby Rose has decided what she wants to be for Halloween."

"I thought you wanted to be a ballerina?" Iris said.

Ruby Rose shook her head, pointed at the TV. "I want to be a Blackwell Belle."

Iris swallowed hard, tried not to notice the

combination of sympathy and uncertainty on Shane's face.

"Will you help me with a costume, too?" Ruby Rose asked as she twisted her hands together.

"I—" The very idea touched her far more deeply than she would have expected. Up until recently, any mention of the Belles was enough to rankle her nerves, but now, seeing the expectation and tempered excitement in Ruby Rose's eyes, she couldn't imagine a more perfect solution to the little girl's costume predicament. "I would be honored, Ruby Rose. Let's get your brother's costume going first, and meanwhile, I'll take some thinking time. We'll get to work on yours tomorrow, yeah?"

Ruby Rose's entire face glowed. "Okay!" She raced out after her brothers.

Shane grinned, stepped forward and dropped an unexpected kiss on her lips. "Thank you."

"It's just Halloween costumes," she told him, enjoying the sweet taste he left on her mouth.

"Oh, I think it's more than that." He caught her arms and pulled her close for another longer, deeper kiss. "I'm just going to say this now because I think you're in the right frame of mind to hear it, but I love you, Iris Blackwell." One more kiss to silence her as her head spun. When he set her back on her feet, she blinked up at him, trying to shake off the shock. "It's up to you to decide what to do with that."

"Iris!" Miles raced back in, stomped his foot in frustration. "We have to go to bed pretty soon. Hurry up!"

"I'm coming." She stumbled a bit, blamed it on her injured ankle, although it didn't so much as twinge in pain. "Yeah." She followed the kids outside. "I'm coming."

"I SAY WE put a lid on the morning, son." Butch galloped over to where Shane stood at the edge of the herd, taking some comfort in the familiar sounds of the cattle. "Time to head in and get some food."

"Good idea." But Shane didn't move. The past two days had been a bit of a whirlwind. Big E and Denny, along with Flora, had taken off in the RV to explore some of the neighboring towns, including Claxton. Big E had said it was his itchy feet wanting to get out and explore, but Shane supposed it had more to do with wanting to give Iris some time and space away from her mother.

Her mother. Shane scowled. His plea to Flora hadn't worked out as he'd hoped. She'd gone off with her in-laws without so much as a goodbye. He shouldn't be surprised. It was easier to run away than confront the possibility of change. Or own up to mistakes.

Shane tugged on Outlaw's reins, turned the horse toward the east. "I want to check on something first, Dad. Come with me?"

Butch shrugged. "If you can stand listening to my growling stomach, so be it." He clicked his tongue. "Come on, Sundance!"

The dog pivoted from his place guarding the cattle and raced toward them. Shane nudged Outlaw into a gallop and didn't stop until they reached the abandoned barn. He kicked a leg over and jumped down, headed to the rusted-out metal door and pulled it open. A damp, musty smell exploded out at him. Inside, he stood and looked up into the rafters where birds' nests and cobwebs had taken over.

"It's still in pretty good shape," he told his dad as Butch joined him. His voice echoed, as the barn was nearly twice the size of the stables. "Been empty a lot of years."

"The new one Wayne had built is a lot more practical," Butch said. "You're right, though." He planted his hands on his hips. "Seems a waste to just let it sit here empty. Guess that's my way of saying I'll get on board with this sheep idea of yours."

Shane's lips curved. Could his father have sounded more reluctant? "Thanks. I appreciate that, Dad. But I think I've changed my mind." He turned in a slow circle, his mind filling in the blanks of what was possible. "I have another idea for how this space can be used."

"After all these months…" Butch's frustration came out with a grunt. "Whatever. You going to share, or do I have to guess?"

"I told Iris I love her."

"Did you?" Butch's brows went up. Sundance joined them and started exploring. "Well, good on you, son. You've fallen for a good woman."

"I think so." He'd never met a better one. "We can give her what she feels she missed out on. A family. A home." He gestured to the building. "A home base for her work."

"You want to give the barn to Iris."

Shane nodded. "The sheep can wait. I think this could be more important."

"I think you're right, Shane. You believe she'll say yes?"

He hoped so. "If all goes according to plan, she won't be able to say no."

His own stomach rumbled. "So you're okay with it?"

"I'm more than okay with it," Butch agreed as they headed back to their horses. "I'm going to help you pull it off."

"Thanks again for the assist." Iris climbed out of Shane's truck. "When I called Carver and said the table was ready, he wasn't sure when he could come get it." She circled back and dropped the truck gate. "He apologized for asking me to deliver it, but honestly, I can't wait to see his and Edith's faces." Given that she'd been so focused on trailers of late, this was the first custom piece of furniture she'd done in ages, and she was beyond proud of how it had turned out.

"I'm just glad we could find a place to park," Shane said, gesturing to the countless trucks and cars in the Depot lot.

"Never seen it so busy." She untied the tarp on one side, while Shane undid the other. "Is there something going on?"

Shane winced. "I probably should have said. It's the twenty-eighth of the month."

"And what happens on the twenty-eighth?" She whipped the tarp back.

"Carver does a storewide discount on the twenty-eighth of every month. Good time for locals to stock up on supplies for the rest of the year. It's probably standing room only in there."

"Oh. That's nice of him." And not surprising. All of her interactions with Carver Wittingham and the patrons she'd met on her trips into town had been friendly. Cottonwood Creek definitely had a lot going for it.

"Also a good way for him to clean out old stock. You got it?"

"Yeah." She wrapped her hands around the

edge of the table and pulled it out, along with the blankets protecting it. This took some effort. The table was solid maple and with the added resin a bit bulkier than planned. Once again, her Belle training paid off with her upper arm strength.

The rumble of voices inside the store echoed loud enough to be heard wide and far. The double glass doors swung open as she and Shane gently got the table free and carefully tipped it upright on its beveled legs and set it on the ground.

"You're early!" Carver's excited voice carried across the lot. "It's done?"

Iris nodded. "It's done."

"Oh, I can't look at it without her. Hang on! Just…" Carver held up his hands as if they were going to run off. "Wait there! Edith! Edie! Come out! Iris is here with your table!"

Shane ran his hand over the top of the varnished table. "You really did a spectacular job, Iris."

"Yeah?" She beamed. "Thanks."

She'd taken a few chances with the design, but after speaking with Edith Wittingham, she let herself think beyond the basic specifications. Length, width and height were one thing. It had been hearing about the Wittingham home and property, especially the creek that ran behind the house, that had caught her imagination. Add to that Edith's desire for her entire family to be able to sit around it and celebrate the holidays had made the long hours of careful sanding and varnishing worth it.

"Iris!" Edith was a petite woman with dark hair and a spark in her eye that was all for her husband of thirty-three years. Wearing her trademark plaid flannel shirt and boot-cut jeans, she hurried out, the smile on her face as warm as the golden autumn leaves falling from the trees. "What a surprise! You know Carver and I would have come to pick it up. I didn't expect you to come today!"

"Carver said he wasn't sure when he could come out." That was what he'd said, wasn't it? Maybe she'd misheard.

She'd been run ragged the past few days, finishing the table, fixing up Cassidy and working with the kids on their costumes. Plus, tonight was pumpkin carving night. Her time with the Holloway family was fast running out. But she could worry about that later.

"Well?" Iris stepped away from the table. "What do you think? I know it's a little different from what you probably expected…"

"Oh, Iris." Edith clasped her hands to her mouth, tears filling her eyes. She walked slowly around the table, touched gentle fingers to the polished wood. She shook her head in awe. "It's spectacular."

"Like I said, I took a few liberties." Iris pushed her hands into the back pockets of her paint-spattered jeans as the crowd grew and more people moved in to take a closer look. Carver circled around to stand behind his wife. Both their faces were filled with gratitude. Iris cleared her throat, uncertain what that bubble in her chest was. "I know we didn't talk about color, but when you told me about the creek, I couldn't get blue out of my mind. So I did this resin inlay here." She pointed to the narrow band of blue meandering through the natural grain. "Since you wanted to be able to use it indoors or outside, it kind of felt right. I know it wasn't what we discussed—"

"It's better than what we talked about." Edith smiled warmly. "Iris. You did the beveled edges."

"And rounded corners," Iris added. "You said you have a lot of little ones around during the holidays, and I didn't want there to be edges. Oh! I made something else, but if you don't want them, I can probably sell them somewhere. Shane? Would you help me?"

"Sure." Together they retrieved the four picnic style benches from the truck bed. The benches matched the table, including a thin line of blue resin meandering across the length.

She heard gasps and *oohs* and *ahhs* from the crowd as they set them on the ground. "Once I got going with the resin I didn't want to stop.

There's four benches, two on each side the same length as the table. I know you have chairs—" Edith threw herself forward and hugged her, squeezed her so tight Iris squeaked when she laughed.

"They're wonderful! They're perfect, and we are absolutely going to take them, aren't we, Carver?"

"I—" Carver blinked, still staring at the table. "Yes. I have no words. You're beyond talented, Iris. You're an artist. Folks, Butch and I told you, didn't we?" Carver called over her head to the crowd. "Just look at what this woman can do!"

"All it took was one conversation and look what she made us?" Edith touched the table again.

"You are truly gifted," one woman in the crowd said, grinning.

"How long is your waiting list for custom pieces?" Another voice called from the back of the crowd.

"I've been wanting a special hutch for my dining room for the longest time." An older woman touched her arm. "Would you come out and give me an estimate?"

"My…" Her eyes went wide. "I don't have a waiting list. This was…"

Other voices chimed in as everyone admired the table, then gathered around Iris, chattering away and asking for appointments and details.

Causing Iris to feel overwhelmed, a bit panicked and more than a little loved.

"THINK THAT WORKED?"

Carver pulled Shane aside as the crowd continued to filter in and out of the Depot. Iris's craftsmanship was quickly becoming the talk of the town.

"Time will tell," Shane said. "Thanks for agreeing to this. I know you're swamped, but we're running out of time, and she means so much to me. To all of us, really."

Carver nodded. "Anything Edith and I can do to help show this woman she belongs here, you've got it."

"You've already helped so much. You gave her something to help spread her wings. I think she may very well be soaring just about now." He turned his attention back to Iris, who was headed straight for him. "Hey. You're like a rock star or something."

"Or something." She eyed him in a way that had him squirming. "Seems like a little birdie's been talking in people's ears. Telling them I've got an open schedule for custom orders when in fact I'm going to be leaving."

"That wasn't me." Shane held up both hands. "That was all Dad. And him." He jerked his thumb toward Carver, who looked far from apologetic.

"Work like that demands careful attention," Carver said. "And I couldn't fit everyone in my house for a look-see. You ever run out of orders, you feel free to set up a corner in the Depot. I'd be happy to feature you as an exclusive artist from Cottonwood Creek."

Iris swallowed so hard Shane saw it. "I don't know—"

"Maybe you don't," Carver said quietly and touched her arm. "But we do. Thank you for this, Iris. You've given us something to be truly thankful for."

Iris stood there, in front of Shane, practically tearful.

"You, okay?"

"You set me up."

"I played a small part," Shane admitted. "I told you I wouldn't stop trying to find a way to convince you to stay."

"You didn't tell me you planned to fight dirty."

Shane wrapped his arms around her and tugged her close. He dipped his head, kissed her as if it might be his last chance. "You should have seen that coming."

She shook her head. "You're backing me into a corner."

"I'm showing you what's possible," he countered. He'd prepared for every argument, every word she'd throw at him. There was nothing she could say that would deter him from continuing to show her how important she'd become to their lives, and how much they cared about her.

She rested her forehead against his chest. "Can we go, please? I need some space and time to think."

Space and time to think might work against him. "Might take a while to get the truck free." The table was still acting as a showpiece. "Give me a few minutes to get clear of the crowd, okay? Then we'll head out."

Eventually, they were back in the truck and headed home, and he could hear the gears grinding in her head.

"Anything you want to talk about?"

"No."

For the first time, he couldn't get a read on her. Up until now he'd been pretty good about figuring out her moods or even what was on her mind, but she seemed determined to lock herself away from him for the moment.

He supposed he understood that. She'd been mobbed at the Depot and inundated with requests that, as she'd planned things, she had no real way of fulfilling.

Shane turned the music on but kept it low during their drive back to the ranch. The optimism and hope that had been building these past few days suddenly popped when he caught sight of the RV parked by the main house again. He'd really been hoping for another few days before the Blackwell contingent returned.

"Did you know they were coming back?" Iris asked.

"Denny said they wouldn't leave without saying goodbye," Shane admitted. "But she didn't say when."

"Looks like today's the day."

"Iris…"

"Time and space, Shane." She swung open the door without looking at him. "Time and space."

IRIS'S REUNION WITH Big E and Denny was brief.

On the assurance she'd keep in touch, Iris said her goodbyes and quickly retreated to her trailer, Cos leaving his canine companions to follow her.

The promise of solitude had her pace increasing as she approached Wander. Pulling open the door, she had just breathed a sigh of relief when the light over the table clicked on.

"Heard you were quite the hit in town."

There was a time hearing her mother's voice would have stopped her cold, had her turning around and leaving. But this was her home. Her trailer. Her life.

"How was Claxton?" Iris asked as Cos went immediately to his bed in the corner.

"Quiet, actually," Flora admitted.

A host of responses came to mind, but she was too exhausted for a more in-depth conversation.

"We should try to talk." Flora twisted her fingers together in an uncharacteristic show of nerves. When only silence followed, Iris walked to the refrigerator for a beer.

She set a second bottle on the table in front of her mother and sat down.

"It's a difficult thing," Flora said in a tight voice. "To realize your child hates you."

Iris set her jaw and took a pull of beer. "I don't hate you, Mom." She looked out the kitchen window, saw the open door to the Holloway stable and heard the horses stomping and moving about. "Maybe I did at one time, but it's a waste of energy." Energy she wanted to use elsewhere.

"I'm sorry about how you were treated. It wasn't intentional. I know that's no excuse, but I wish that I'd seen it then." Flora flinched as if she wasn't sure she was sounding believable. "It was wrong and it broke something between us we may never get back."

Iris watched her for a long moment, then nodded. "Apology accepted."

"That's it?" Flora asked cautiously. "That's all it took?"

Instead of reminding her of the years they'd lost, Iris let the resentment move through her like mist. "I don't want to live in the past anymore, Mom. It's been holding me back for too long. So yes, that's all it took. But that's all this is. A truce. I'm not performing with the Belles at your ceremony."

Disappointment flashed in her mother's eyes. "There's nothing I can do to convince you?"

"Like I said." Iris took another drink. "I'm done with the past."

Flora's gaze flicked to the saddle display over Iris's bed. "As I was sitting here, I was looking for something, anything that represented us. The Blackwells. Your sisters. The Belles. Other than that." She motioned to the saddle. "There's nothing."

Iris didn't comment.

"Shane called this my apology tour," Flora said with a weak smile. "That man. I'll tell you, he loves you something fierce, Iris."

"I know." It was the first time she not only admitted it, but also believed it.

"Maggie and Violet, they said no at first, too. He was right. You girls aren't making it easy on me, but I really am trying."

"You're trying because you want something from us." Done playing games, Iris gave in. "What is it you want from me, Mom?"

"The saddle." Flora practically gulped. "Maggie said she'd come back and perform at the Hall of Fame ceremony if Violet gave her Ferdinand."

"Ferdinand's still alive?" Iris couldn't help but balk. That bull had to be almost, what? Fifteen by now? Older probably. "Wow. That's..." She broke off, catching on. She spun in her seat, looked at the saddle behind the custom case she'd built for it. "Violet wants the saddle."

"She'll give Ferdinand up for it." Flora flexed her fingers. "I know it's important to you. You've built your brand around it. And it was your aunt Dandy's."

Iris's breath hitched. The pressure in her chest built. "This is why you really came, isn't it? To ask me for the saddle."

"And to see you again," Flora said, insisting. "I know you probably don't believe me, and I understand why. I've missed you, Iris. And maybe I didn't realize how much I would until you were gone. All those years, I thought you didn't need me. You were so self-sufficient. So independent. It didn't dawn on me that you needed something from me."

Iris couldn't stop staring at the saddle.

"I've had some time to think, to reflect. And my frustration with not understanding you, not having as easy a time communicating with you as I did with your sisters, it was just easier to pretend there wasn't a problem and leave you on your own. That doesn't mean I didn't, that I don't, love you."

Iris turned back around.

"I do love you, Iris." Tears glistened in her mother's eyes. "And the fact you've gone most of your life believing otherwise is something I'm going to have to accept and deal with. Yes, Violet wants the saddle, but I'm not in a position to ask you for it. Even though I already have."

Iris's lips twitched. Always the same Flora.

"I just wanted to be open about everything with you now. You deserve that much at least." She got to her feet, looked around the trailer. "I wish there was something here of us for you to carry with you moving forward, but I understand why there isn't. Do me a favor, though, Iris?" She walked to the door. "Don't let the mistakes I made stop you from loving someone. Or from letting someone love you. If you walk away from that, from him, from them, I'm afraid you'll never forgive yourself, and trust me, that's not a feeling you want to live with."

Iris didn't move after the door closed. Her mother's words, possibly the kindest and most thoughtful Flora had ever uttered to her, sank slowly into her, coating her wounded heart with hope and forgiveness.

Iris set her bottle aside, slid out from behind

the table and pulled open the drawer beneath the bench seat her mother had occupied. The long, deep drawer was as organized as it had been from the day she'd stashed her Belle mementos inside. She lifted the carefully wrapped costumes out, then the photo box, and lastly, the bright pink cowboy hat studded with rhinestones. She stared down at the hat for a long moment, a smile coming to her lips as she thought of another little girl who would love to wear it. A little girl who had snuck into Iris's unsuspecting, lonely heart along with her brothers, PaPa and uncle.

She sat on the floor, popped open the lid of the photo box and flipped through the images inside.

A knock sounded on the door before Shane poked his head in. "You okay?" He stepped up, petted Cos when the dog shot forward to greet him. "Hey, boy." He crouched, looked at Iris. "I saw your mom come out of the trailer. Everything all right?"

"Today seems a day for ambushes," she said. "Don't worry," she added at his frown. "Everything's fine. I was just…" She pulled out a stack of pictures, tears blurring her vision.

Shane sat beside her, took the pictures from her hand. "These are of you and the Belles." He sorted through them, laughing at some of the funnier, more candid shots. "I thought you got rid of everything."

"I lied." She'd forgotten about the good times. About her sisters and the fun they'd had. Everything had been tainted by the pain she'd felt growing up, but not everything had been bad. "I miss them." Tears plopped onto another picture she pulled free. This one of her and Magnolia and Violet and J.R. and Willow, all on horseback, lined up together, arms tight around each other's shoulders, show smiles firmly in place as they beamed at the camera. "I miss my sisters, Shane." The tears wouldn't stop and only increased as he slipped his arm around her shoulders and drew her in. She leaned into him, gave in to the emotions she'd been fighting for so long. "I don't want to be alone anymore."

He pressed a kiss to her head. "You don't have to be, Iris. Stay with us. Stay with me. I promise, you will never be lonely again."

She squeezed her eyes shut. "I can't give up what I've built, Shane."

"Of course, you can't." He set her back, looked at her as if she'd sprouted two heads. "I'd never ask you to."

"But—"

"Do you love me?"

She sighed, touched his face. "You can read my mind, Shane. You know I do."

"I suspect that you do," he teased. "There's a difference."

She kissed him, surprising them both, and kept kissing him until she felt his body relax. "I love you, Shane Holloway. And I love your cranky father and your wonderful children and this place." Her heart swelled and filled at the same time. "I love everything about all of you. But I don't know who I am without Saddle-Up."

He stared at her for a long moment, and she wondered, for a split second, if she'd said too much. Shane got to his feet, set the pictures on the table and pulled her up.

"I need you to come with me."

"What, now? Don't we have to carve pumpkins or something?"

"Later. You need to see something. Grab your hat. And your coat. We're going for a ride."

Iris joined him in the stable. He'd saddled Calamity for her once more and was getting Outlaw ready.

"Where are we going?" She hauled herself into the saddle, kicked Calamity gently and eased her around.

"You'll see." Shane took the lead, immediately switching into a trot until they reached the edge of the homestead. She rode beside him, the wind in her hair, a rush of adrenaline surging through her system as they crossed over pastures and around to the west end of the property.

The old barn was one she hadn't seen before,

but, given its state and location, she realized it was the future home of the sheep Shane intended to herd. The structure was enormous, almost aircraft hangar size, with rusted metal siding, a rounded dome roof and ancient rickety doors that whined and squeaked when Shane opened them.

"Come on." He held out his hand, and she dismounted, slipping her fingers through his. A tiny thrill shot through her as she realized nothing had ever felt as natural or right. "I want you to see this."

"Shane, it's your father you have to convince about the sheep, not me."

"We aren't getting sheep. At least not for a while. Dad and I decided a couple of days ago. We have another idea in mind for this place." He looked up and around, then back at her. "A home base for Saddle-Up Designs."

"A…what?" Iris gasped.

"Think about all you can do with this space, Iris. You wanted to do a TV show, you can expand your online channel with your own video studio. Plenty of space for that and a workshop. You can fit multiple trailers in here at one time, and there's sliding doors over there and there. It's perfectly set up for a design and custom furniture business."

She couldn't stop blinking. He'd thought all this out, hadn't he? "But what about traveling?"

"You can travel as much as you want, as much as you need. Maybe we can even go with you sometimes. You and me in Wander, Dad and the kids in Cassidy."

"An RV design caravan?" She laughed, pulled her hand free so she could cover her mouth. "I can't believe how much I love that idea."

Shane beamed. "Does that mean you approve of the space? Do you want to hang out your shingle?"

"That depends." Iris faced him, reached up and caught his face in her hands. "Do you come with it?"

"Afraid so. I love you, Iris. I want you to stay. We need you to stay. I don't think any of us can imagine life without you anymore."

She smiled, her chin trembling, and she nodded. "Okay," she whispered. "We'll have to work some things out, but I think for the first time in my life I'm ready to be happy. With you. As a Holloway."

"Is that a proposal?" he challenged.

"Maybe. If you can stand being married to a Blackwell... Belle." Iris frowned, her stomach lurching. She stepped back, let him go. "I need to do something. Back at the... I have to catch them before they leave."

"Who? Big E?"

Shane ran after her as she catapulted herself onto Calamity's back like the old days.

"No! My mother. Come on, Calamity." She kicked Calamity into full speed, hanging on to her hat as they raced back to the ranch. Outlaw's hoofs pounded beside her, and the knowledge that she wasn't alone, not anymore, surged through her.

They didn't slow until they reached the house, coming to a sharp stop at the front door. She looked around for Big E's RV.

Butch and Ruby Rose stepped outside. The door banged shut behind them.

"Where are they?"

"You just missed them," Butch said.

"How long?" Iris demanded.

"Not even five minutes. Wait… Iris!" Butch called after her, but she was already racing off.

This time she didn't pay attention to whether Shane was with her. She had to catch up, had to close that final door on all the resentment and anger she'd been carrying around for years. The RV was put-putting its way down the road, was nearly at the turnoff when she kicked Calamity to go faster. "Stop!" she yelled when she got close and pulled just far enough ahead to wave them down. "Stop!"

The brakes screeched. The RV came to a dust-swirling stop. Iris backtracked with Calamity and leaped off as Denny powered down her window.

"What in tarnation are you doin' girl?" Her grandmother scowled at her.

"I need to talk to Mom." She pulled open the door and found Flora clinging to the cabinets, half seated on one of the cushioned benches.

"Iris, what on earth—"

"The saddle." Iris couldn't even wait to catch her breath. "I'll give you the saddle and I'll perform at the ceremony."

"You will?" Flora's face lit up like a Christmas tree. "You mean it?"

"What's this?" Big E demanded as he shoved out from behind the steering wheel.

"I mean it." Iris nodded. "I'll do it. But I have one condition."

"Oh, yes." Denny sighed and wedged herself in front of her brother. "Well, let's have it."

"Aunt Dandy's bracelet. The charm bracelet J.R. got when she left. I want it back." With her proposal made, she sagged in relief. "That's my price."

"Is that doable, Flora?" Denny asked.

Flora smiled wryly. "I don't know. But it's worth a shot. If Iris came around, then anything's possible."

"I didn't come—oh, never mind. Hey, Shane."

Shane climbed into the RV behind her, a perplexed scowl on his face. "Did you install jet-packs on that horse that I missed, because you practically flew out here."

"I told you she's magic on a horse," Flora said proudly. "The saddle for the bracelet." She gave a quick nod, as if the exchange was already complete. "I can make that work."

"Okay, then there's just one other thing." She looked over her shoulder at Shane. "Don't go yet, folks. Stay. We're carving pumpkins tonight, and we have celebrating to do."

"What kind of celebrating?" Denny eyed the two of them.

"The kind where I'd like my family with me," Iris said. "Come on back to the ranch." She prodded Shane through the open door, jumped down, then poked her head back inside. "You can follow us home."

EPILOGUE

"As you can see." Iris's voice filled the interior of Big E's RV, coming through the laptop speaker loud and clear. "The completion of Cassidy came with an extra set of rewards."

Big E, Denny and Flora all crowded into the dining cubby to watch Iris's most recent video. They'd stayed at the ranch long enough to see the finished product, but they'd been anxiously awaiting the online reveal.

In the video, Iris stood outside the finished trailer, which was sparkling with a new coat of paint and the trademark SaddleUpDesigns.com logo. She'd taken the old, rusted-out trailer and made it shine like a newly born star.

"I was able to do a bit of unexpected personalization with this one." Dressed in jeans and a gray tank top, Iris stepped inside to show off the triple sleeping compartment at the front end of the trailer. "And here are some guests who are going to be enjoying this trailer for years to come."

"Look! There's Eric!" Flora pointed at the screen. Big E chuckled, and Denny pushed her hand away so she wouldn't block the view.

"This is Eric." Iris pointed at the bottom bunk where Eric stuck his head out and waved at the camera. "He asked for a cowboy-themed cubicle and even drew the lasso along the back here himself.

"And Ruby Rose," Iris continued as Ruby waved and blushed. "She's all about pink and cowgirls these days."

"She's wearing Iris's Belle hat!" Flora gushed. "Look how cute she is!"

The camera aimed up. "And here is Miles," Iris said. "He wanted to match his bunk with his car costume from Halloween that won him first prize at the Cottonwood Creek Halloween Fair."

"Hi, internet!" Miles yelled as the camera panned away.

"She really did an amazing job with that trailer," Denny said, as they watched the full tour. "You should hit her up for a remodel when this apology tour is over, Big E."

"Already on her schedule," Big E confirmed.

"For those of you who follow me on the road," Iris said and walked to the door. "I'm taking a bit of a detour in life." She turned her hand around to show off the engagement ring on her finger. "I got me my very own cowboy!"

"Kinda tiny," Flora grumbled and leaned between the two of them, squinting.

"That was Butch's wife's ring," Big E boasted. "He gave it to Shane to give to her."

"That boy never stops surprising, does he?" Denny said with a wide smile.

"Keep your eyes on this channel," Iris said, and she tugged Shane out from behind the camera to join her. The dogs barking in the distance added a special and familiar soundtrack. Zinni hopped up on the bench as if to say hi to her left behind friends. "And on the town of Cottonwood Creek... I'll have a brand-new workshop and custom furniture business opening after the first of the year, and for one-of-a-kind pieces, visit the Lone Star Depot, which will have exclusive distribution rights for all my pieces. Coming to you from Cottonwood Creek at the Holloway Ranch, along with my family." Shane pulled her in for a side hug and waved at the camera. "We'll see you online soon with Saddle-Up Designs! Bye!"

"Bye!" Flora waved and earned an eye roll from Big E. "Oh, stop. I know she can't see me."

"Coulda fooled me." Big E closed the laptop and sat back, eyed his traveling companions. For the first time in a long while, he was feeling like they might succeed in their grand plan to unite these Blackwells. Three sisters down, two to go. Once they each made a stop back home to check in on ranches and loved ones. "Anyone planning on giving J.R. a heads-up that we're comin'?" he asked as he made his way back to the driver's seat.

"Not yet," Flora said. "But we will. Right, Zinni?" She pushed her face into the dog's fur.

"When we get close enough that J.R. can't make a run for it," Denny added. "Onward, Big E! Family awaits!"

Big E grinned and turned the engine back on. "Denny, you just said the magic words."

* * * * *

*Don't miss the next installment of
The Blackwell Belles! Coming next month
from acclaimed author Amy Vastine
and Harlequin Heartwarming!
Visit www.Harlequin.com today!*

and sometimes more perfect solu-